ABANDONED

Books by Edwin Silberstang

Fiction

RAPT IN GLORY
NIGHTMARE OF THE DARK
SWEET LAND OF LIBERTY
LOSERS, WEEPERS
SNAKE EYES
ABANDONED

Nonfiction

PLAYBOY'S BOOK OF GAMES
LAS VEGAS, AN INSIDER'S GUIDE
PLAY CHESS TONIGHT
PLAY BRIDGE TONIGHT
PLAY PINOCHLE TONIGHT
SMART CASINO PLAY
WINNING POKER STRATEGY
HOW TO GAMBLE AND WIN
WINNING CASINO CRAPS
WINNER'S GUIDE TO CASINO GAMBLING
PLAYBOY'S GUIDE TO CASINO GAMBLING (4 volumes)

EDWIN
SILBERSTANG

ABANDONED

1981
DOUBLEDAY & COMPANY, INC.
GARDEN CITY, NEW YORK

For John Capman

Grateful acknowledgment is made to the following for permission to reprint copyrighted material:

Lines from "In Memory of W.B. Yeats" copyright 1940 and renewed 1968 by W.H. Auden. Reprinted from *W.H. Auden: Collected Poems* by W.H. Auden, edited by Edward Mendelsohn. By Permission of Random House, Inc. and Faber and Faber Ltd.

Library of Congress Cataloging in Publication Data

Silberstang, Edwin, 1930–
Abandoned.

I. Title.
PZ4.S5718An [PS3569.I415]   813'.54
ISBN: 0-385-15978-1
Library of Congress Catalog Card Number 80–1071

In the deserts of the heart
Let the healing fountain start.

W. H. AUDEN

PART I

1

In the courtyard one flight below my window, two young women in bathing suits were sitting in plastic chairs, sunning themselves and talking. They were talking about movies they had seen. The words filtered up the same way the sun came through the smoggy skies of LA, indistinctly. They had nice figures and I stood by the window watching them for a few minutes, but there is only so much you can take of movie talk, especially in Hollywood.

I moved away from the window and turned on a small portable radio that had been left in the apartment, turning the dial till I caught a classical music station. The music was unmistakably Mozart, but the sound coming out of the cheap two-inch speaker was pure tin. I listened for a couple of minutes and then turned it off.

I was staying in a small studio apartment on North Orange Grove, in a cheap residential area of Hollywood, within shouting distance of Santa Monica Boulevard, which must be, by any standards, one of the most dismal and depressing streets in the world. It has no redeeming social value whatsoever. All day long the sounds of the cars shooting the stop sign at the corner assaulted my ears.

In harmony with those sounds, my neighbors' stereo sets blared out James Brown and Marvin Gaye music at all hours. Buildings are built in Hollywood one on top of the other and it is impossible to find a place that is quiet and peaceful, unless you live next to a cemetery, but I don't know of any in this town. The last apartment I lived in was at Western and Santa Monica, which is the pits as far as Hollywood is concerned, with its string of porno stores, discount houses, and massage parlors. The rent was cheap there, however, but I had one problem, and that was I couldn't even pay it, so I was kicked out.

At that time, which was two months before, I still had my VW in operation. It was ten years old and had no insurance as required by California law, but I took my chances, because basic insurance is at least $400 a year in Hollywood. Right now the car was laid up with brake and clutch troubles at Bug Builders on La Brea, and the bill amounted to $144, which I didn't have to my name. In another couple of days, the mechanic informed me, they were going to charge me for storage.

But the car had served its purpose. I had been able to move all my things to this apartment before it gave out. There really wasn't much to move, but what I did move was essential. I was keeping this apartment on borrowed time, for I had sublet it from a woman named Phyllis Millard, whom I had met on Larabee, over in West Hollywood, while we were both watching a Redd Foxx film being shot. We got to talking, and then went out for coffee and then over to my place on Western. It turned out that Phyllis was a photographer, had just been in LA for a month, and that morning had to leave the apartment she had been crashing at. That same afternoon she moved into my place until she could find her own apartment.

She was young, just about twenty-four or so. Phyllis came from a rich family in Pennsylvania and had gone to Bryn Mawr, but she came out West to try and make it on her own as a photographer. After she had been with me for a week, she found a job at an advertising agency for $1,000 a month, and then she moved into this apartment on Orange Grove. I helped furnish it by going around to garage sales with her, and that's how she got most of her furniture. Also, she was a charmer. Phyllis had a pert, pretty face with big brown eyes and all the men fell for her and did what they could to help her out. Some gave her furniture, and the landlord threw in an old couch and a dresser, all for nothing.

In a way, I was sorry to have her leave my place, because it was nice to have a home of some sort, to have a woman to come home to, to eat meals with another person, someone I could talk to and hold at night in bed. It was very pleasant for a while, but I'm a writer, if I may use that hackneyed term, and I needed my privacy, for I was working on a screenplay at the time, and in a way I was glad when she moved out. We stayed friends, however, and although she found herself a few boyfriends, we continued to be occasional lovers.

A few months after she took this place, her parents sent her an airplane ticket to the East, and she flew back to spend a short vacation with them. She wrote to me from Pennsylvania, short chatty notes, telling me she had become involved with a young man there. Then she wrote that she was staying with him at his place on the campus of Penn State, and would I mail back some things for her.

Since she no longer had any use for this apartment, and since I was on the verge of being bodily thrown out by the sheriff for nonpayment of rent, I asked if I could sublet it. Phyllis agreed, and that's how I moved in. The rent was pretty cheap, $155 a month. If the landlord knew it was really mine now, he'd have raised it to $200.

My problems were mostly financial, but when you're down and out, then the spirit cracks, and financial and money matters can quickly become spiritual matters. My spirit, along with my finances, was splintering fast. Right now there were two letters just forwarded to me from the Western Avenue address sitting on my desk, unopened. One was from the Commonwealth of Massachusetts, and the other from my ex-wife. I decided to open them.

The Commonwealth letter told me I owed more than two thousand dollars in back alimony, and that the matter had been turned over to the State of California. This was stale news for me, since I already knew that an order of arrest had been issued and it was just a matter of time before the sheriff found me here. I put the letter to one side and opened the other one, thinking I was foolish to have my mail forwarded, but I needed some contact with the outside world, with my agents and friends. I had to keep in touch.

This one was from my ex-wife. I opened it carefully, since I could reuse the stamp. She wrote the usual thing about what a lousy person I was, and how I was neglecting my obligations and how I only thought of myself, and that one of these days she'd tell my mother just what a selfish, cheap bastard her son was.

I dropped that letter on the floor and closed my eyes, thinking not of my ex-wife, but trying to get a mental image of my mother, whom I hadn't seen in over a year. All I could see, however, was my ex-wife's sour face and the face of the man she was living with. That was the rub. She was living with a professor at Boston U, and I was still paying alimony. It had been a terrible financial burden for me, and had put me into debt, and into my present bind. I had tried for months to reason with her to drop the alimony, but with all her liberal women's rights thinking, she wouldn't budge.

It wasn't just the alimony that had knocked me out. It was a screenplay I had written, which my agent here, Al Hunter, had shown to a few people. Finally he got

Lawrence Walker Productions interested in it, and when
Lawrence Walker himself asked the price, Hunter told him
$300,000. Walker was agreeable but wanted some changes
made. For five months I met with Walker and his staff and
worked on the changes, always with the three hundred big
ones blazing a hole in my head.

After a couple of dozen meetings, the whole thing fizzled
out one day. From $300,000 to zero, while during that five-
month period, I had gotten nothing for my efforts, not even
carfare. To do the screenplay, I put aside all my other writing, and as the months went by, my money drained away.
In the end, I blew work with three local magazines that had
supplied me with a decent living, and couldn't even go on
unemployment.

All that lovely money had flown out of my eager hands.
That was the trouble in Hollywood. There was no middle
ground. You either hit it big, enormously big, or you made
nothing. That was the goddamn film industry in a nutshell.
I would have been happy with ten grand for my screenplay.
It would have put me on my feet, given me some breathing
space. If it had been a matter of ten thousand, Walker
would probably have taken a chance on my work. But for
three hundred grand he got cold feet. I had no track record,
he finally said. Where was my track record? That was one
of the favorite terms here in magicland, that and "block-
buster." A writer with a track record that wrote a block-
buster, well, that was the living nuts all right. And block-
busters came from fresh concepts. Jesus, it was a strange
world out here, a world suited for hacks.

Well, who was I to talk? I was a hack now. Otherwise,
why would I be writing screenplays? I knew what I was
trying to do, and that was to make the big bread, the real
big bucks, that movies and TV offered. I used to write serious novels at one time, and right now, in my closet, I had
four novels, each in manuscript form. A couple of them had
come very close to being published, and the ironic thing

was, they were my poorer works. The really good work had received form letter rejections. I still had a New York agent, because I had actually been published in national magazines; three stories five years ago. Five years ago is a long time, a long, long time. Before I was sandbagged by Lawrence Walker Productions, I had been grinding out copy for all kinds of second-rate publications, getting paid anywhere from twenty-five to a hundred and fifty dollars per article.

Now I had blown those outlets, and at the moment, I was really in deep. I had paid the rent from the last of my published articles, and had exactly fifty-five dollars left to my name. There was still the phone bill to pay and I'd be going out to get a money order in Phyllis' name to take care of that. The phone and the mail were my two lines to the outside world, and I hated to give them up. After I paid the phone bill, I'd have about forty dollars left, with no money coming in, and for all I knew, the sheriff due any moment.

There had to be something I could do. I had already gotten into crime in a minor way, boosting some things from the local supermarket, things like tuna fish cans and wrapped steaks, but I knew it was stupid to leave myself wide open for such petty crimes. And I hated myself after stealing the stuff. My other boosting was minor. I got lemons and oranges from trees in my long walks around the neighborhood, and I had about a dozen avocados ripening on my windowsill from the tree next door, which was dropping fruit all the time. But what the hell, if I didn't take the avocados, they'd just lay on the ground and rot. The people who owned the tree didn't give a damn about them, so why couldn't I grab them while the grabbing was good?

I sat in a rocking chair and rocked, thinking of what I could do. I thought of all the people I knew in LA, and then thought of my film agent, Al Hunter. If things got really hairy, I could probably borrow a couple of hundred from him. I nearly earned him thirty big ones some months before. He owed me for the lousy five months I had wasted, when he didn't lift a finger to get me some money, any money at all. Yes, I had been so close, so goddamn close, I could weep with the frustration. So close, I had already smelled that money . . . money, money, money, oh yes, that's what ruled this town, that's what brought me to this dead land in the dying sun in the first place.

Then the phone rang.

2

"Hello, hello, is this Mr. Tom DeWinter?"

"Yes," I answered. The voice was unfamiliar and foreign sounding.

"Mr. DeWinter, this is Max Hildendorf. Of Kansas City."

He was waiting for some kind of recognition. "I'm sorry," I said, "I don't know who you are."

"Didn't Mr. Brundage speak to you?"

"No." He was referring to Ralph Brundage, my literary agent in New York, who never phoned me these days. In fact, he hadn't called in over a year. The last call was to inform me that he was sending along eight rejections of one of my novels by mail.

"I'm terribly sorry. I thought he had spoken to you."

"Well, he hasn't. But what can I do for you?"

"It's difficult to speak about without your agent having called you. I'll tell you what . . . well, let me see. Yes, I'll get in touch with Mr. Brundage again, and then I'll have him call you and explain the matter to you."

"What matter?"

"If you don't mind, Mr. DeWinter . . . let's leave it at that. If that's all right with you?"

"Sure." What else could I say? I didn't have the faintest idea who he was or what this was all about.

"So I'll wait for your call, then," I said.

"Yes, I'm terribly sorry to have disturbed you."

"You didn't disturb me at all."

He said good-bye and hung up the phone. I put down the receiver and wondered how he had gotten my number, since the phone was still listed under Phyllis' name. Then I remembered sending a short note to Brundage giving him my new phone number and address, just in case something came up. Outside of Brundage, Hunter, my mother, and a couple of friends, all my mail was being sent to the old address on Western and forwarded here. The California courts and sheriff's office still hadn't found out about my new address, otherwise I would have already been in the slammer for nonsupport.

I thought about the caller, Hildendorf. It was probably all a lot of bullshit anyway, because Brundage hadn't done anything for me since I had him as an agent. Yes, probably all bullshit, for this was the first indication in over a year that my agent knew I was even still alive.

The sun was still shining, despite the smog cover. I went to the window and looked down at the courtyard. The young women had left, and an old lady, one of my erstwhile neighbors, was sitting and fondling her white poodle. Since she thought no one was watching, she goosed the dog, who whimpered and jumped off her lap. That was life in Hollywood, one of those vignettes which reinforced the charm I felt about this city. I wondered where the two young women had gone or who they were. I hadn't seen them before. Maybe friends of the guy who lived below me. He walked around with an unlit pipe in his mouth, and a pencil mustache, trying to look like James Brolin's imitation of

Clark Gable. I had never really spoken to him, just exchanged hellos. My nearest neighbor lived just across the
hall. Her name was Merle Oldham, and she had been a
friend of Phyllis'. She was a self-styled actress. When she
heard that I wrote screenplays she became somewhat interested in me, at least to the point of inviting me in for coffee.

We had talked about movies and screen acting and writing, but it was all small talk, meaning nothing at all. Merle
was sort of attractive, with a slim figure and a good nose
job, but though she dressed in the uniform of the day, jeans
and denim shirts, and tried to look twenty-one, she appeared to be in her late thirties. Not that it mattered to me.
Maybe it did. I don't know. I'm thirty-four myself, and I
wonder why it bugged me. I look like thirty-four, a little
overweight from eating crap and not having enough exercise. That was my trouble.

I decided to get out of the apartment for a while. There
was nothing doing here, I couldn't think clearly, and I
needed some fresh air. I put on my one pair of hiking boots
and took along a pack of cigarettes. I had been off cigarettes
for five years up to three months ago, but had started up
again. Was it nerves or lack of spirit? Whatever it was, I
tried to keep my cigarette smoking down to a minimum, but
it was turning into a losing cause, along with the doughnuts
and coffee I was having instead of meals. Hell, I could go
into Winchell's and have a breakfast for about seventy cents.
That was cheap enough and filling besides, but I knew I
had to stop doing this.

Sometimes I went whole hog the other way, buying lettuce and salad vegetables and mixing them with vinegar
and pepper and eating only that for days at a time. But then
came a craving for something substantial, and since I
couldn't afford anything but cheap hamburgers, I'd have
some more doughnuts. It was turning into a lousy scene,
and descending the stairs, I thought how much more intelli-

gent it would be for me to get out of Hollywood, and California.

Just get out and disappear for a while, and forget about writing, which was a million-pound weight on my back. Everything I wrote was being rejected. How long could I go on like this?

If only that screenplay had been taken. Goddamn. Three hundred big ones. I used to stay up at night with my dreams, when Walker was seriously thinking of buying it. Three hundred big ones. I'd think of the tax situation and how I'd invest the money. Quality bonds and growth stocks and some of it would go in the bank. Or maybe I'd buy myself a house somewhere, a place with privacy and a den and a room for books and files and manuscripts. Pipe dreams . . . dreams that blew up in smoke when Mr. Walker shook his head at the last meeting and walked out, leaving the screenplay on the glossy teak table.

That bastard. My agent, Al Hunter, had been no help. Shit, I had been so weak in the situation. I needed the money, I could almost taste it, I was willing to do anything for it, but Hunter should have been firmer. All those meetings, and all that rewriting. He should have gotten me something for it.

I was out in the street. Still thinking. I really needed room to think. I needed to get away and think things out completely, think about my future, because right now I was going nowhere.

I walked down to Santa Monica Boulevard, walking slowly in the dull sunshine and breathing the exhausts of the cars going by. There was no end of cars in LA. I had been in other cities in my life, but there was no traffic like the traffic here. Cars and more cars. Old cars and funky cars. In this town if a dude had three grand he didn't buy a new Toyota, he bought an eight-year-old Porsche, and then, a month later, the engine would blow out and the finance company would repossess it.

I wish I could get a loan on my car. But the damn heap had 120,000 miles on it, and was worthless except as basic transportation. Foul black smoke poured out of it when I started the engine cold. It was a sick car all right. And would probably die in the Bug Builder hospital, because there seemed no way to get the money to bail her out. But, I thought, you're dead without a car in LA. You could get old waiting for buses in this town.

LA is a lousy place for walking. There's nothing to look at, and the crowds look spaced out and dull, and the goddamn fumes from the cars choke you. And there's no place to sit and relax without spending money. But I had to get out of the apartment, so I decided to take a walk, to brave the fumes and the smoke and the people I'd see on the streets.

I took a long walk all the way to Plummer Park, and sat on the grass and watched the old people sitting there in a daze. Near the tennis courts a bunch of old men were playing cards and I sat near them in the shade. I wondered if I'd end up like them, sitting and killing time like this. I couldn't stand cards. I had some interest in chess, and at one time even belonged to the USCF, but that's when I could spare fifteen dollars a year, and had a more or less permanent address. Now, I had no magazine subscriptions. I had moved to about twelve places in the last few years. It was enough of a bother to let friends know where you were, let alone magazines, with all their postage dues when they had to be forwarded.

Over the last few years, I had gotten rid of a lot of things, a lot of excess baggage, and then, some baggage got rid of me. Bankamericard and Master Charge dumped me along the way, and had judgments against me. Household Finance and Bank of America were also on my trail. My debts were mounting day by day, fed by that great fuel, interest.

But why think about things like that? I got up from the bench and watched the tennis players. There were a couple of cute women playing in a foursome, and I recognized one of the male players in the group. He appeared on TV quite a lot in commercials, and he strutted across the court like a peacock. Big man in a small place. Very small place.

I once had a good tennis racket, but the gut strings broke and I never replaced them and one thing led to another and the handle got warped or busted or something and that took care of tennis. One by one my pleasures had been taken from me. I still had my doughnuts and occasional sex . . . but even writing, the joy of writing, that had long gone.

It was working on screenplays that had done it, that and my editing jobs and writing half-ass articles about subjects I couldn't give a damn about. Once, a long time ago, not so long ago really, I loved to write. I'd lose myself in my novels, in a world of my own characters and situations. I didn't care about anything else when I was writing my serious books.

But no one else cared about them . . . that was the trouble. Whether they were good or bad, I didn't know anymore. I only knew that I was unpublished as a novelist, and now was one of a million people in Hollywood writing screenplays.

Even the mailman was writing screenplays, and the other day I overheard two pizza delivery boys talking about their screenplays. Talk was cheap in this town, everyone talking about the movies, about their acting or writing or directing, and everyone in a common pit of failure. And I was also in it, greasy from the effort of trying to keep alive, trying to breathe.

I left the park a little while later, and it was already getting dark. The sun was having its trouble in the West, where the blue Pacific was, where Marina del Rey beckoned, and Malibu Beach glistened.

I walked along Fountain to avoid the boulevard's fumes, but traffic was picking up there also, and I began to cough and choke after a few blocks. I kept up a steady pace though, and by the time I got home I was fatigued.

3

The next day I got up early, my purpose twofold. I'd try to find a job, and failing that, try to borrow some money. My one drawback was lack of mobility. I needed a car, and I racked my brains trying to think of someone who would lend me one. Maybe Al Hunter? No, I needed him for a loan. He was my ultimate tapping prospect.

I thought of a couple of other people, but I wasn't that friendly with them. I did know a director of small theater that I had done a couple of favors for, and he would gladly have lent me his station wagon, but he was up in San Francisco right now, trying to get connected with A.C.T. there. I then thought of Merle, but I had already been turned down by her a couple of times. She needed the car for her rounds to agents and auditions.

So there was nothing to do but get dressed. I put on my pair of tan Levi's. I was down to two pair of pants, the blue Levi's and the tan ones. Then I put on a short-sleeved shirt and my walking boots. This was an acceptable LA costume

for anything. When I had my first appointment with Walker
at his studio, I put on a jacket, but found Walker and all his
associates wearing raggedy jeans and denim shirts. It was
the reverse phony style of Hollywood.

I flashed on a party Hunter had taken me to, up in the
Hollywood Hills, when I first hit this town. When I came by
Hunter's house, Al was wearing a western shirt and slacks,
and he told me he had to change for the party. He changed
to a greasy sweatshirt and torn Levi's. That was Hollywood
all right. It was a crazy mixed up place.

But all this nostalgia wasn't adding a penny to my
bankroll. I went down to Santa Monica and bought a *Times*
at a newsrack, and looked through the want ads, but it was
depressing to do so. I didn't know what I was fit for
anymore. Executive type? Shit, no. Salesman? Commission
work? No way. Jesus, I thought, this is like a time warp.
When I left college I went this route, but today? I just
couldn't go through it again.

No, there must be another way. There must be something
else I could do. If I got a shitty job here, I'd be stuck all
over again. I began the tedious walk to the Winchell doughnut shop. It was that or walk further to McDonald's, but
McDonald's wasn't open yet. I'd settle for one doughnut
and coffee. Instead of putting another nail into my coffin,
I'd stick a doughnut on top. And while there, I'd have my
first cigarette of the day. I really wanted that cigarette and
coffee now, and walked a little faster.

I ate the doughnut slowly and drank a couple of cups of
coffee with it. Then I had my cigarette. I savored the smoke
curling around my lips. Basic enjoyments and pleasures, like
orgasms. At least orgasms were free, but not necessarily in
this town. They were free when you handled the situation
yourself, but otherwise, it was a hassle. Everyone here was
on the make, especially women. They didn't want to give it
away when they could use their vaginas for better purposes,

like cash, or an audition, or a TV part. Maybe I was getting too jaded on this scene.

Now that I had my coffee and cigarette, I turned my thoughts to leaving LA. That would probably be the wisest thing to do. Go away somewhere, to a college town, and get a cheap room and an easy job, maybe in a bookstore or something like that, and write my next novel. Get back to serious work again. Forget about screenplays . . . I'd leave that to the Hollywood hacks with their golden shitty touches.

All I needed to get away was some money. Not too much, but enough to bail out the VW and drive it up to Oregon. Eugene, Oregon; that's where I'd go to. Six months before, I had met a woman named Sarah at the County Museum. She was a painter and we got to talking and had coffee in the little restaurant at the museum and spent the day together. She was from Eugene and had invited me up to visit her sometime. At that time I was still involved in my big deal with the Walker organization and was noncommittal. Sarah had a handsome face, strong and intelligent. She seemed like a good woman. From time to time she wrote letters to me, telling me about her life in Eugene, about her paintings and her aspirations. I rarely answered the letters, but that was what I would do now. Go and visit her, crash with her till I found my own place.

I had new energy. I walked quickly to my apartment and called up Al Hunter. I'd put the touch on him. But he wasn't in, and his answering service took my name and number. I'd wait for his call. If he called back soon, I'd make plans to pack and leave by tomorrow, when I could rescue my car. I'd put my few things in and be on my way to the great Pacific Northwest. Everything I owned would fit into a suitcase and a duffel bag, for over the last few years I hadn't bothered to hold on to books. I didn't want anything cluttering up my life, and books cluttered things up. They took up space and were heavy as hell to move. All

I had was a cheap dictionary and a couple of volumes of Chekhov's stories, which I had been rereading lately.

A few days passed. Despite the care I took, my forty dollars had dwindled down to thirteen. The telephone bill was paid, by money order with Phyllis' name on it. No sense in arousing the telephone company. Every day I tested the avocados on the windowsill, but they were still firm and green. It would be a couple of weeks, I figured, before I could eat them.

I had heard from my Hollywood agent, Al Hunter, or rather from his secretary. He was in New York for at least two weeks, negotiating some deals. Well, they weren't my deals. That narrowed the field considerably for my going-away money. I had called a couple of people I knew but got the same response, "Gee, Tom, we'd love to, but you know how it is."

Yes, I knew how it was. That left only my family to borrow from, but that wasn't so easy. My brother worked in Iran, for an oil company. Once a year I got a card or letter from him, with a picture of his wife and kids on it, wishing me a Merry Christmas. Help from him was out of the question.

And that left my mother, who was living on social security down in Florida. She'd send me money, I knew, but how could I impose on her? She had barely enough to get along with. There were some cousins and uncles I could call, but what was the use of going after them? They were all on another wavelength, all stuck in middle-class poses along the Eastern Seaboard. Some I hadn't seen in over five years, since my divorce. No, they were definitely out of the question.

There were a couple of old friends from the East, but I didn't have the energy to contact them out of the blue, to ask for money. Too much anxiety for that. Well, there I was, nowhere, with my back to the wall.

There were no phone calls at all coming in. No calls from Brundage or from this mysterious guy in Kansas City, what was his name again? Hildendorf. Who the hell was he? I thought of calling Brundage but the bastard never contacted me, and if I called collect and he refused to take the call, I'd be screwed and lose more face. No, I wanted to hold on to what little dignity I had. It was bad enough with the rejections and all. The other night I had pulled out what I thought had been my best writing, a novel I did six years before, but I couldn't read it. Too many emotions welling up . . . it was written during the trouble with my wife, when I poured everything I had into the story. Nothing much had changed in my life since then. Still the same struggle. Still the same bullshit.

Oh, I had been with other women, and had even fallen in love again. With a married woman, but that was hell itself and why think about her now? I had better things to think about; in fact, anything was better to think about.

I looked at the avocados again. No change. What did I expect from an hourly perusal? And no change in me. I had to get some money. Lately I had been eating salads again, lettuce and onions and whatever else was cheap, mixed with Wesson oil and white vinegar. I guess it was healthy after a fashion but it wasn't filling me up or slacking my appetite. I needed something more substantial.

I decided to walk over to McDonald's. A Big Mac would do the trick. One of those and some coffee would hold me until evening. I left the apartment and saw the old woman with the dog sunning herself. She was weird all right. I walked by her quickly. I was surrounded by weirdness and bullshit and avocados that took forever to ripen.

I took my usual stroll down Santa Monica Boulevard, memory lane to me, past the familiar landmarks, Winchell's doughnuts and the Arco station and the used furniture places and a couple of porno bookstores, and of course the traffic. Cars were out like insects today, blowing horns, shuffling slowly from light to light.

I walked all the way to La Brea and the McDonald's there, but decided against having a Big Mac. The hell with it, I had to get myself into good physical shape, and to do that, I had to get out of LA, away from the stinking air and noise and traffic. I had to get away to green places where there were trees and mountains, not backfiring Porsches and burnt-out people.

I'd go back to my apartment, sit down, and go through all the names I knew, all the people I could call, and get that money. I'd get the $144 for the car and an extra one hundred and that should do the trick. I'd get rid of the apartment some way. I'd call Phyllis and tell her what I was doing. Maybe I could sell her stuff and take the money in the meantime and then send it to her when I got on my feet.

I'd tell no one where I was going. The hell with them all. What difference would it make whether or not I got a Christmas card from my brother or a letter from my agent, telling me of fresh rejections? And the sheriff wouldn't be able to find me. When I got back on my feet, I'd make a deal with the courts, pay off the arrears slowly, and in the meantime get an attorney and fight my wife's right to alimony. Yes, greener pastures ahead, movement ahead, sunlight and fresh air ahead.

I had a couple of road maps in the apartment. I'd study the best route to Eugene. The car might make it . . . I knew the rubber on the tires was fair, fair enough to get me up to Oregon.

I could probably get a cheap room or crash there with Sarah. It was a college town and I had always felt comfortable in college towns. It was going to be OK. I felt it in my bones.

When I turned the corner into North Orange Grove I

stopped short, because there was a sheriff's car parked right in front of the house. No one was in it. I sauntered up the block, putting on my dark glasses, and walked past the car and the house from across the street.

A few people were outside on the street, but they didn't know me by name. A woman walking a dog said hello to me, but all she knew was that I was an anonymous neighbor. I was just a shadowy figure to her. I said hello and smiled, keeping my eyes on the car. I glanced at my watch, and five minutes later the sheriff came out, carrying a paper in his hand. He looked up and down the block, but obviously he didn't know me. I lit a cigarette calmly and blew out the match, and then walked up the street a little further, not turning around. In fact, I walked all the way up to Fountain, before turning around.

The sheriff's car was gone. I retraced my steps, still keeping on the opposite side of the street. No use taking any chances. I went past my driveway and kept on walking to the corner of Santa Monica. Yes, I was going to be supercautious about this. Then I turned around, crossed the street and went to my building, walked down the driveway, but no one was outside.

I went up the steps, and as I got to my door, Merle's door opened. She was wearing a kimono and was barefoot.

"Hey," she said, "what's happening?"

"What do you mean?" I could see a note taped to my doorknob. I untaped it.

"The fuzz was here looking for you. They rang my bell."

"What about?"

"They didn't say. They only asked if you lived here and when you were around."

"What did you say?"

"I told them a man lived next door, but I didn't know who it was."

"Good. Thanks."

"That's OK." She stood there barefoot, shifting from one foot to another.

"You want to come in for a minute?" I asked.

"OK."

I opened the door, then carefully locked it, putting the chain in place, something I rarely did. If the cops came back they'd have to break it in, because I wasn't going to open up. I tried to think of an alternate way to get out of the apartment, but there was no way except to drop to the alley on the north, and that was a precarious fall available only through the kitchen or bathroom window.

"What's going on?" Merle asked.

"Wait a minute. I want to read this note."

The note was simple and told me to call Deputy Sheriff Dave Warren to avoid being arrested for back alimony.

"Something to do with alimony," I said. "It's my goddamn former wife putting the screws on me."

I offered her a cigarette, which she took. We lighted up. The cigarette tasted good, relaxing.

"You know," Merle said, "I was offered a job in a massage place, one of those domination scenes. You know what I mean?"

"Sure I know."

"Some weird things going on there. I was interviewed by the owner, and we got talking. If you wrote her story, you'd make a million dollars. The stories she told . . ."

"Maybe that's the kind of writing I should do."

"I told her about you. I could put in a good word if I see her again," Merle said.

"What's her name?"

"Crystal Waters. Isn't that weird, to have a name like that."

"Crystal Waters," I repeated.

"I could speak to her again, you know. I liked the things you showed me. That screenplay. You have talent. They should have taken it."

"Harry Cohn used to say he kissed the ass of talent, but Lawrence Walker didn't want to kiss my ass."

"That's funny," she said, "really funny. Harry Cohn ran Columbia, didn't he?"

"Yeah."

"You ever work there?"

"No. I never worked for any studio. I free-lance. I work for my closet. It's filled with my material."

"Don't get so bitter," Merle said. "You look terrible when you get so bitter."

"No kidding."

"That's right, you look so . . . your mouth gets so tight and your eyes narrow. Have you looked at yourself when you're this way?"

"No."

"Well, don't get bitter. Listen, I have to get going. Got an appointment with a dude in Beverly. But I'll speak to that woman again if you want."

"What woman?"

"Crystal Waters, from the massage studio."

"Oh . . . you really think there's anything in it?"

"She told me some fantastic stories. They'd blow your mind if you heard them. When I get a chance, I'll tell you a couple of them."

"OK. Do that."

I walked her to the door and she gave me her cheek to kiss, a peck that I administered while she pursed her lips and kissed the air. Merle could be too much sometimes.

After she left, I sat and pondered my fate again. I looked at the note, together with the deputy sheriff's card and phone number. They were closing in, all right. I had to delay them, stall them. No slammer for me right now. Time to get my ass out of town, get moving, but I needed money. Where could I get hold of some bread?

I went into the bathroom and washed my hands and face. I was really wet from perspiration. I combed my hair, then brushed my teeth. I was getting hungry, so I made a lettuce salad and poured vinegar on it and ate it like a goddamn rabbit, and washed the lousy thing down with some hot tea. But it wasn't satisfying. Nothing was satisfying these days.

4

I decided not to call the sheriff that day, and slept uneasily that night, worried about a sudden intrusion into my apartment, handcuffs, the whole bit, the whole "Adam-12" shtick, with my hands bound behind me. I got up a few times during the night, imagining that police cars were parked downstairs, that cops were ascending the stairway, that there was pounding on my doors. But it was all nothing, and the dismal smoggy sky greeted me at seven in the morning. Business as usual.

I dressed and got out of the apartment quickly, walking through the driveway with a bit of anxiety, but I told myself I was getting paranoid and to settle down. I bought a pack of cigarettes and walked around for a while, but that was getting me nowhere, this aimless strolling through barren streets. I needed some course of action.

After a three-hour walk in which I accomplished nothing but the deterioration of five cigarettes, I returned to the apartment and called up Dave Warren, the deputy sheriff who had left his card with me.

He was on patrol, but the desk sergeant knew all about the case and asked me where I was at the moment.

"At a friend's house in North Hollywood," I said.

"Well, Sheriff Warren will be coming around to your apartment this morning."

"Look, isn't there any way I can straighten this out?"

"No, it's too late for that. Once we have you in custody you can contact the probation department of the court."

"Can't I do it now?"

"I guess you could."

I called the court next, and after being disconnected three times I got hold of a clerk who told me they didn't seem to have my file; that the order must have emanated from a California court, but they just couldn't find my file.

I hung up. I knew what that meant. That meant, after I was busted, I'd spend sixty days in jail while they searched for my records, and meanwhile I was going to be behind bars. No way. "No way," I said aloud to the unhearing walls.

Now I knew I had to get out of here. I was in a desperate situation . . . wolf at the door in the guise of uniformed sheriff. I started to pack my things.

First I pulled out my manuscripts and tied them with rope and put them into the duffel bag. Then my clothing, then my toilet articles. It didn't take but a half hour for me to be packed up. But how was I going to transport all this? And to where?

The phone rang. I picked it up quickly. An editor I knew asked if I was willing to do some temporary work. A couple of his people were out with the flu, and he needed some rewriting done. It would be a couple of days' work.

"I can start right now," I said.

"Come on over."

So, the phone call held me over for two days. I was in an office atmosphere, with other human beings again. I realized my isolation these last six months, during which time the last of my money had drained out, while I sat at home with the stupid screenplay and my other dead projects. This was a real pleasure, sitting at a desk, surrounded by other people, hearing voices and joining in conversation.

And best of all, I got sixty dollars for my work. That wasn't much money considering the work I was doing, but it was money and it came at a perfect time. I tried to talk the editor into a two-hundred-dollar advance, telling him about my car being laid up, but he wouldn't bite, so I took what I could get.

There was another note from the sheriff awaiting me on my second day's return from work, but now I didn't care. I slept well, after taking in a movie, *Women in Love*. It was a dual Ken Russell bill along with *The Devils*, a real bomb. But *Women in Love* was good, and Alan Bates was terrific in it. It lifted me up. Art, life . . .

The next day I got a call inviting me to a preview of a play written by some people I knew over in West Hollywood. Two were young women and the third was a former Broadway character actor down on his luck. They were putting on three one-act plays at the Matrix on Melrose. It was for the following night.

Yes, things were picking up a bit. Money in my pocket again, involvement in art, hearing from creative people I knew. Still, the sheriff's specter haunted me.

Then, finally, that afternoon I heard from Ralph Brundage in New York. His secretary came on to tell me in a snooty voice that Mr. Brundage wished to speak to me; then I heard my agent's voice.

"Hey, what's happening, Tom?"

The voice was so upbeat and friendly it surprised the hell out of me.

"Nothing much," I said.

"Jesus," he said, "we haven't spoken to each other in a long time."

That's right, you prick, I said silently.

"Well, Tom . . . I'm sorry I didn't call earlier. I was out of the country. In England. Spent three weeks there. Just beautiful. You heard from Max Hildendorf?"

"The guy from Kansas City? Yes. What's this all about?"

"It's a long story, really. But he wants to meet you. He has something he wants you to write. It could be very, very big . . . very big for you."

"What do you mean, very big?"

"When I say big, I mean big."

"Who is he anyway?"

"He's a rich businessman who wants a book written and I've suggested you as the writer."

"I see . . ."

"So, time is of the essence because of my trip. I didn't know this was coming up or I wouldn't have taken it, but now time is definitely of the essence. He wants to meet you right away. So, here's what's happening, and you tell me whether or not this is OK with you . . . ready?"

"I'm listening."

"If it's OK with you, Hildendorf will fly out to LA tomorrow. I've already made a reservation. We'll both be in LA by early afternoon. He wants to meet you tomorrow night. We have reservations at the Beverly Wilshire . . . you know where that is?"

"Yes."

"Let's all plan on dinner. Come over and ask for him at six tomorrow."

"Tomorrow night . . . Beverly Wilshire. Can't you tell me more about this?"

"I don't know that much about it. He's going to first tell me about it when we meet in LA. But it's big, believe me."

"Then there's money in it for me?"

"Tons and tons. Believe me, Tom."

"Then I'll see you tomorrow. At six."

"Beautiful." And he hung up.

Before I could even digest all this, I could hear the tread of footsteps coming down the driveway, and there was the sheriff, holding a paper in his hand. This was it. I thought of bolting the door, but that would be a giveaway. I had to hide somewhere.

I could hear him come up the steps. God, he had a heavy tread. Boom boom boom up the steps, and then the pounding on the door.

"Mr. DeWinter . . ."

More pounding.

"Mr. DeWinter."

I didn't move a muscle. I heard him fooling with the knob. He could easily have smashed the door in, but what was the point to that, if I wasn't home. He was putting something on the door . . . another note. . . .

The phone rang. My first instinct was to pick it up, but that would be a giveaway. I let it ring. It rang twelve times, and only after it stopped did the sheriff leave.

That might have been Brundage with more information . . . or maybe canceling the trip, informing me that it was all a joke in the first place, another joke on me. That damn sheriff. Of course if he had come a few minutes before while I was on the phone, that would have been the end of my freedom.

I really had to get out of here, make myself scarce. I started unpacking, till I found my jacket and good pair of blue jeans to match. Then a clean sport shirt, fresh underwear, and my good boots. This was what I'd wear tomorrow night, and I wasn't going to take any more chances. I wasn't going to spend another night in this place. I wanted to meet my benefactor, the mysterious Hildendorf, before I landed in the slammer.

Again the phone rang. I picked it up this time. The sheriff was gone, only the echo of his cloddish footsteps remained.

"Hello," I said very softly.

"Hello, is this Tom?" It was a woman's voice, then I realized it was my former wife.

"Yes."

"Well . . ." The long pause to pour in the guilt.

I didn't say anything and was tempted to hang up, but who knows what this call was all about? Maybe she was getting married again, and called to tell me the good news.

"So, I finally got to you. You have a habit of disappearing."

"I'm right here."

"Did you hear from the sheriff?"

"Yes."

"How come you're not in jail?"

"Because I straightened it all out. I paid half of what I owe. You'll be getting the money any day now."

There was a long silence.

"Are you serious?" she asked.

"Absolutely. I got a nice contract with a studio, and things are chipper, definitely looking up."

"Are you really serious? Is this for real?"

"Absolutely."

Again a stunned silence.

"How is the professor?" I asked, taking the offensive.

"What do you mean, the professor?"

"The man you're living with. Are you still living with the professor?"

"What difference does that make?"

"I'd like to know."

"Yes, I'm still living with Franklin."

"And everything is OK between you?"

"Yes, everything is fine."

"Then why don't you waive the goddamn alimony and let me get on my feet?"

"I don't want to discuss this anymore."

"What did you want to discuss?"

"I wanted to make sure this was your number . . ."

"You wanted to make sure I was hounded by the cops, isn't that so? You wanted to see if I was in jail. Is that why you called?"

"I have a lot of expenses. The bills . . ."

"Well, since the professor is living with you he should provide for you. If he's screwing you, he should at least take care of you. I'm not screwing you anymore, nor do I care to. Nor do I care to support you, do you understand?"

"For God's sake, stop acting like a baby," she said.

"Like a baby . . ." I repeated in a shouting voice.

"All this childish temperament . . . that's the way things are and accept them. Grow up, will you."

"Look," I said, "you sic the cops on me and want me to sit here with my legs crossed taking afternoon tea, thanking you for doing that to me. Well, I'm not going to take this shit lying down. Just don't call me again, and don't bother me anymore."

I slammed down the receiver. I knew later I'd regret all this, but I had to let some of it out. It was all boiling inside me.

I sat for about ten minutes after the stupid call, shaking, then got my energy together to take a shower and change into the clothes I'd wear tomorrow night. I took my electric typewriter and put my manuscripts in the suitcase with my toilet articles, and left the apartment. These were my essentials. I might never go back there again. At least I had the things that were important to me.

5

After I left the apartment I walked down to Santa Monica Boulevard, lugging the suitcase and typewriter. I was tired and sweaty after half a block and stood at the corner. My shoulders were sore and I didn't know where to go. Then I decided to splurge, and I took the bus all the way to West Hollywood, stopping at the Tropicana Motel near La Cienega. I checked into their cheapest room, which was $9.50, and stowed my things. Relieved of that burden, I went into the restaurant downstairs, which I knew to be one of the best eating places in LA, and treated myself to coffee and their homemade carrot cake.

The place was filled with unemployed actors and actresses all talking shop. I knew a couple of them by sight and exchanged hellos. I ate the carrot cake slowly, savoring each bite. I felt homeless without my apartment, and I knew I couldn't last too long in motels, not with my bankroll. Well, whatever was going to happen tomorrow night better be good. Already I was formulating plans. I'd get on the bus to Oregon, if my limited money could buy such a bus ticket. But first I'd see what was going to happen at the Beverly Wilshire.

After killing time over a third cup of coffee, I went over to Larabee Street and rang up my friends there, but they weren't in. Probably at the Matrix Theater setting up things.

Having nothing better to do, I wandered over to the library on San Vincente and sat down and read the latest magazines, looking over the stories and pictures of the celebrities. As far as I could see, none of these people were interesting, but somehow they had caught the public's imagination. There was a story about a writer who had signed a million-dollar deal for his last book, and I knew the book was shit. Jesus, the world was upside down, it was truly a dream world, but I was in it, and that was my main problem.

I knew I was killing time with my life. And right across the street was a sheriff's station, with patrol cars parked all around. But I felt safe. . . . Who would guess that this bookish, nondescript person was in reality a wanted criminal on the bottom rung of life? I sauntered past the station, then crossed the street and went into a nearby playground. A couple of basketball games were going on, and I wished I was wearing sneakers instead of boots; I'd have loved to play.

I watched the games till they broke up; and then I headed for Melrose and took a long walk down toward the Matrix Theater. The plays were going on at eight and I got there about forty-five minutes early, so I bought a late edition of the *Times* and sat and read some of it in the lobby. At eight I went into the theater. There were only about fifteen people in the audience, and I recognized two of them as actors' agents. I sat and watched the three one-act plays.

I rooted for the players and the plays but they were bad.

Absolutely rotten stuff. If I didn't know the people involved I'd have left as did half the audience after the intermission. During the break I heard a woman, who was an agent, telling a friend that she was going to pull her client out of the play that night.

"It'll fuck up his career," she said.

I looked at her, fortyish, tight mouth and eyes surrounded by crow's feet. She needs a good orgasm, I thought, that's what was the matter with her. Probably her motto was "just tread on everyone's dreams."

After the plays ended, I went backstage to look up my friends. They looked harried and unhappy; they knew they had bombed.

"Good seeing you, Tom," said Kurt Johnson, who had been a featured actor on Broadway.

"Fine performances," I said. "Thanks so much for inviting me."

They were busy taking off makeup, and they also had to put away the scenery afterward, and I was in the way, so I stayed only a few minutes. The theater and the lobby were deserted except for the agent and her actor, who had played a young man in the plays but looked much older in street clothes.

She was haranguing him and he listened with his head cocked to one side.

"Look, this will fuck up your career. They're nowheres. They're no-talent people. You got to get out."

"What'll I tell them? They open tomorrow night." His voice had the whinish quality of a child's voice.

"You don't have to tell them anything. I'll take care of it. I'll call them and tell them what I think of their so-called plays."

And they left the theater ahead of me. I walked into the cool LA night and headed back to my motel room. I wished I had brought along the Chekhov books. I wouldn't have

minded reading them tonight, but instead I put the remnants of the LA *Times* under my arm. I'd have to settle for
that.

The Beverly Wilshire is the kind of hotel I hate, because not
only is it fancy but it is ostentatious as well, pukey in the
way that Beverly Hills can be pukey, everything out in the
open, all flash and no depth. I arrived early for my appointment, my goods still stored at the motel. This was going to
be my absolutely last night in the city, because, if nothing
worked out, then I was leaving LA. That was my resolution.
I had already blown twenty dollars on the room, including
taxes. That was enough. Twenty dollars probably repre-
sented a couple of hundred miles by bus, and that was
down the drain. My plans were to leave town as fast as possible, and alternative plans suggested themselves in case
Hildendorf was just full of shit. I was definitely going to put
the touch on my agent in front of him. I needed bus fare
out, or better yet, money for my car. So, that was plan number two.

No need to save face in front of Brundage, since my goal
was to put him right to the wall. I had been humiliated by
his failure to keep in touch. I had no further need of him except for instant money, and I'd wheedle and annoy him till
I got it, and I'd do it right in front of his Kansas City mil-
lionaire.

At six sharp, I went to the front desk and asked them to
ring up Hildendorf. They hemmed and hawed and got his
room, and I got on the phone and introduced myself.

"We'll be right down," he said. I guessed he meant Brundage and himself, so I sat down in an overstuffed chair and
examined my fingers. The fingernails were clean. I had
taken a beautiful hot shower before leaving the motel and
put on my last pair of clean underwear. I was sparkly,
squeaky clean. I sat and waited, looking over the rich types
walking by me, well-dressed men and perfumed, beautiful

women. Somehow I had missed out on this aspect of life. I was denied the grand hotels and the elegant women . . . why? But that was too mind twisting a question to answer on the spot, so I tried to clear my head while waiting. I meditated for a few moments, then I saw my agent, and with him, a sixtyish, stout man, rather tall, who walked with his legs spread apart to better balance his belly. Aha, the fair Hildendorf.

I stood up and was introduced to Max Hildendorf by Brundage. Then the three of us stood awkwardly.

"How about a drink?" suggested Hildendorf. "You're not terribly hungry right now, are you?"

"No," I said.

"I must confess," he said, "because of the time difference, I was famished, so Mr. Brundage and I just had some hors d'oeuvres up in the room."

I walked with them to the hotel bar, and we sat in a semicircular room draped in red. I ordered a bloody mary to keep in touch with the decor, and they ordered martinis.

I could see Hildendorf examining me closely, but I lit a cigarette nonchalantly and took the stares. Finally, after we had been in the bar about five minutes, he broke the silence and spoke.

"Your agent tells me that you're a fine writer," he said, paused and continued, "but you've rather had a run of bad luck."

"You could say that," I agreed.

"I read one of your novels. Ralph took the liberty of Xeroxing it and mailing it to me. Very fine."

"Which one?" I asked.

"*The Mirrored Wall.* Very fine indeed."

Aha, I thought, he wants to publish it. Beautiful.

"Yes, I was very impressed," he continued. "You may be just the man I want."

"Want for what?"

Ralph was leaning back watching me. He had turned

gray and fat in the two years since I had seen him last. His face had that overblown look that big drinkers got when they moved into their forties.

Hildendorf, when he spoke, had rather an English accent or an accent that suggested he had learned English somewhere besides the United States. He looked very rich, with a pinky ring made up of glistening stones, emeralds, and diamonds. That ring would have kept me going for five years.

My question still hadn't been answered when the drinks arrived. Hildendorf raised his glass and gave a toast to the success of our future project together. I drank to that. The bloody mary was classy, with a piece of celery for a stirrer. Vitamin A with my schnapps.

"I know you're curious," he said, "about what I have in mind. First, let me tell you this. I'm in the automobile and real estate businesses. I was one of the early Volkswagen dealers . . . so you see, I was fortunate in my foresight when the car was first introduced into America. Now I'm interested in publishing. Mr. Brundage was kind enough to recommend you for this project."

I drank most of the bloody mary and a waiter materialized and we ordered another round of drinks. I hadn't eaten much that day and was getting a little dizzy from the liquor.

Hildendorf fingered the second martini and paid close attention to it, drained it quickly, and then carefully wiped his mouth. He had a gray mustache, neatly trimmed and clipped, a square mustache, which gave him a rather Prussian look. Then he spoke to me. "Let me ask you, Mr. De-Winter. Have you ever read *Robinson Crusoe?*"

"*Robinson Crusoe?*"

"Yes, the same."

"Sure, I read it. It's a classic, but I must have read it . . . I don't know . . . in college."

"What can you remember about it?"

"It's by Defoe. Daniel Defoe. About a man who's shipwrecked on a desert island in the Pacific, I believe . . . and . . ."

"The Atlantic," interrupted Hildendorf, "in the West Indies, off Brazil. For twenty-eight years."

"For twenty-eight years. Yes." I had some more of the second bloody mary, trying to think of Robinson Crusoe. "Yes, there was another man he found on the island, named Friday. My man Friday, and he became his assistant . . . but I don't remember how it ended."

"That's not too bad. Not too many mistakes. You have a fairly good memory," said Hildendorf. "Actually, he lived alone on the island, and was near the mainland, and there were savages, cannibals, who brought their victims to the island to eat them, and the savage called Friday escaped from them, and Crusoe rescued him. Then they rescued others, and finally a British ship docked nearby with a mutinous crew, and Robinson Crusoe rescued the captain of the ship and the captain took him back to civilization."

"Really?" I said. "I had forgotten all that."

"I continually reread the book. It is one of my most dear possessions, the great novel of Defoe's. You might be interested to know, Mr. DeWinter, that many scholars consider it to be the first novel ever written, the very first. It was published in 1719 when Defoe was sixty years of age."

I took in all this information. Hildendorf was transformed by the story. His eyes lit up . . . the light of true love. Well, what had all this to do with me?

"You might also be interested, and not many people who have read the book remember, that the main character, Robinson Crusoe, refers to himself, not as of English descent but of German descent. Do you recall?"

I shook my head.

"Yes," he continued, "definitely. His family name was actually Kreutznaer, his family having come from Bremen,

which is of course a German city. The name was corrupted
in English to Crusoe. Interesting, what?"

"Very interesting." A third round of drinks was ordered.

"Oh, yes," said Hildendorf, "the book has a long history
and many fascinations. I have read it so many times. I never
tire of his adventures. Imagine, abandoned on a desert island, alone, carrying on by oneself. It sends shivers down
my back to just reread some of the passages. The early life
. . . the shipwreck, his first days on the island. A true masterpiece."

We started on our third drinks, and Hildendorf was off
again on the subject.

"In many ways, I feel similar to Robinson Crusoe. My
name is German by origin, but I was educated in England.
My father brought the family there after the war, that is the
First World War. My uncles, my father's brothers, all became British subjects and changed or corrupted their names
to Helms, to make it sound more English. Interesting,
what?"

I agreed that it was interesting.

"So, that is why we meet," he said to me. "I've spoken to
your agent, and I've read your work, and I think you are
just the man for me."

I was getting the message now. It was slowly seeping in.

"I would have, to tell you the truth, preferred one of my
nephews for this project. I'm a lifelong bachelor you see,
but I have five nephews, two of whom would have been
ideal. But they are not writers, alas, and the important thing
is that this be written. You are a writer, and that makes all
the difference in the world."

By now, the light was shining strongly in my brain.
Robinson Crusoe, desert islands, my agent smirking, this
madman sitting before me. I waited for the proposition.

"I want to publish a book about a modern-day Robinson
Crusoe. You would be the author, but I'd want to go on the

television talk shows and radio shows and present this as my idea. I want to show that my interest in this book has modern implications. It has been my dream for many years, and if it weren't for circumstances beyond my control, which I'll not enter into now, I personally would have relived the adventure. Alas, age has withered me, as the saying goes. It is more for a younger man, a man preferably even younger than you, but you will do very well."

"You want me to go on a desert island?" I asked.

"Yes."

"For twenty-eight years?"

"Oh, no . . . No, my good man, no. Nothing like that. I was thinking for a limited time, and then you would keep a journal and write a book from the journal. Then I would publish it personally and publicize it."

"How long did you have in mind?" I asked.

"Aha, that's the rub and crux of this whole idea. Why don't we have dinner now, Mr. DeWinter, and we'll discuss it over a good meal."

And so we left the bar and took a cab to a French restaurant on the other side of Beverly Hills, and it was there that we went on with this insane idea.

6

"So," said Hildendorf, "I'm curious. How do you support yourself? Are you able to make a living just by writing?"

I thought carefully about my answer. If I said I was desperate, I'd possibly lose any bargaining position in this mad venture; on the other hand, I didn't want to appear affluent, because sure as hell I was going to put the touch on that rat bastard Brundage.

"I do what I can," I said. "I do some free-lance writing and editing, and occasionally have to show up at an office somewhere when times are hard."

Very diplomatic. Hildendorf chewed his pâté thoughtfully.

We had soup next, and then I had veal medallions. The food was altogether too rich for me, since it had been months since I had eaten in a restaurant like this, and I was beginning to feel queasy. After the dishes were cleared, Brundage suggested that we continue the dialogue about Robinson Crusoe.

ABANDONED 41

"You asked me how long you'd have to be on an island?" said Hildendorf. "How long do you think you could stay on an island by yourself?"

"I didn't say I was going on an island by myself," I replied.

"Oh . . ." His gray eyebrows arched. My answer had definitely put a crimp in the conversation.

"Now, Tom," said my agent, "doesn't this idea intrigue you at all?"

"Not what I've heard so far."

"Now, Tom . . ."

I was thinking that I'd ask them for five hundred dollars. I'd ask for money to think it over; option money. All my brain could think about was money now, getting-away money.

Brundage was talking but I faded out on his words, then faded in again.

"Look," the agent said, "we both flew out here to meet you. We're very serious about this project. When I told you over the phone that it was big, I meant big. Mr. Hildendorf has many fine ideas and this is only one of them. With this project, you stand to make a lot of money, a great deal of money, isn't that right, Mr. Hildendorf."

"Well, it's up to the young man."

"Tom, at least listen to what he has to say."

"All right, I'll listen. I didn't say I wouldn't do it. I simply said that I hadn't agreed to do it."

"That is so," said Hildendorf.

"Let me make myself clear," Hildendorf continued. "Not only do I expect to have a fine book to publish, a modern-day classic, but I feel that it could be a motion picture and possibly a series on television. I must confess to you, Mr. DeWinter, that I am not an artist like you. I have artistic pretensions, like so many other men, but basically I am a businessman, an entrepreneur, with hopes of becoming an impresario. Do you understand what I'm getting at."

"Yes, you're trying to give the impression that you're not really in it for the bucks, for the money."

Hildendorf chuckled mirthlessly. "Ah, my good man, you have a wonderful wit, and so penetrating. Right to the core, to the very heart. Yes, well . . ."

He cleared his throat and continued.

"I must confess, I'm a businessman at heart, and although it is a work of art we're talking about here, for I feel that somehow this project will definitely elevate mankind, if you'll forgive my cliché . . ."

He had become so bound up in this wordy bullshit that he lost his trend of thought and had to drink some water to clear his throat and perhaps his mind, once again.

"Anyway, please forgive me. Let me continue. I have on many occasions been approached to invest in motion pictures as a tax shelter . . . it's quite common, as you must know . . . and I've turned them all down. I wasn't interested in them for two reasons. First of all, I didn't intend to support trash on the screen, and secondly, there was no real money to be made, merely a hedge against taxes.

"I'm not one who's interested in losses, tax losses or otherwise. Here, we have an ideal situation. A classic can be made with a project that's very dear to my heart. And, just as well, the project can earn millions. We can all become rich from it. You will have a book and a motion picture screenplay to your credit, and I will produce and have the profits from its distribution, and our mutual friend here, Mr. Brundage, will get ten percent of all we earn.

"And imagine, as we are counting our money, that we will not have given the public another junk picture, but a classic, a modern-day Robinson Crusoe. We will have satisfied the public's taste for quality at the same time that we are gathering in enormous profits for ourselves. And even better, we will do this with a project that no one thinks can be done.

"For, after all, where could one become shipwrecked

these days, completely out of communication with the outside world? It just couldn't happen. Planes go down at sea,
ships still break apart in storms, but due to modern com-
munications the whole world watches and knows. Just the
other evening I was watching the television news and the
announcer was discussing a shipwreck off Madagascar.
Imagine that. In the eighteenth century, how would anyone but the shipwrecked sailor know what was happening.
Today, with radio, with telecommunications, with satellite
pictures . . . with airplanes, I could go on and on, but I
don't want to bore you with information you already know;
it's just impossible."

The long speech had left him breathless. He drank some
iced water, and then a glassful of the fine Pinot Chardonnay
he had ordered, and wiped his mouth and mustache carefully with a starched napkin.

"And of course," he continued abruptly, "there are the
shipping lanes and the air lanes practically encircling the
world. Yes, everyone thinks that a modern-day Robinson
Crusoe is impossible."

"Is it impossible?" I asked.

"Aha, such a fine question . . . yes, that is the crux of the
situation . . . I repeat myself, forgive me . . . but when I
first thought of this project, that was my first concern. But I
solved it. I know an island . . . you see. I have an island,
isolated, out of reach, uninhabited, containing fresh water.
In other words, ideal."

"Where is it?"

Mr. Hildendorf smiled. "That's the rub, you see. I've been
on the island; I've inspected it, but I won't disclose its
whereabouts, because that is where the modern-day adventure will take place."

"Let me ask you something, why have you selected me?
Why couldn't you put an ad in a newspaper or national
magazine? There are many writers . . . you'd get an overwhelming response to an ad."

"Yes, don't think I haven't thought about that," said my host. "But unfortunately, such an advertisement would attract publicity, and though I want publicity, it is not for now. Publicity will be very helpful after the project is complete; I don't want to interview a few hundred people and let the word out on what I intend to do. For the present we must keep this just between us. Now, assuredly, I don't know what your decision will be, sir, but if it is negative, I would assume you'd keep this confidential. Do I have your word on that?"

"Yes," I said, thinking again that this was another opportunity to ask for money.

"I know that you are a man of your word. Mr. Brundage has vouched for you and, I might add, has only the highest respect for you."

My agent nodded sagely, sipping wine, as if his goddamn opinion meant anything to me.

"Now," said Hildendorf, "our little talk has gone afield. . . ."

By this time, we were handed dessert menus. Both of my overweight companions avoided the dessert, but I ordered chocolate mousse and espresso.

"You asked me how long you'd have to spend on the island? Right?"

"Right."

"You're still interested, I assume."

"Absolutely," I said.

"Good. Well, to tell you the truth, it has been a problem that I haven't solved, just how long such an undertaking should be. Ideally, it should be for many, many years, but of course, how could I get anyone for that, and anyway . . . there is the factor of age. I'm not a young man. I don't want this book published when I'm a doddering old man. I was thinking in terms of a few years."

"Three years?" I asked.

"Three years, yes. Or even two years. Two years to four years. Two years as a minimum and four years as a maximum length of time. I have felt, with my conditions . . . that is, conditions I will present as essential, that we would create the same kind of isolation that Robinson Crusoe endured."

"Two to four years," I repeated.

"Yes, exactly. In complete isolation. So, you see, we're not talking about that much time. Two years, they fly by, nowadays. You turn around and a decade is gone, and you don't even know where it went. It's been thirty years since I opened my first automobile agency, and let me tell you, my dear Mr. DeWinter, I don't know where those years have fled to."

I thought to myself, two years. Two years didn't sound that bad. Two years away from this so-called civilization. But what were the conditions? I posed the question.

"Complete, and I mean, complete isolation," said my host. "The island, and this is all I'll disclose about it, is in the tropics. It is uninhabited, near no other island, on no shipping or air lane, has fresh water and some vegetation. There are some palm trees and other tropical trees. Some plants grow wildly, but I don't know if they're edible. You see, what I have in mind . . ."

We were interrupted by the coffee and my mousse. I spooned some and let it melt in my mouth as he spoke.

"As I was saying. Isolation. You would spend the required time alone on the island. During that time, you'd not only see no other person, but you would have no way of reaching the outside world."

"No radio," chimed in Brundage.

"That's right, no radio, no wireless, no way whatsoever to contact anyone."

"What about an emergency?" I asked.

Hildendorf shrugged.

"I mean, a medical emergency."

"No outside contact. You would definitely have to give up that option."

"So, if I had an appendicitis or a heart attack, I would be finished."

"Yes."

"Or a gall bladder attack, anything like that. I'd be a goner."

"Yes."

"You wouldn't allow a radio just in case, and used only in that event."

"No. There's no point then in the whole undertaking. The man must feel absolutely and irrevocably, for that time span, isolated, helpless, and alone. He must fend for himself and hope for the best."

"And pray he doesn't get a burst appendix," I said.

"Why, Mr. DeWinter, are you in poor health?"

"No. I'm in good health."

"I assume you have your appendix."

"Yes. And my tonsils. I have everything I was born with."

"I would think," he said, "that a physical would be a prerequisite, for your sake, before you undertook this project," and he quickly added, "of course, if you do decide to undertake it."

"That would be wise," I agreed.

"So . . ." He paused, as if to collect his thoughts. "Where was I? Yes. No communication . . . you would be completely isolated without any hope of seeing anyone during that time, or in any way communicating with anyone. Then, there's the matter of supplies and provisions. If you recall, Robinson Crusoe got many supplies from the ship, which was foundering in the bay offshore, and he spent about two weeks taking what he could. You would also have supplies. Food, shelter, tools, whatever you needed."

"Robinson Crusoe had animals on the island, if I remember," I said.

"Yes, a good point. There are no animals on this island, however. It's much smaller than the one that he was on. Just a matter of economics. It's hard to find many uninhabited islands of that size nowadays. But you could take a pet with you, a dog or cat or bird. There are probably birds that visit the island, but there were none when I was on it last."

"When was this?" I asked.

"Oh, let's not discuss that aspect. Suffice it to say I've been there recently."

"So," I said, "I'd have provisions, food, tools, and a pet."

"Yes. What more would you need?"

"Books. Things to amuse myself with."

"Like what?"

"A chess set. I love to play chess."

"That would be all right." He paused while the waiter filled his cup with more coffee, then he asked me if I cared for a brandy. I asked for a grand marnier, and he ordered cognac for himself and Brundage. Brundage was sitting all the while in silence, turning his head from side to side as either one of us spoke. His eyes were half shut. He looked in terrible condition.

"You must remember," said Hildendorf, "that, though this is the modern era, I wouldn't want any electrical or electronic gear on the island. You'd have fishing gear, also can openers and such things. But nothing run by electricity or batteries."

"What about weapons?"

"Weapons?" That shook Brundage awake.

"Yes. Robinson Crusoe had muskets and sidearms and a sword I believe. He walked around that island well armed."

"But . . ." said Hildendorf, then he closed his mouth and sat in contemplation. "Of course . . . that would be all right. Dangers may crop up. To be unarmed would be foolish and Robinson Crusoe's weapons were important to the story, when the rescue came. What would you want?"

"A rifle, pistols, a few good knives and ammunition."

"What kind of rifle?"

"An M-16, I have a fondness for that weapon. And a .45 and a .38 with a long barrel."

"You know something about weapons, then?"

"Something. Yes, from the army."

"Aha. All right, that would be agreeable. How much ammunition?"

"Several hundred rounds."

"Yes, agreeable."

Now it was Brundage's turn to speak. "Tom, what do you now say to the project?"

"I don't know. I'm just finding out things. But we haven't discussed,"—and here I was about to say "the most important part," but I held myself back from being overly concerned with money. So I simply said, "another important aspect of this project, and that is my payment."

"Ah yes, I was about to bring it up, Mr. DeWinter."

I had more coffee and waited as he stared down, thinking. I felt he was putting on an act, because this must have been thoroughly discussed with Brundage.

"Here's what I have in mind. If you stay two years, you will receive fifty thousand dollars. And an additional twenty-five thousand for every other year you care to stay on. If you stay the full four years, you'd get one hundred thousand dollars."

Well, the number was out of the box. I stared at him.

"Are you serious?" I asked.

"Why do you ask that?"

"I'm going to be isolated; I'm going to risk death; and for the same money any junior corporation executive can make in America?"

"All your provisions and supplies would be paid for. You'd live rent free and food free for the time."

"Rent free in what?"

"A tent."

"Wonderful. No, it's out of the question." Now I was ready for my pitch to Brundage for the money. "Ralph, I'd like to speak to you for a moment."

Hildendorf took this to mean I wanted to discuss something about this project with my agent in private, because he excused himself and said he had to go to the men's room. So there I was alone, without my trump card, Hildendorf, when I made the pitch.

Brundage shook his head after we were alone. "I think you're making a big mistake, Tom."

"Why is that?"

"That money would be just front money. You'd share in royalties, in movie and TV rights, and he'd take you along with him around the country when he publicizes the book. It would be great publicity. It would make you a celebrity, a world-wide celebrity."

"If I didn't have appendicitis on the island."

"That's a very remote possibility."

"But it could happen. Anything can happen."

"Well, what do you have in mind?"

"I'll think it over, and make a counter-offer if I'm interested. And that's also a remote possibility. This guy may just be a nut for all I know."

"He's very serious about this."

"Did you work out these figures with him?"

"No. I couldn't get any numbers out of him at all."

"Why'd you think of me for this project?"

"Well, I know you've had some hard luck."

"How did you know?"

"I'm your agent, and I know you're getting nothing big published."

"Yes, you would know. Anyway, before he comes back, Ralph, I need some money. I'm broke right now. I don't want him to know, but I'm tapped out."

"I really am in no position to help you."

"What do you mean, you're in no position? I'm flat broke. I need just a couple of hundred bucks."

"That's out of the question."

"Is it? Then this whole fucking project is out of the question. I won't even think about it. And when our mutual friend comes back, I'll tell him why. Because I have an agent who's so cheap he won't lend a client a lousy two hundred. Jesus, man, you think I'd ask you if I wasn't flat out? I haven't heard from you in a year and I never bothered you. I'm busted . . . fuck it. Just fuck it."

That's how matters stood when Hildendorf came back to the table. I sat glumly, and Brundage sat just as glumly. Hildendorf immediately sensed the change.

"What's the problem?" he asked.

"There's just one problem," I said. "And that's money. I think your terms are too low, and I'm going to think it over. But I'll need some option money. I want you to give me twenty-four hours, till tomorrow night to think it over, and I want you to give me five hundred dollars to make up my mind. If I accept, you'll apply it to the payment. If not, it's mine."

"What is this?" Hildendorf asked Brundage. "I never heard of anything like this before."

"I don't know," said my agent lamely.

"I just don't understand. What does this mean . . . option money? Just to think things over? I never heard of it."

"Forget about it, then. I better be going." I stood up.

"Wait a moment," said Hildendorf. "Does this mean you're not interested at all?"

"Take it any way you like. Let my agent tell you all about it."

"Tom, now take it easy," said Brundage. "Just take it easy. Let me talk to Mr. Hildendorf for a moment, would you. Alone. Why don't you come back in five minutes. OK?"

"No, I'd rather not right now. I better be going. Thanks for dinner," I told Hildendorf.

"For God's sake, Tom, take it easy."

"Well, so long."

"Tom, I'll call you at the apartment later," said Brundage.

"I'm not there anymore."

"Where are you staying?"

"At the Tropicana Motel. But I don't have a phone in my room."

"The Tropicana? Where's that?"

"On Santa Monica, near La Cienega."

"Look, let's have breakfast tomorrow. I'll come by at nine, is that OK?"

"All right. I'm in room four." I said good-bye to Hildendorf and left the restaurant. I was anxious to get back to the motel and think about my future plans. I walked over to Santa Monica Boulevard and waited for a bus, seething. Those cheap bastards. Those cheap, lousy bastards.

7

I was already dressed when Brundage arrived the next morning. He had come fifteen minutes early, and I opened the door and stepped out. The room I occupied was dark and the bed unmade. I had been up half the night, restless and thinking. Thinking about the money offered and about Hildendorf's proposition, at turns accepting and rejecting it. It's so easy at 3 A.M., in a desolate lonely room, broke and sleepless, to think of any proposition as wonderful. In the cold light of day, however, things look much different.

Brundage was dressed in a sporty outfit, without a tie, dressing down to my level, I supposed. I had on the same outfit I had been wearing for the last three days, ever since I left the apartment. My blue pants were creased and had a couple of stains on them. My jacket was wrinkled and my shirt was starting to stink. I had until noon to renew the room for another day, and I knew I'd have to make my decision before then. Accept a crazy plan, or somehow scheme to get money out of these two. I'd see what happened.

Brundage had leased a car, a shiny new Ford, and we drove back to Beverly Hills, to Wilshire. There was a coffee house near the hotel and we went in and sat in a booth. All this time, during the trip, Brundage never shut his mouth. He told me a long rambling story of the last time he had been in town and met a starlet and screwed her. I sat frozen lipped next to him, not commenting.

Once in the restaurant, we ordered our breakfasts. I ordered pancakes and Canadian bacon, and Brundage had a bowl of Special K, with skimmed milk.

"Well," he said, watching me as I lit a cigarette after the first taste of coffee, "I must say, despite what happened, you made a distinct impression upon Hildendorf."

"What kind of impression?"

"He liked you. He told me you were a man of spirit."

"No shit."

"I just don't understand you, Tom. You think I would have flown out here, or had Hildendorf fly out here on a fool's errand. We have a big deal here. We can wrap up a really big deal. And when I say big, I'm talking mucho money."

"What? Twenty-five Gs for every year I rot on some crummy island."

"Don't worry about that number anymore, OK? We're going to get you more. Here's the deal. We get fifty percent of all motion picture and TV deals, and seventy-five percent of all paperback resales and book club resales. And . . ."

"Look, Ralph, don't jerk me off, OK? First of all, before we talk about this madness, I want to ask you a couple of questions."

"Shoot," he said.

"First of all, I don't hear from you for a whole year or more. You do nothing to promote any kind of work for me. Nothing. Now, suddenly you're here with some nut . . ."

"He's serious, I told you."

"All right. I've been thinking. Why me? You knew what my situation was, didn't you? Otherwise you wouldn't have bothered with me."

"I don't get what you're driving at, Tom."

"Look, any writer in his right mind would tell you and your friend to fuck off. But you knew I'm not in my right mind. I'm in a bad bind. The only way you could have known this is by speaking to my former wife."

"Tom . . ."

"Right? Come on, level with me."

"All right. Yes. She called me a few months ago, and wanted to know if I heard from you, and where you were. I didn't tell her anything, then she went into a long song and dance about how you were in arrears, and she was taking legal action against you. Then she called again last month, with the same tune."

"So here I was, you figured, someone ripe for this nut."

"Why do you keep calling him a nut?"

"What is he then, with this Robinson Crusoe bullshit?"

"He's what he said he was, a businessman. He has big ideas for this project, that's why I'm telling you, you're foolish to turn it down. He's talking big bucks. He's talking about a million-dollar deal here."

"A million dollars for whom? Not for me."

"Tom, take it easy. Listen to me, hear me out first. Look, you met the guy. He's no idiot. All he knows how to do is make money. He's swimming in money. And he wants more. He sees this as a way to make millions, to make himself a power in the entertainment world, to produce a whole string of pictures, to get his own studio. Listen to me, Tom, he had me up all night. I've been listening to his dreams for the last month.

"There are millions to be made, according to him. He can smell money and power a mile away. And you go along with him, Tom. You'll do the book and then the screenplay.

You'll be on his payroll for a couple of thousand a week after this deal is over."

"So far I haven't seen a fucking penny."

"Be patient. You were picked by him, and these deals take time."

"The point is, he didn't pick me. You picked me because I'm desperate. What established writer is going to drop everything to live on a goddamn desert island alone and risk his life?"

"All right, you're in a bad spot, Tom. But I can't get a guy making a hundred grand a year for this. On the other hand, look at it this way. I need a good writer. You're a good writer."

"No kidding. When did you come to that conclusion?"

"I always had faith in you."

"Bullshit."

"Say whatever you want. Don't take it, then."

"It all sounds crazy to me, Ralph. Being paid to sit on a goddamn island for two years . . . and you talk about a million-dollar deal."

"No, you're all wrong, Tom. You're not going to be paid for sitting on an island. You're going to be paid for writing a good book about those years on the island. That's the essence of the deal. If you write a lousy book, there's going to be just pennies in this for everyone. You won't get much, Hildendorf will get nothing, and I'll get nothing."

"What are you talking about?"

"Just this. I was up with him till five this morning, getting the deal put together. And it's a good deal. All right, first, let's talk about money. You're going to get fifty thousand dollars for each year you stay on the island. Fifty big ones. That's his new offer."

I leaned back and took a deep breath. These were numbers that sounded interesting for once. Two years, one hundred grand. Freedom. Escape from problems; a villa in Europe; space, movement, freedom. Freedom.

"So, if you even stay the minimum two years, that's one hundred grand for you. Plus, he's paying for all the equipment and food for the two years, and getting you there and back again. That's a damn good deal, Tom. And that's not all."

"Go on."

"I know your problems. You have to pay all that money for alimony. For the two years you'd be away, that's what . . . close to ten thousand or so? He's agreed to put the money in my bank account, and the interest, on a two-year certificate of deposit, will easily cover your payments and give you some money besides when you get back. So, in essence, you're getting all these things . . . it's a terrific deal. And Tom, forget about the book. There's going to be a film here; that's definite. That's where the big bucks are, and he wants to make the big ones. And that means a screenplay. And you're going to have the first crack at it. Another hundred grand against a percentage of the gross on the film. You'll be made, Tom. You'll be one famous fucking writer after all this is done. It's a sure movie or TV sale. It's going to be one or the other. It can't miss. A mini series on TV or a feature movie. But he's going to push it for a movie first. And we get a big percentage of the gross against one hundred grand for the screenplay.

"It's terrific no matter how you look at it. If you don't want it, I swear, I'll get someone else. And one day, when it all breaks, and you're still grinding out magazine copy, you'll say, that could have been me."

I sat and absorbed what he had said. Jesus, it sounded good right now. I could come out of this with a million dollars if it was played right.

Brundage's words interrupted my thoughts. "But the main thing is, Tom, you can't go there and play with yourself. You're going to have pens and paper and pencils . . . reams of supplies. You have to produce a good book, a modern-day *Robinson Crusoe*. You ought to read the book again."

"Now what?" I asked.

"What do you mean?"

"Suppose I agree . . ."

"Well, he has the contracts all drawn. You sign and it's a deal."

"When would I leave?"

"Within the week."

"Within the week? That soon?"

"That's it. That's why we're both on the West Coast. He doesn't want any advance publicity. He wants it done fast. And remember, Tom, it has to be a good book. The deal is based on his accepting the book. If he turns it down, you're not getting any hundred grand."

"Wait a minute. What's this, now?"

"If he turns down the book, and he can't be unreasonable about it, and we have the right to hire an impartial editor to dispute it, you're going to get $25,000 for your time on the island, period. I want you to know that. Know it right now."

"That doesn't sound good."

"Listen, Tom, it's OK. Just write your usual book. He likes your work, and I have faith in you. And the biggest thing we have going for us is he loves this concept. He loves it. He wants to publish it. He's got nothing but money, and he'd rather put money into this than into anything else. Remember, he'll deposit the money with me, in a special account. We'll have his dough. You just write a decent book and we're in."

"Let me go back and think about it. And Ralph, I'm out of money. I need money for the motel room for another night."

He took some bills out of his wallet.

"Here's a hundred dollars. Keep it. It's not even a loan. And remember what I said, Tom. It's a tremendous opportunity for you. It's the biggest thing that could fall into your lap."

"OK, I'll really think it out."

"When will you make your decision?"

"I'll let you know by four o'clock."

"That's fair. You want me to pick you up?"

"No, I'll come by the hotel. If I decide yes, then what?"

"We sign the papers, and he'll then explain everything to you. You'll decide what you want on the island, and within a week, you'll be there."

"It's crazy, you know," I said, as he paid the check at the cashier's.

Brundage shrugged and put his arm around me. "We're going to be millionaires from this, Tom. If that's crazy, then it's crazy."

I paid for still another night at the motel with Brundage's money. Then I counted my assets. I had about $105 to my name. I walked out of the motel office and looked up the Greyhound number in the phone book, but didn't dial it. Instead I went to my room and lay on the bed, putting my hands underneath my head, thinking. I thought of the new proposition. A hundred thousand dollars. Jesus, that was a lot of money. That was a fortune to me right now. I guess I'd be paying taxes on the money, but for the last few years I had practically no income and I knew I could income average the money and still have about sixty or seventy thousand to my name. Maybe a little less.

Then I'd take off for Europe, out of reach of sheriffs and my former wife. And that might not be all the money I'd make on this deal. Ralph was right. If there was enough publicity, it could be very, very big. I might be set for the rest of my life. For once I'd be welcome at the fancy hotels; I'd have the elegant women and everything I ever wanted and craved in my life. And all for two years on an island by myself.

Well, even that could be an adventure. I wasn't much of
an outdoors person. Other than the Army experience, I had
camped overnight a few times with friends, but I was basically a city person, having lived in cities most of my life.
Still, it could be a great adventure. I'd have fishing gear, I'd
have rifles and ammunition, a tent . . . I could write the
Robinson Crusoe story and also write another novel at the
same time.

And there was another intriguing aspect. Two years by
myself. It was a terrific opportunity to get myself in perfect
shape. I could exercise every day, running and swimming. It
was a good chance to harden my body, really lose weight
and be in perfect condition. I'd take no candies or sweets
with me, or tobacco either. I'd come off that island a new
man, strong and lean and in top shape.

Yes, that was the good part of it. The other side was . . .
well, what would I be missing? First of all, women. Other
human contact. Well, I could do without them for two
years. It wasn't as if I would be in solitary confinement. I'd
have an island to roam around on. And a pet. I liked cats.
But a dog sounded better. A good trained dog would be
perfect.

The one bad thing was the medical situation. What if I
got sick, or got some internal attack? I'd be finished. But I
was in good health, relatively speaking. I had a couple of flu
attacks, but in the last five years I'd been almost free of
sickness. I could take along medicines . . . Aureomycin,
penicillin. Alcohol. Aspirins, codeine in case of pain. Maybe
even morphine . . . if I could get hold of that. And Valium.
That would be it. I'd have to carefully think of what I
needed.

I went down and had some coffee and carrot cake in the
restaurant. I lingered there, thinking of what medicines and
drugs I'd need. Maybe I'd get a physical and ask the doctor
who examined me for a few prescriptions. That would be

wise. I'd also ask Hildendorf. He probably had connections and could get me whatever I wanted.

At four o'clock I was back at the Beverly Wilshire. I rang Hildendorf's room and he told me to come right up.

He had a two-bedroom suite, one bedroom occupied by Brundage. They greeted me cordially, and Hildendorf offered me a whiskey, which I accepted.

"Well," he finally said, after we were seated, with the drinks in front of us, "have you made your decision?"

"Yes," I said, "the answer is yes."

Hildendorf smiled. He raised the glass. "To our venture, to excitement and adventure and riches."

I drank to all that.

8

To tell the truth, the decision to accept was a great relief to me. It was as though a load had been taken from my mind, and now I could look forward to an adventure. Instead of the aimless life I was leading, there was now purpose. I had a book to write; I would be transported to a secret island; I would be starting on a marvelous adventure, a unique undertaking.

I drank a second glass of cognac, and Hildendorf produced a sheaf of papers. The average book contract is no more than four pages in length, and though I hadn't signed any, I had seen a few in my time, dangled in front of me, only to be snatched away at the last moment.

This contract was much more intricate. I read it over carefully at first, but after a couple of pages of legalese, I started skimming. The essential points caught my attention. I was to receive $50,000 for each year I was on the island, and the number of years was fixed at two. The $100,000 was to be given to my agent this very day to be deposited in a special escrow account, subject to the following provisions. First, I was to produce a book of not less than 80,000 words, based on a journal I was to keep on the island. That upon completion of my two-year stay, I was to be given $25,000 at once, with the additional money to be given to me, as follows: $50,000 more upon acceptance of the manuscript, and $25,000 upon publication.

I objected to this clause, and it was rewritten. I wanted the $75,000 upon acceptance of the manuscript. Whether or not he published it was Hildendorf's business. I would have done my work by that time, and would have given up two years of my life in solitary confinement, as it were. So, this change was agreed upon.

Also, the interest on the monies deposited for the two years was to belong to me, so that, in essence, even if I didn't produce a word of copy, I would make $39,000 for my two years on the island.

The other matters were quickly disposed of. I was to, as agreed, receive 50 percent of both TV and motion picture monies, plus $100,000 for the screenplay if a movie was to be made. Also 75 percent of the paperback sales and book club sales. And Hildendorf agreed to spend at least $50,000 in publicizing the work.

So far so good. The next item was both interesting and time consuming. What was I to take with me on the island? This was to be written out and agreed upon. All equipment, food, and supplies of any kind, including transportation to and from the island, were to be furnished and paid for by Hildendorf.

We started listing the weapons. One M-16 rifle or equivalent with 300 rounds of ammunition. One .45 automatic, magazine loaded, with 100 rounds. One .38 revolver with six-inch barrel and 100 rounds of ammunition. Also, oil and cleaning supplies for the weapons. That much was easy.

Then, other things. I was to get a variety of knives—

bowie, hunting, and otherwise—six in all, plus an oiled whet-stone to keep the knives sharpened. Agreed upon easily.

One pair of binoculars, 35 power. One telescope, 100 power. One magnifying glass. Four pairs of sunglasses, polaroid type, both optic gray and green. So much for the optical equipment.

Clothing came next. I wanted several hats, including a pith helmet. I needed both cool and warm clothing. Jeans were included, as well as fatigue pants, shirts of all types, sweaters, down and leather jackets, and a pea coat. Boots and sneakers, and thirty pairs of assorted socks. All easily agreed upon.

Hildendorf and I went over the items, and Brundage wrote them down on a pad. We had another round of drinks, and were very serious. These decisions were final. What I forgot now, I might not remember within the week, and once on the island, it might be too late.

One animal. I decided to get a German shepherd to be my companion. We would select him the following day.

Writing supplies. I'd pick them out myself. I wanted notebooks, plenty of pencils and ballpoint pens, plus a good Parker 61 fountain pen and a dozen bottles of blue-black permanent ink. Hildendorf told me he'd give me cash to get whatever of these supplies I needed.

While we were on the subject, he told me I'd be limited to five books for my stay. I tried to talk him into more, but he was adamant. That number had been on his mind for years.

"Do you want me to tell you what I want now?"

"No. You have a week to pick them out."

This was a Thursday. "When will I be leaving?" I asked.

"Wednesday night. That is takeoff time. You should be ready to leave by five P.M. on Wednesday. So you have time to think about the books you want."

"All right. Will I buy them?"

"If you like. The more you can select and buy yourself, the easier it will be for me."

"Fair enough. Five books, then."

"Yes. And one other thing. No books that are primarily picture books of people. If there are illustrations that are incidental, that's all right. Otherwise, whatever you want to take, you may. And by a book, I mean just that. One book. You can't pick a set of encyclopedias, for example. Is that clear?"

"Fair enough."

"Put down vitamins," I told Brundage. "I don't want to forget vitamins."

The idea of making these lists was exciting me. Here I was, finally, master of what I'd be wearing and reading and eating for the next two years, all picked out in advance.

After going over pots and pans and other cookware, we finally got down to the basic item, food.

"Any limitations?" I asked.

"Not really," said Hildendorf. "We don't expect you to pick caviar and pâté de foie gras, things like that. A can of pâté would be all right, but you know what I mean."

"Well, I've made a decision," I said. "This will be a perfect opportunity for me to give up a lot of crap. I'm not going to take any junk food or chocolate or sweets with me."

"You could take some," said Hildendorf. "An occasional piece of chocolate would be good."

"No, I'll get that sugar out of my system once and for all. When you see me after two years, you'll see a man in top condition, healthy, perfect weight, all muscle and bone."

"Beautiful," said my agent.

"Yes, so no chocolates or sweets of any kind. And no cigarettes."

"Beautiful."

"And what about coffee and tea?"

"Yes, I want that. But I'll limit myself. We can get teabags and instant coffee, right?"

"Without sugar, though," Ralph said.

"Absolutely."

"What kind of coffee?" my agent asked.

"I want . . . let's say, Taster's Choice and Yuban instant. Enough to last two years. And tea . . . some herb teas . . . Orange Spice, Lemon Mint, Jasmine. Earl Grey, Darjeeling, Oolong, and some regular tea. That will cover it. Enough again for two years."

"We're going to give you two and a half years' supply of everything," said Hildendorf, "just to be on the safe side."

"Wonderful," I said.

"Now for food. Most of it, Mr. DeWinter, will be canned and packaged, you understand."

"Yes."

"You will have fishing gear and snorkeling equipment, if you want, so you can supplement your food supply with fresh fish."

"I'm not familiar enough with that equipment to buy it," I said.

"I'll take care of it," said Hildendorf.

I agreed he would select that equipment.

"I'd want a chess set and chessboard."

"You pick one out, then," he said. "Now back to food."

He asked me what I didn't want to eat.

"No cakes or pastries or anything like that. I'd want dried fruits. I like dried apricots, dried pears, dried peaches, dried papaya, and dried pineapple, raisins, but none with sugar added."

"I can arrange to get that, in equal amounts. All right?"

"Yes, that would be fine, Mr. Hildendorf."

"Now for more staple things. Do you want dried milk?"

"No. Something like Coffeemate for my coffee would be fine. I never drink milk."

"And canned meats. Any preference?"

"I don't want things like pigs feet. Mostly meat that is un-adulterated if possible. Also canned vegetables and dried soup mixes, a lot of those, but none with an excess of salt."

"All right. What about salt and spices."

"Salt, pepper, mustard . . . I don't think ketchup will keep. Yes, they come in individual packets. Ketchup also. I'm not much for spices."

"Canned fruits."

"Yes, things like canned pineapple in its own juice. Nothing in syrup. A wide choice of that."

"What else?"

"I don't know. Let's see. We go from appetizer to soup to main course . . . canned tunafish. Bumble Bee tuna, solid in oil. And plenty of can openers and bottle openers."

"You won't be having any bottles, really. Unless you want cans of soda."

"No."

"Liquor?"

"I'm not much of a drinker. But I would like an assortment. Maybe a mixed case of drambuie, grand marnier, amaretto, and cointreau."

"Three bottles of each?"

"Yes."

"Hard liquor?"

"Uh . . . no. All right. Maybe a bottle of Johnny Walker scotch, black label."

"You have exceedingly good and expensive tastes in liquor," Hildendorf said.

"Well, that's because I'm not a drinker. What about glasses and cups and forks and knives and such."

"We'll give you that. Instead of glasses, we'll give you cups, all right?"

"Yes, and a canteen or two for water."

"Yes, that would be important."

"And a compass."

"A compass?"

"Why not?"

"The island is small."

"But in my description of storms and events, I'd want to know the right bearings."

"Yes, a good point. All right, a good compass."

"And an ammunition belt, holsters . . ."

"All right."

The list was mounting up. Brundage had to stop and shake his hand.

"Matches, lamps . . ."

"All right. We'll give you two storm lamps and a supply of kerosene for them, but that's all. And you'll have a tent, which I've already selected. It will be quite spacious and allow you to walk underneath it. Leave that to me. And I'll supply you with air mattresses, a couple of hammocks, and two sleeping bags."

"All right."

"Have we forgotten anything?" asked Hildendorf.

We decided to go down to dinner and then resume the list making when we came back, with full bellies and clearer minds.

This time we ate at a Chinese restaurant on West Pico. The food was extraordinarily good for Chinese food in LA, and during the meal, I thought of how I'd miss food like this. Ethnic meals. Chinese and Japanese, French and Italian, and even Jewish hot dogs. But this deprivation was all very minor compared to the money I'd be getting. A hundred thousand dollars was a sum I could only imagine having. I studied Hildendorf during the meal. He had become much more relaxed and affable, but my main thoughts were about why he had money and I didn't. Why did the money-makers rule everything and the artists nothing but their own bankruptcy petitions?

It was a futile line of thinking, I knew. This had gone on from time immemorial. Mozart turned into a lackey, Rem-

brandt went into debt, Van Gogh was driven to insanity
. . . it was nothing new, and I wasn't even comparing myself to those giants, but I was an artist anyway.

When Hildendorf went to the bathroom, I asked Ralph
about taking care of my pressing debts, mainly the two
thousand in arrears to my former wife.

"That's a big nut," he said.

"Couldn't you speak to Hildendorf about it?"

"I suppose so. I'll ask for authorization to take care of it.
I'll do it right away. After all, the papers are signed and he's
happy that you're going through with this."

"I have some other judgments against me," I said.

"Let them wait. They can wait, can't they?"

"I guess so. OK. But I want to leave with a clear mind."

When Hildendorf came back to the table, it was dessert
time. We all had ice cream and fortune cookies. My fortune
was the usual nonsense and I crumpled it up and threw it
away.

"Mr. Hildendorf," said my agent. "Tom has one pressing
bill that he'd like to have taken care of before he leaves.
It's a matter of two thousand dollars for his wife . . . alimony payments. I wonder if I could take that out of the
monies you gave me so that it could be paid as soon as possible."

"No problem. When are you going to deposit the checks?"

"When I get back to New York."

"I'll give you written authorization for that. No problem
at all."

I took a deep breath. That really cleared up matters for
me. I could leave with a somewhat clear conscience. Now
there was the matter of Phyllis' apartment. There was no
way I was going to return there and risk arrest. I'd call
Phyllis and then ask her if Merle could sell off her things.
That should be no problem at all. If there was any loss, I'd
make it up when I returned, flush with money.

After supper, we returned to the hotel and went up to

Hildendorf's suite. Back to business. The lists were gone
over and additions made, notably in the way of waterproof
clothes, blankets, bags, and containers: The papers had to
be protected during a storm, and the supplies as well. That
was no problem, Hildendorf repeated. Nothing was a problem anymore. Things just sailed along smoothly.

It was finally agreed that I should buy all kinds of drug
supplies, but Hildendorf, through a local contact, would get
me the medicines. And I was to have a physical as soon as
possible. He had lined up a physician for that purpose and
the appointment was for the next morning. Hildendorf gave
me the doctor's card and told me not to eat breakfast, for
there were going to be a lot of tests taken.

I was also going to buy my books and supplies for writing, the chess set, and various other things. The food, I now
found out, was already on order from a wholesaler in the
LA district, and would be shipped out to await us on the island. Things were moving along rapidly.

The evening came to a close. Hildendorf took out his wallet and peeled off five hundred-dollar bills.

"This is for your supplies."

I thanked him, pocketing the money.

"Keep whatever balance there is," he said. "Do what you
want with it."

I again thanked him and got to my feet. We shook hands
all around and I went downstairs and ordered a cab. I got
back to the motel in fifteen minutes.

While there, I relaxed and thought about things. There
must have been items and provisions I forgot. What were
they? I couldn't think clearly. Too much food and too much
cognac. I knew I'd have to notify people of my leaving. And
I had to be sure and tell my mother about my trip, and ask
her to call my agent if she didn't hear from me within two
years. That was essential. And I should notify other people
as well.

But it was ten o'clock LA time, and that meant one in the morning in Florida. I'd call tomorrow. I undressed and went to sleep, and for the first time in weeks, slept a peaceful, deep, restful sleep.

9

The next morning I took the bus over to Century City for my doctor's appointment. I was kept waiting in the office for almost an hour, consuming *Time* and *Newsweek* and *Vogue* magazines. I realized that one of the things I would be relieved of during my island stay would be the news of the world. What difference would it all make to me? It was so stupid, unimportant, and dull anyway. I closed my eyes and waited my turn.

The doctor was an older man, who, if I didn't know he was a doctor, I'd have sworn was a tailor; he just had that look. He sat me down and asked me about my general health, took my blood pressure, pulse, examined my heart, checked me out for rectal cancer, and then drew blood, had me urinate into an immaculately white plastic container.

"Your blood pressure is a little high. Not that high but a little high."

"What is it?"

"It's one forty over eighty-five."

"Well, I'm a little nervous."

"That's usually the case. And you smoke, don't you?"

"Yes, about a pack a day."

"Well, I don't have to tell you how bad smoking is, do I?"

"No, in fact I'm giving it up. Absolutely."

"Good. That would definitely be a good idea, Mr. De-Winter. Your pulse rate is higher than I'd like to see it in a man your age. It's eighty-eight."

"That's from the smoking and inactivity. I'm going to . . ."

I was about to say go on a desert island, but I quickly checked myself. "I'm going on a regimen of diet and running. I want to get back into shape."

"You could also lose some weight. Not a lot, but ten or fifteen pounds would help."

"That's also part of my plan."

"Well, you do those three things, and you'll be in fine shape. The tests will be back from the lab Monday or Tuesday. Why don't you call me Tuesday?"

On the way out, I found that the bill had already been paid by Hildendorf. I whistled a pop tune in the corridor, waiting for the elevator, looking at the sick types standing there. At least I was young and fit. In a short while I'd leave this city for an exotic adventure. I whistled happily.

I called the Beverly Wilshire and spoke to Hildendorf after the exam. I told him I had taken it, and also mentioned things like soap and toilet paper that I'd need on the island. He suggested that I leave all these things to him, because he'd spent years planning this project, and had thought of everything. Why didn't I just take care of my personal things, like books and drugs and things like that, and leave the rest to him.

I looked up car rental agencies after the call. It was important to get around the city, and I couldn't move on buses. I didn't want to get my car out of hock . . . let it die there over the next two years. But I wanted mobility. There was a budget agency on West Pico, and I arranged to see them. I took a cab over, and then negotiated a five-day lease on a Datsun.

Now I had wheels. It was a real relief to drive wherever I pleased. I stopped off at a restaurant for a late breakfast and ordered eggs and bacon and toast, things I wouldn't be eating for quite a long while. The food tasted good after my long fast, and I wolfed it down together with three cups of fresh coffee, something else I'd be missing.

While sitting in the restaurant I thought of the five books I'd take with me. When I was in college, my roommates and I would often make up such games. Five or ten books or records or whatever to take to a desert island, that was just food for bull sessions. This was different. I had to make a definite decision and I was going to be stuck with it.

The first obvious choice always is the Bible, but I thought I might reject that out of hand. Then there was the complete works of Shakespeare, but again, I would keep an open mind. *Robinson Crusoe* had to be a choice. I wanted to carefully read it and pattern my own book after it, so that I'd please Hildendorf. After all, I had to have an acceptable manuscript.

That was one book. Now I thought of chess. I loved to play, but had little chance to do it the last year or so. When I was writing I hated to read, since I was afraid of being influenced by other writers' styles, but chess terminology was an abstraction without style. I wanted a big book. I decided upon Bobby Fischer's *Chess Games*. It was a huge volume containing about 750 games by the greatest player of my era. That would be a good book to pass the time with. I could play out all his games at my leisure, and considerably strengthen my own game. That was book number two.

Third, a dictionary. I felt that I could enhance my own vocabulary and learn a great deal about the English language, and it would be an invaluable tool, since I couldn't

communicate with anyone else during my stay, and my vocabulary would thus deteriorate. First and foremost, I had
to write that book, and I wanted the words to adorn it with.

Three books. I thought again of the Bible. There was
beautiful language there, and solace as well for my long
solitary encampment. I decided I'd take a Bible. I had never
really read it from cover to cover, completely, and it was
the book which formed the basis of Western civilization.
Book number four. As for a fifth book, I rejected Shakespeare. I didn't think I'd be that interested. Something in
prose or perhaps poetry. A good anthology of poetry. One
that I could read and reread and memorize. I had always
liked the Oscar Williams anthologies. An anthology of great
poetry, the biggest I could find. Or perhaps modern poetry.
Modern poetry would be better. Modern poetry it would be.

Five books, then. The Bible, *Robinson Crusoe,* a big dictionary, an anthology of modern poetry, and Bobby
Fischer's *Chess Games.* A wide selection. I wondered what
other people would take. What another writer would take.
Well, it didn't matter, really, because this was going to be
my selection, a selection I'd be stuck with. I wrote down the
titles, finished my coffee, and left the restaurant.

Shovels, tools of all kinds, spades, hammers, and nails. I
made out a written list. Also more foodstuffs. Wheat germ
. . . I needed vitamin B complex. Crackers, things like that.
The list grew.

I called my mother on the phone but there was no answer. I tried several times during the day, then gave up.
Then I called Merle a couple of times. Finally, Friday night,
I reached her, but she told me that she had to rush to a date
and for me to call her the next day.

That night I didn't meet with Hildendorf or my agent. I
went to a movie and saw a couple of Charlie Chaplin films,
Modern Times and *City Lights.* Just beautiful films. The

last scene in *City Lights*, the tentative revelation of a man's soul—there was no other scene like it in the movies.

I slept well again, and fortified by another solid breakfast, I went out to buy my books and chess set. I found the chess set in a store on West Pico, along with Bobby Fischer's games. I might have preferred Alekhine's games, but they were in several volumes. I got the anthology in Beverly Hills, along with a good Random House dictionary and a copy of *Robinson Crusoe* in Penguin books. That left a Bible. I went to a couple of bookstores and bought a hardbound copy, which was a waste of money to me. How often had I, in the past, had my choice of the Gideon version in hotel and motel rooms, only to pass it by. Well, what did a few extra bucks mean now? I had my books and chess set. I thought of other games I might buy, but nothing seemed to interest me. What good would scrabble or word games be on the island? I'd have no one to play with, no one to test my skill against.

I spoke to Merle on Saturday afternoon. I told her I was leaving town for a long time and that she should try and sell Phyllis' things. I told her I'd mail back the keys.

"Where are you going?" she asked.

"I don't know yet. I'll contact you when I get there."

"Keep in touch. So you're giving up on film writing?"

"Who knows," I said. "You never know."

Then I called Phyllis' number. No answer. Time was running out. I tried my mother again. Finally I got her in, but it was a bad connection, and we had trouble speaking to each other.

"I'm going away, Mom," I told her.

"Where? Where?"

"To Asia, on a writing assignment. I might not be able to write to you while I'm away, but listen closely. I'm going to write you a long letter and I want you to carry out the instructions."

"What's wrong? Where are you going?"

"There's nothing wrong. It's a big chance for me. I'm going to make a lot of money, but I have to be away for a while."

"Now, Tommy, you're not going to prison, are you?"

"No, Mom, don't be foolish."

"Swear to me."

"I swear."

"Tommy, it's nothing dangerous, is it?"

"No, Mom, it's just an assignment. A writing assignment, but it's going to take a long time."

"What's in that letter you're sending me?"

"I'm going to tell you what to do if you don't hear from me in two years."

"Tommy, what does this all mean? What's wrong?"

"Nothing's wrong, Mom. Nothing. But I'll be away writing. All I want you to do is contact my agent after two years, that's all. Don't forget to do it."

"What's his name?"

"It'll all be in the letter."

"All right, I'll do what you say, Tommy."

"I love you, Mom."

"I love and miss you terribly. I hope I'm around when you come back."

"Why, what's the matter?"

"Nothing. Just a little sugar in the blood. But the doctor says he can get it under control."

"Are you feeling OK?"

"Yes, Tommy."

"Are you sure? Tell me if anything's wrong."

"No, nothing's wrong. My, this call must be costing you a lot of money. Maybe I should hang up."

"No, don't worry about that." The operator had just come on asking for more money for the second time, and I told her I'd take care of it after the call was completed.

"How are you doing?" I asked.

"I'm getting by."

"Have you made any new friends?"

"Yes. But a couple of my friends died recently."

"Oh. Are you depressed about that?"

"Well, you know how those things are, Tommy."

"Now, take care of yourself, Mom."

"And you too, Tommy. You sure everything is all right?"

"Couldn't be better. I love you, Mom."

"Love you, son."

We hung up the phone together. The operator came back on and I deposited a whole bunch of coins, then walked away from the payphone outside my motel. I felt depressed by the call. I missed my mother, goddamn I missed her. And I was going away for two years. What would happen to her?

I went back to the room and lay down on the bed. Then I went out to the movies.

The next day I spent writing a long letter to my mother explaining what I was going to do, and telling her to keep it confidential, but to definitely contact my agent if I didn't show up in two years. Then I tried to call Phyllis and couldn't get her in, so I wrote another long letter, telling her I was leaving town and that Merle would be selling her things.

The rest of the day I went over my needs on the island. My mind was so full of lists that it became overloaded and went blank.

Monday morning went by, and I called Hildendorf, who told me that the supplies were already ordered and being shipped in advance, to be on the island before our arrival. He informed me that both he and Brundage would accompany me there, and he still wouldn't reveal whether or not it was in the Pacific, Atlantic, or Caribbean. He asked me about the books I had selected. I told him I already had bought them and named them to him. He said it was a good selection and that we'd get together Tuesday night and then finalize all the plans for departure Wednesday. He asked me how I felt. . . . I said I was looking forward to the trip, which pleased him a great deal.

10

At ten o'clock on Tuesday morning, I called the doctor, and
his secretary told me to call back in a half hour. In the
meantime, I went to Walgreen's Drugs and looked around
for supplies. I didn't pick and choose, I just chose. Whatever I could see that would be useful, I took. Vaseline, oint-
ments, splints, gauze bandages, Band-Aids, shampoo, soap,
toothpaste, a few toothbrushes, a couple pairs of scissors,
nail clippers, cotton, vitamin pills by the bottle, combs,
brushes, dental floss, rubbing alcohol, and the list went on
and on.

I spent over seventy-five dollars in that drugstore alone
and carried out the packages to the car. I figured that what
I had bought would hold me for two years. Of course, there
weren't any real medicines in there; nothing for specific ail-
ments, but if I remained healthy, these would be sufficient.
Having bought all kinds of supplies for my teeth, I knew it
would be wise to see a dentist, and resolved to make an appointment with one after my call to the doctor.

The doctor told me that all the tests had come back. My blood tests were normal, but there was a slight abnormality in my urine test, something to do with my kidney function.

"How serious is it?" I asked.

"Uh . . . not serious at all, but it is there. It could be just a temporary thing, or . . ."

"Or what?" I was now getting concerned.

"The way I look at it, Mr. DeWinter, your physical examination showed no abnormalities. You've been in good health for a long time, and my feeling is that this just could be one of those things that show up from time to time. Perhaps a change in the diet; the kidney is throwing out more urea than usual. Are you eating a great many rich foods and sweets?"

"Not that much in rich foods, but a lot of doughnuts and things like that. And starches, doctor. But I'm going to cut them out soon, as I told you."

"Well, nothing to worry about, then. My feeling is that if you get yourself in shape, and we take more tests in six months, everything will be perfectly normal."

"You feel that way?"

"Yes. Other than this minor irregularity, I see nothing wrong. Nothing else has shown up. You eat the proper foods, stay away from sugar and rich, starchy foods, and you should find yourself in tip-top shape."

Well, that took care of the physical. I called a number of dentists, including the UCLA dental clinic, but received the same answer. No possible appointment for at least a month, unless it was an emergency. There was no emergency, and thus I wouldn't be seeing a dentist. I rubbed my tongue around my teeth. They felt strong and secure. I was only missing one tooth, in the far right side of my mouth. Otherwise I had had no trouble from my teeth. They were white and reasonably healthy and strong.

While meditating about my mouth, I thought of some other things that it would be handy to have on the island,

and stopped at Mays Department store on Wilshire, and bought a number of candles and a few candle holders. Also a couple of hand mirrors. I piled these things up with my drugstore goods in the trunk of the Datsun.

My next stop was for some cigarettes. I'd have my last smokes for a long time. While at the counter, I purchased three Cricket lighters and put them into my pocket. They would take the place of a hell of a lot of matches. I bought a fourth lighter as well and lit up with the last one purchased, a blue lighter. I had bought a red, green, yellow, and blue one, and felt that I'd use them in sequence. My mind was turning more and more to survival on the island.

Next came a stationery store. I bought ten large notebooks, two reams of lined paper, a few dozen ballpoint pens, two Parker 61 pens, and eight bottles of Sheaffer's blue-black ink. I also bought pencils and erasers and a pencil sharpener.

Then I looked around, thinking of what else I might need. I got some rubberbands and paper clips, though I didn't know if I'd use them at all. I got a dozen large folders that closed with string and a couple of small notebooks for my personal use. I blew another $105 in the stationery store, but this material was the key to the trip. Without pens or paper I couldn't write. Then, after stowing the things in the car, I went back in and bought a diary and a calendar for the year. It was now August, and none of the new calendars were out for the next year, but the diary recorded three years on its inside cover, the past, present, and future years. I realized that this was important information. When I got to the island, I'd update the calendars and keep my own, all the way ahead for two years or more.

I drove down Fairfax and stopped at Canter's restaurant and treated myself to pastrami and eggs and some coffee. I might as well get in all the ethnic foods I could. While I sat over my coffee and lit a cigarette, I thought of one more thing it would be nice to do, and that was to have a woman.

However, I knew of no woman offhand I could just call up and sleep with that afternoon. A hooker would have to do. I had money. Perhaps a masseuse. I left the restaurant in a hurry and bought a *Free Press* and looked at the sex ads.

The first thing I noticed was Crystal Waters' big ad . . . "torture room, domination, water sports, enemas," well, that wasn't for me. I circled a couple of ads that seemed interesting, "young girl, 18 and hot, wants to give you a massage." I made eight calls but all the lines were either busy or no one answered. Finally, I called a massage place over in my old hunting grounds, on Santa Monica near Western. I remembered passing it many times, an oriental massage studio. The woman told me in broken English to come right over. No appointment necessary.

I drove there like a demon and then made a stupid mistake. Crossing a small side street, I didn't quite stop for a stop sign, and the next thing I knew a sheriff's car was behind me, its red lights flashing. I pulled over to the side.

Oh, no, I thought, my heart pounding. This is it. I could be arrested now with the warrant against me, and that would be the end of everything. How dumb, how utterly fucking stupid I had been.

There was only one cop in the car and he was calling in. I could see him through my rear-view mirror, bent over and speaking into his radio microphone. I waited. The car I was driving must be clean; it was a rental car. The fun would come when he asked for my license. Maybe this was Warren, the sheriff who was looking for me. If it was, good-bye, paradise island; hello, county jail.

It was so stupid, just sitting there in the car, waiting for him to make a move. Finally he came out and sauntered over to the car door.

"Could I please see your license, sir?"

"Yes, officer. What's the problem?"

"Well, just a ways back there was a stop sign. Did you see it?"

"Yes."

"Well, you're supposed to make a full stop at a stop sign."

"Didn't I? I thought I did."

"No, you didn't. Lucky for you there was no cross-traffic."

"I looked carefully both ways. I guess the car moved. I'm not used to an automatic. I rented this car, and I have a standard shift on my regular car."

"I see." His words were noncommittal. I passed over my license, and he looked over it, looked at the picture of Thomas A. DeWinter, and looked at my face. There seemed to be a resemblance, though my harried demeanor might have made me look like a person out of a space probe.

"Where do you live?" he asked.

"1114 North Orange Grove."

"The license says 2305 Western."

"Well, officer, I just moved there about a week ago, and I mailed in a letter to the motor vehicle department telling them I moved."

He looked me over and looked the car over.

"Where are you going now?"

I knew all this was none of his business but I stayed polite. I had to get out of there alive and free.

"I'm a free-lance writer, and I'm supposed to meet a couple of people at Musso and Franks, on Hollywood Boulevard."

"That's a pretty good place to eat. You a screenwriter?"

"Not a successful one. I wrote a couple of novels, and they want to talk about one of them."

"Anything I might have read?"

"Perhaps. *The Mirrored Wall.*"

"No. Never read it."

"It's in the main library, I believe."

"OK. I'll try and remember the title. And look, watch the stop signs, will you."

"I'll be super careful, believe me."

He went back to his car, and I turned on the ignition and

slowly slid away from the curb. I was drained out from the encounter. I drove slowly, very slowly, to my rendezvous with the Japanese masseuse. I stopped ahead of time for every red light, even for yellow lights, and each stop sign got my full attention.

On Santa Monica, I parked in the Sears lot nearby and walked to the massage parlor. A thin Japanese woman was sitting at the front table, and she gave me a bright smile. "Wish a massage, sir?"

"Yes."

"Thirteen dollars."

"OK." I took out my wallet and paid her and then followed her to a cubicle. She told me to undress and she left. The masseuse was in her middle twenties, I guessed, not really my type of woman, but I'd take what I could now. About twenty-four hours left to me in LA. I undressed and lay face down on the table, and she came back and asked me if I wanted oil or powder.

"Powder. Can I take a shower afterward?"

"Yes, sir. Shower included."

She gave me a light rubdown, then turned me over, looked down at my erection, and smiled. Her hands, after ten minutes of patting my body, moved down there, and she jacked me off. It ended quickly, and I felt depressed. This wasn't what I had in mind at all for my last encounter with a woman. I needed someone who cared about me, who loved me. Of course, if there was such a woman around, why would I ever leave her, even for the big money of this so-called Robinson Crusoe venture?

I took a quick shower, just enough to wash away the powder, and then put on my clothes. My underwear was wet with perspiration. I had bought a couple of T-shirts and undershorts the other day to replace the ones I had been wearing for several days. The nylon shirt I wore felt sticky and uncomfortable next to my skin, and the underpants

were also moist. I wished I could dry them out, but there
was no time right now.

So that was done. My orgasm had been had at the touch
of a woman. Sexless and futile. The heat of the day now got
to me, I rolled down the windows of the car to let the air
circulate, and drove down Santa Monica, heading for West
Hollywood. I didn't know where I wanted to go now or
what I wanted to do. I drove to the motel and put the
things in my room, and then drove a few blocks down to a
coffee shop and had a couple of cold glasses of water and
coffee and a sweet roll.

I sat over another cigarette and thought of what else I
needed. I had my books, my stationery supplies, my drug
supplies, candles, cigarette lighters, what else? The dog. Of
course. I forgot all about the hound that would be my loyal
companion, my only companion.

I paid the check and called Hildendorf. He told me he
was on his way out to purchase a few more things to send
out, and I reminded him of the dog.

"Weren't we supposed to pick up a German shepherd?" I
asked.

"Oh, yes, Mr. DeWinter. I forgot to tell you. I spoke with
the owner of the kennel, and he told me that German shep-
herds had too heavy a coat for tropical climates. He
suggested a shorter haired dog, and we found a brindle
colored one. They breed them in Barbados. He's a mongrel,
not a purebred, but very well trained and friendly. And a
good watchdog. I'm sure you'll like him."

"When will I see him?"

"Not till you get to the island. I had to ship him separately. I hope you don't mind."

"Did you see him?"

"Oh, yes. He weighs about forty pounds, I should say, a
nice medium-sized dog, very alert. About two years old, a
fine dog."

"All right. That sounds good. I've been buying supplies."

"Oh."

I named all the things I had bought and he reminded me that we were going to meet for supper that evening, to go over the final plans. Would I bring the supplies over that night, and he'd make sure they were packaged and put on the plane.

After the call, I returned to the room and lay on the bed and tried to take a short nap, but sleep wouldn't come. I was restless and anxious, and I tested my pulse. It was over ninety. I had to calm down. This was going to be my last night in the city for two years. I had to relax. But I couldn't sleep, and instead got up and took a long, hot shower.

We were back in Hildendorf's room after another long meal, this time at a Japanese restaurant, a footnote to my massage experience of the afternoon. As usual, Hildendorf served cognac, and we sat around the table.

"What I want to be sure of," I said, "is that I'm not stranded on the island."

"What do you mean, Mr. DeWinter?"

"You know where I am, and I guess you will also, Ralph, but no one else will. I want to be sure that in case anything happens to both of you, that there's some permanent record somewhere of where I am. I don't want to spend forever on the island."

"Oh, no." Hildendorf laughed. "Don't worry about that. I'm going to write to my attorneys and tell them to keep the envelope sealed unless I'm incapacitated or die. Then they are to open the envelope and read the letter that contains full instructions as to your location, and authorization for my estate to pay you and publish the book in case of my death. Will that satisfy you?"

"Perhaps, Ralph, you should do the same thing."

"I don't even know where you'll be."

"After you do know, put it in a vault or give it to your lawyers, or have some record. Tell your assistants."

"There's no need to worry about that," said Hildendorf. "We'll take care of every precaution necessary to ensure your removal from the island after the two-year time interval is up. No need to worry. I assure you. The last thing we want is for you to be stranded."

"It may be the last thing you want, but it's a matter of life or death with me."

"Now, Mr. DeWinter, every precaution will be taken. I assure you of that. If anything should happen to me, there'll be a full account of your location and position with my attorneys. If it will make you more comfortable, I'll also put it into my will as a codicil, naming this project, telling of your location, and notifying the executors to take you off the island after the two years are up."

"You'll definitely do that?"

"Oh, assuredly. Now, we don't want you to go to that island full of worries. You are to have a clear head to write the book. That is our main concern, the book. We'll do nothing to jeopardize that, believe me."

I leaned back and thought, what other assurances could I ask for? I then asked Hildendorf if he'd send the full location of my whereabouts to my mother.

"No, I'm afraid not. Your mother would start worrying, and the next thing we know, she'd call the coast guard or write to her congressman, and that would put an end to the project."

"All right." I thought of other ways to protect myself, but I guessed they wanted this book done, and they were going to take the necessary precautions. No matter what my feelings were about my agent, after all he was a human being. He wasn't going to let me rot on an island forever.

All the things I had purchased were in the room, and they were examined by Hildendorf, who had cartons and heavy tape ready. He packed them expertly. These supplies were going on the plane with us, he explained, all the other supplies would be shipped separately.

"By the way, I got you codeine. I couldn't get morphine. And also, penicillin tablets. As to Valium, I thought it would be better that you didn't take tranquilizers. We want all your feelings coming out in the book. Unless you need it medically, of course."

"No, that's all right." I thought, this would be another test. Along with no cigarettes and sweets, I'd handle myself without the need of drugs.

"So, we will soon be on our way," said my sponsor. "Tomorrow at five we leave Los Angeles."

"I have a rental car to return," I said.

"Well, why don't you do that in the morning. Take cabs when you need them. Here's another hundred dollars to cover these incidental expenses."

He gave me another bill, which I pocketed.

"What about my typewriter and manuscripts and such? Just a few things."

"I'll tell you what," said Ralph, "I'll keep your typewriter and manuscripts in safekeeping for you. You'll have to get rid of the clothing."

"Well, there isn't much anyway," I said. "OK, the hell with it all."

"Then tomorrow at five, you'll be here?"

"Yes, right at five."

"Perfect. Mr. DeWinter," said Hildendorf, "it will be a great adventure, one of the great adventures in the history of mankind."

"I hope so," I said. He was disappointed with this remark, but the words just came out that way. I shrugged, said good-bye, and went down to get my car.

11

Wednesday morning came on hot and full of smog. It was to be my last day in civilization for two years, and I was like a condemned prisoner with a multitude of choices on how to spend his last hours on earth. In the end, too many choices meant no choice. I decided to keep busy. I packed my manuscripts and the typewriter and told the bellhop at the Beverly Wilshire to deliver them to Hildendorf's room.

The rest of my things were all meaningless and worthless and I dumped them out. I was now free of worldly possessions. I still had some money left over, and I decided to send it to my mother after paying for the car rental. But as long as I had the car, I had mobility and decided to make the most of it. I drove down to the main library and went in and looked up atlases of the world. I perused the world of Micronesia, of the Caribbean, of the west coast of Mexico and South America. After a while, I gave up. There was nothing to see, and the island he referred to might not even show on the map. It might never even have been recorded in a world atlas, any more than a pond on my grandfather's farm in Iowa would be on the state map. And the island could be as big as his pond was.

I wandered around the library thinking of what I could read at the last minute. There was nothing. . . . I couldn't be rushed like this. Then I thought of the cop who had stopped me yesterday. It would be a real joke to run into him, looking for my book in the library. That would be very funny. I decided to get out of there at once. On the way out, I stopped short and thought, why don't I look up Hildendorf in the Kansas City directory? I went to the room where the telephone directories were located and found the most recent one and looked up Hildendorf, Max, in the white pages. No listing. I looked up the VW dealers but there was no listing of Hildendorf Motors. Well, the car dealership could be under another name, or he could have an unlisted number. I tore out the VW dealers section and put it into my wallet and left the library.

I got back into my car and decided to eat something. I thought of what my final breakfast might be. Perhaps pancakes, bacon, and eggs, lots of creamery butter and syrup, then a few cups of coffee. A real gluttony meal. Then I thought it would be best to cut out sugar right then and there, and eliminate my craving for the goddamn stuff. I drove away from the downtown section in a pale haze of yellow-brown smog and went for the last time to West Hollywood. I stopped in a coffee shop and ordered bacon and fried eggs, with whole wheat toast, and tomatoes instead of cottage fries.

I had two cups of coffee and lingered over a couple of cigarettes. This pack was fast running out, and these would be my last cigarettes for the next two years. Then I drove down to the car rental agency and turned in the Datsun.

The rest of the day went slowly. Hildendorf was right, time would move on, inexorably, and it would move swiftly. I wished I was already on the island, so that this could be my first day, and one day would be gone. Seven hundred and thirty days altogether. They would go one by one, calendar leaves falling off the book of time, making me older and perhaps wiser.

Once I was rid of the car, I counted my remaining money, went to a post office, and bought a stamped envelope and a money order. I put the money order in the envelope, addressing it to my mother. I asked the clerk for a couple of note pages and wrote a short note to her, telling her this was my early Christmas present, that she should keep well, and that she should read the other letter I had sent her and file it away in a safe place. After I mailed the money order, I felt down. I missed my mother.

I decided to remind Ralph to send her Christmas and birthday presents each year in my name. I'd remember that, for it would be important for my mother to know that I hadn't forgotten her. Yes, that would be a good thing to do, and I was surprised that it hadn't been one of my priority items and that I hadn't thought of it earlier. Also, I'd tell Brundage to inquire of my mother from time to time and make sure that she was well, but in any event, she was to receive some money for both her birthday and Christmas.

Thinking of these things made me feel better. I should have carried them out more assiduously during the time I was in a position to do so, but it wasn't too late to become a better person. It was never too late.

Five o'clock, that dreaded and fateful and exciting and looked-for hour came and I went to the hotel to meet Hildendorf and my agent. My agent's car was parked in front, and I got into the back seat with Hildendorf while Brundage drove. We headed down to Sunset Boulevard, and then he turned west, heading for the San Diego Freeway. At this point, Hildendorf asked me if I wouldn't mind being blindfolded. The rest of the trip, he said, including the plane ride, all the way to the landing on the island, would be undertaken so that I wouldn't know where I was.

I thought his precautions were out of line, but he had Brundage stop the car, and he insisted on carrying them out.

"Even Robinson Crusoe knew approximately where he was," I said.

"Yes, of course. But he was stuck on an island without any hope of getting off for twenty-eight years. You'll be on this island for only two years. It would spoil the whole thing if you knew exactly where you were."

So, I submitted. I felt the cloth go around my eyes, and then dark glasses, Hildendorf told me, were being placed over the cloth, to make it appear that I was either blind or had had a recent eye operation. I truly couldn't see anything.

As we drove, my whole perspective changed. I was aware of Hildendorf's cologne. When he had bent over me, I had smelled its sickly sweet odor clearly. It was strange how things were different with one's eyes closed. I was more aware of turns and noises, of bumps in the road, of changes in the grade of the road and the surface itself.

We drove steadily, and I lost track of time. It's very difficult, unless you count, to know just how much time has passed when your eyes are closed. It's like waking in the middle of the night and trying to figure exactly how long you've been asleep.

"By the way," I said, breaking the silence. "Mr. Hildendorf, I looked up your name in the Kansas City directory and didn't find it there. Nor did I find your car company."

"Oh yes, well you wouldn't find me in the directory. I have an unlisted number, and I no longer own the agency, which has now changed names."

"What's its name now?"

There was a long silence. Had I struck a deep chord, a false note in his makeup? I waited for an answer.

"German Import Motors, that's the new name. The Krieger brothers own it now."

"I see."

"Yes. My interests are now in other fields. I'm still heavily invested in real property and of course in enterprises like this. . . . I'm moving my investments in artistic directions."

I didn't say anything. I detected anxiety in his voice, or was it my own imagination? It was hard to tell. It was interesting, though, how utterly perceptive of feelings I was becoming with the cloth over my eyes.

Nothing more was said for a while. I was aware of the car turning off a highway and entering another highway. I heard horns blowing up ahead, and then we seemed to be stalled in traffic. My thoughts were reinforced with Brundage's curses as we slowed down to a crawl.

"I hope we're not late," said Brundage.

"No, don't worry," said Hildendorf. "They have to wait for us. There's no other way. They'll wait."

"Where are the things you packed?" I asked.

"What?" asked Hildendorf.

"The packages you packed yesterday. In the hotel room."

"Oh yes. They're in the trunk of the car."

"Where are we going now?"

"To an airport."

"Which one?"

"Please, Mr. DeWinter. I can't tell you that."

"What kind of plane are we going on?"

"No comment."

"Will you and Brundage be on the plane with me?"

"Oh yes."

"Anyone else?"

"Please, don't ask so many questions. You will see what you will see."

"So far I'm blindfolded and can't see anything."

"Well, then, don't worry. Everything is going according to schedule. Aha, we're moving again."

And the car shot forward.

"It was that damn truck," said Brundage. "Did you see that, Mr. Hildendorf?"

"Yes . . . bad accident."

On and on we drove. I sat and scratched my face near my eyes, wanting to rub them. At least my hands were free. If Hildendorf had wanted to tie my hands as well, the whole deal would have been off then and there. But why would he want to tie my hands? I was feeling very anxious and felt my pulse. It was racing. Was this a good idea? Was I crazy? Should I stop all this nonsense right now? I slumped in my seat and thought about my position.

It was the blindfold, I decided. It was making me feel terrible. I never liked to feel helpless and now I was feeling that way, in the hands of two men I neither liked very much nor trusted very much. And yet I was going to trust them, in effect, with my very life, or at least two years of it. Should I take off the bandages and tell them the deal was off?

I was very tempted to do that. Twice my hands reached for the bandages, but each time I stopped short and rubbed my face. I was sure Hildendorf was watching me, wondering what I was doing. Well, screw him. I would make my own decision.

As I was thinking these thoughts, and having no idea of how long we had been driving, I was aware that Brundage was turning the car.

"Now what?" he said.

"Follow the signs with the orange arrow."

"Those?"

"Yes."

This road was not as smooth, and suddenly for a short while it became gravelly. I heard the gravel flying against metal as we bumped and rocked along. Then it became smooth again: we slowed, made a turn, another turn, and stopped. Then I heard a man's voice distinctly.

"Is that him?"

"Yes."

"Well, the plane is ready."

"Good. There are some things in the trunk. Please be good enough to stow them on board."

"Right."

The car moved for a few feet, then jolted to a stop. The engine was shut off. A door opened. I felt a man's hands touching my arm and leading me out.

"Duck your head, pal," he said.

I ducked and could feel his hand on the top of my head as he guided me out of the car. I stood and stretched. I heard shuffling of feet, movements, voices. I heard Hildendorf talking, giving directions to an unknown man. I heard the man's reply. "Right, sir. Yes sir."

I stood and listened to it all. The night was around me, I could feel its coolness and moisture. I stood still, my arms at my sides, feeling awkward and alone. Very much alone, and yet all this activity was centered around me. Finally, a hand touched my arm. I jumped.

"Take it easy, pal," said the voice.

"Where am I?"

"Sorry, pal. Orders."

"Where are we going?"

"To a plane."

"What kind of plane?"

"Sorry."

Then I heard Hildendorf. "Please, Mr. DeWinter, please. No more questions, if you will."

I was led to the plane, then stopped. "Now, pal, put one foot up. A little higher. That's it. Now start taking steps. You'll take five steps. That's it. Now wait a minute."

Other hands got hold of me. I was pushed and pulled and finally placed in a seat. Then a seat belt was fastened over my lap.

"You comfortable, Mr. DeWinter?"

"I guess so."

"We'll be taking off in a few minutes now."

"OK."

I heard an engine roar, then another, then both going simultaneously. The whole seat shook. Piston engines. Two-engine plane. A door was shut. A voice shouted something indistinct. Then the plane started rolling. The whole seat was vibrating. The plane was turning, still turning. I felt it move faster, increase its speed. I felt the speed through my body, and suddenly I was pushed back. The plane was airborne.

"Beautiful," said Brundage.

"Amen," said Hildendorf.

We were airborne. I thought of counting but that was useless. Too much to think about and observe to bury myself in numbers.

"Will this be the plane that takes us to the island?" I asked.

"No. We'll be transferring to another plane."

"And that will take us to the island?"

"It will all become clear to you, don't worry, please. How are you feeling?"

"OK."

"Would you want some water? Some coffee?"

"Both. My coffee with a little cream and sugar if you have it."

"That can be done."

A cool glass of water was placed in my hand. I drank it down. It had a metallic taste and I didn't like it. Then the coffee. It was warmish and bitter. I sipped a little and then held it out. It was taken away without explanation.

We flew at what seemed a steady altitude. Now and then we were subject to a sudden wind change, or a change in the air patterns. We dropped a few times, and I felt a sinking in my stomach. I felt helpless.

I asked if my seat belt could be taken off.

"Why, do you have to go to the bathroom?"

"No."

"Then leave it on. We all have them on."

12

I dozed off for a while, then awoke with a start, and automatically reached for the bandages on my eyes. Then I realized where I was and stopped. The dark glasses were still on my bandages. I heard Hildendorf speaking to someone, and then I recognized Brundage's voice.

"Ralph," I said aloud.

"Yes. Excuse me, Mr. Hildendorf. Yes, Tom."

"What time is it?"

"It's a little after ten. We all ate, but didn't want to disturb you. You want something to eat?"

"OK. What do you have?"

"Sandwiches. Ham and cheese, and coffee."

"OK."

Brundage handed me a sandwich. I knew it was from my agent by his odor. It was remarkable how I was quickly differentiating the various sounds and smells around me. There was the roar from the engines, the air being pumped into the cabin, the squeaking of the chairs, the movement of metal under the strain of flight, my own breathing, the voices of Hildendorf and Brundage, and occasionally, another man's voice, from far away. Perhaps that was the pilot.

The sandwich was wrapped in paper of some kind. I undid the paper and felt around and placed it on the empty seat next to mine.

"You want your coffee now?" Brundage asked.

"I'd appreciate some water. Also, where's the bathroom? I want to wash up."

I held the opened sandwich in my hands, and realized how clammy they felt. I held out the sandwich, and it was taken away from me, then I heard the paper rustling, then the seat belt was loosened.

"Now, take it easy, standing up. Easy."

I was helped up and walked stiffly and awkwardly following Brundage to the rear of the plane. A door was opened and I was guided into a smaller room, obviously the bathroom.

"The seat has no cover," he said. "The toilet paper is to the right of the toilet and the sink is to the left. After you're done, I'll help you wash up if you want. You turn on the water by pressing down on the faucet. Don't worry about which one you turn on. The hot and cold are both the same, lukewarm. And you flush the toilet by reaching behind you . . . anyway, there's a pull-chain kind of device that's a couple of feet above the back of the toilet."

The door closed behind me. I felt around. No one was in the bathroom except myself. Now was the time to get these damn bandages off and see where I was.

I first took off the glasses and placed them in the sink. Then I examined the bandages with my hands. It was double knotted in the back and rather tight, but it was possible to pull at the cloth in front and inch it down. There was a little pressure and pain to my right eye, but I got it lowered so that I could open my eye and look around.

I was in a narrow plane restroom. The signs were in English and French as to the use of the toilet facilities. There was no window in the room, the only light coming from a fluorescent lamp above the sink.

I looked at myself in the small mirror. I looked strange with one eye unclosed and the other bandaged, like a man from a distant planet, or more aptly, an escapee from an insane asylum. I had to urinate, so I turned around and did my business but waited to flush the toilet. I didn't want to leave yet. Maybe there was some clue as to my whereabouts or what kind of plane I was on. I looked around and examined what I could, but there was nothing to detect, so I flushed the toilet and then took my glasses out of the sink while I washed up. I dried my hands on a paper towel and left it in the sink. Without sight, I wouldn't have been able to find the disposal slit in the side of the sink.

I tugged at the bandage, keeping my eyes shut tightly, and got it back into its original place, and replaced the dark glasses. Then I rapped on the door, calling for Brundage. I heard him coming down the aisle, and he pushed the door open slowly and led me out.

"Everything go all right?" he asked.

"Yes. I even groped around and found towels. At least I hope it was towels. I left them on the floor or in the sink or somewhere."

"That's all right. Don't worry about it."

"Ralph, how much longer till we land?"

"I understand about midnight. In a couple of hours."

"Where are we, over water, over land?"

"I can't tell you anything; you know that, Tom."

"Ralph . . ."

"Yes."

"Never mind." I wanted assurances that this whole thing was legitimate, but who knows where Hildendorf was at this time. He might have been five feet away, or hanging over us, listening to every word I spoke. Instead, I kept my mouth shut and let myself be led back to the seat.

After a while, we were gradually losing altitude, and there was scurrying around in the plane. The engines were changing pitch, and the plane was slowing up. I could feel it. I tried to calculate. It was about seven hours from the time I met Brundage and Hildendorf. It had taken a couple of hours of driving, I guessed, to get to the airport and to take off. We must have been flying about five hours then. Five hours at about three hundred miles an hour in a twin-engine plane. Fifteen hundred miles. That meant that we didn't traverse the continental United States. If we went west, we'd probably be in Hawaii. If we went east, southeast, how far toward the Caribbean would we be? I should have examined the atlas more closely, looked at maps, tried to do some calculation.

We were coming in for a landing, then the wheels hit with a big bump, bounced, and landed again. A lousy pilot. The plane came to a halt after a few more minutes. No sound at all from anyone. Then a door was opened, and a new voice was heard in English. Hildendorf replied to a question I didn't hear by saying "yes," then "no."

I could feel the draft of night air (was it still night? I wondered). Then scraping and movement. I was tempted to open the bandage. Perhaps I was alone in the plane.

I decided to try. I took off my dark glasses and rubbed the bandages, then slowly tried to loosen the right side.

"Mr. DeWinter, just what are you doing?" asked Hildendorf.

"My right eye is bothering me. The bandage is too tight."

"All right, we'll loosen it. Come with me. We'll go to the back, to the toilet, and there I'll retie it."

So, once more I was led down the aisle, and once more groped my way to the bathroom. Inside, it was too small for both Hildendorf and myself, so I was in the restroom and he was jammed against the door. He opened the bandages.

Again I could smell his cologne, recently administered in strong doses. Its sweet smell was powerful and sickening.

The bandages were off. I opened my eyes but could only see Hildendorf, and beyond him, a blank cabin wall. There was nothing else to see.

"This is a relief," I said. "I want to wash my face and put some water on my eyes."

"Go ahead."

It was truly a relief. I looked at my face in the mirror. There were lines from the bandages and my eyes were bloodshot and weary looking. I was dead tired and clammy from all that sitting and inactivity. I lingered as long as I could, rubbing and throwing water on my eyes. Then Hildendorf told me he had things to do, and would I please hurry up. So I dried my face and hands, and submitted to the bandage again. Hildendorf was wearing a watch, but I couldn't make out the time. My own watch had been taken away from me before we got into the car, and I was sorry that I hadn't hidden it. It would have given me some sense of how far from civilization we would be going.

I was led back to my seat. The short rest from the bandage had been refreshing, and I felt a lot better. I was put into the same seat, and then the seat belt was strapped on and buckled.

There was plenty of activity around the plane then. Hildendorf told me we'd be at the airport for a while, a few more hours, before taking off again.

"We'll remain in this plane," he said. "We're not going to change planes. I decided it would be too inconvenient moving you and the packages to another aircraft."

"That's OK with me."

"Good. Just cooperate with us a little while longer. I know how inconvenient it is for you to be tied down this way and blindfolded. But just bear with us. Soon, your bandages will be removed and you'll be back to normal."

"What do you mean, back to normal?"

"My command of English is a little awkward, as you must have noticed, Mr. DeWinter. I simply meant, we'll remove the bandages and then . . . well, then you'll be on the island."

"How much time till we're there?"

"I can't tell you."

"You mean, you don't know?"

"I have an approximate idea, but I don't want to tell you."

"I see. Are the supplies there now?"

"Oh yes."

"All of them? I mean, won't others be sent after I'm there?"

"No. By now they're all in place. That was the first priority."

"You got all the food?"

"Yes, everything. Now, stop asking so many questions. There are a few things I have to do. Mr. Brundage . . ."

I heard my agent stirring.

"Sit with Mr. DeWinter awhile. I have to take care of a few things."

Now it was Brundage's turn to hold my hand, or rather to make sure I was a good boy and didn't know too much. I tried to get some information out of him, but it was all in vain. He wouldn't even tell me the time.

I grew bored with his grudging silence and fell asleep again. When I awoke, the plane was moving and the engines humming once more. We were soon aloft. I again fell asleep. I kept waking, hearing the engines going full blast, but no longer did I feel like taking off the bandages. I didn't want to play games. What would be, would be. I was aware of light, however, strong light that permeated the edges of the bandages. It was bright and sunny outside. I could not only sense the light but feel the heat of the sun's rays.

We flew for a long time in the sunshine. Then Hildendorf came over and asked me if I was awake.

"Yes."

"Want something to eat?"

"Not another ham and cheese sandwich."

"No, we have coffee and pastry."

"I don't want a pastry."

"Coffee and a bologna sandwich, then?"

"Where did you get this gourmet food?"

"I'm sorry, Mr. DeWinter. We took what we could get. That's all they had at the stopover."

"I'll have the bologna."

"Here it is. One moment."

I chewed on the tasteless meat and stale bread and then put it on the seat next to mine. The coffee was again luke-warm, and I could only drink a few mouthfuls. I asked for more water. I drank three glasses of water, then got them to loosen the seat belt so I could get up and stir.

"What time is it?" I asked Hildendorf.

"The time now is meaningless, since I've reset my watch according to the time zone here."

"Well, what time is it here?"

"It's morning. I could tell you ten or nine or eleven A.M. Would it really matter?"

"No."

"Then why ask? I'm sorry . . . I don't mean to be abrupt, but we've all had little or no sleep and so many things to do, you must understand."

I didn't reply. I didn't feel like feeling sorry for Hildendorf.

I tried to sleep again. I dozed off, then abruptly opened my eyes. We were losing altitude, the engines had a different sound to them.

"What's happening?" I asked.

"We're landing."

"What's the matter?"

"Nothing. This is where we must refuel."

"And then what?"

"Then we fly some more."

"Oh."

The refueling didn't take very long. We were soon in the air again, and the sun's rays were weakening. Then we were landing once more.

This time I was taken out of the plane. A fierce breeze was blowing, and my hair was tumbling over my face. The wind was a hot one, and the air felt somewhat stifling.

I was led by hand for about two hundred yards, then told to sit down. I sat in a wooden chair in some kind of enclosure. Around me I heard planes landing and taking off. Brundage sat next to me.

"Where are we?"

"Tom, to tell you the truth, I don't know myself."

"Is this an island?"

"I can't tell you."

"You mean you won't."

"That's right."

"Where's Hildendorf?"

"He's around somewhere . . . he'll be back soon."

"Ralph . . . you'll take care of things, won't you?"

"Yes, of course."

"I mean, the payments to my ex-wife, and the money to my mother . . ."

"It's all been taken care of."

"And the Christmas and birthday presents to my mother. On the note I gave you."

"Everything will be taken care of."

"And you're going to inform people . . . right . . . I mean, about my being on an island . . . you're going to find out just where I am, aren't you?"

"Sure."

"Hey, just don't say it to please me. If you don't know where we are, how the hell will you know where I'm going eventually?"

"I already know that. I have that written down."

"The name of the island?"

"The longitude and latitude readings. I told you, don't worry."

"But I am worried. I don't like this idea of a blindfold at all. What's the purpose?"

"You have to . . . well, you know, you have to be kept ignorant of where you are."

"Why, what the hell would I do?"

"He's worried that if you knew where you were, you might somehow make side trips . . . I don't know."

"Side trips to where?"

"I don't know. When I get back, I'll look at a world map and spot your location. I don't even know the name of the island, just its location."

"He gave you the right location, now, didn't he?"

"Hey, don't worry, Tom. Don't get paranoid."

"Why not? I want to make sure you know where I am. That other people know where I am."

"His lawyers will know about it, and I'll let my assistants know about it, and my lawyers also, is that OK? And I'll put the location in my safe deposit box. What else do you want?"

"I don't know. I just don't want to be stranded forever."

"You'll have adequate supplies, don't worry."

"What do you mean, for a twenty-year stay?"

"No. Goddamn, Tom, don't put words in my mouth. For the two-year stay. There's nothing to worry about. We're all very interested in your safety."

"Suppose you come back in two years and I'm dead?"

"You won't be dead. You're strong as a horse and healthy as one. Now, stop worrying."

"Ralph . . ."

"Shhh . . . here comes Hildendorf."

"Well," said my sponsor, "how are you doing, Mr. De-Winter?" He sounded very cheerful.

"Can't I take these bandages off now?"

"Soon, very soon. Well, we're ready." My arms were grasped by both men, but I shook loose, and then only Brundage led me across a gravelly field. Or I thought it was gravel. It could have been loosely packed sand. It was hard to tell. I heard, in the distance, a loud whirring sound, and soon I felt an incredible wave of air assaulting me.

"We're going on a helicopter," Brundage shouted to me.

"What?"

"A helicopter."

I was helped on and strapped, facing the rear, since I felt completely unbalanced as the thing took off. Hildendorf and Brundage were with me. I decided to time this, since I figured it could go about a hundred miles an hour, and that would tell me just how far I was from the island.

I tried to count, then lost track. The noise was deafening, and we were continually jolted by air currents. We flew longer than an hour, however, I was sure of that. We flew on and on.

Then we slowed down and circled. I could feel my heart beating fast, my pulse racing. This was it. There was no more turning back. I was committed. Remember, I told myself, don't let them leave till you make sure there's fresh water on the island. Make sure of that.

We were coming down for a landing. Then the motor stopped. A door opened, and I was helped out. Finally, I stood on solid ground.

"Is this the place?" I asked.

"Yes," said Hildendorf.

I ripped off the glasses and the bandage, unraveling it, and blinked. It was almost dusk. I couldn't make out much of the island. All I saw was an indistinct hill, some palm trees, and the endless ocean in front of me. I was on an elevated portion of ground, and I could see a sandy beach below.

"So, this is it," I said aloud.

"Yes," said Hildendorf.

"Where is the fresh water?"

"Yes, certainly. Come with me."

He already had to use a flashlight, and I followed him across sandy stubble.

"Here, here is a freshwater spring."

I bent down and inspected it. A flow of water was coming out between two worn-away rocks, forming a small pool about four feet across. I bent down and tasted the water, cupping it with my hands. It was cool and clean, definitely fresh water.

"And the supplies?" I asked.

"Yes. Well, your packages are being unloaded now by the pilot."

"I mean the food supplies. What about the dog?"

I suddenly remembered the dog.

"The food and all . . . yes . . . see that large mound over there? Actually three mounds, covered with canvas. Your supplies are there."

I peered into the gathering darkness and could barely make out the things he was referring to.

"And the dog . . . his name is Sam," said Hildendorf. "Why don't you call him?"

"Sam, Sam . . ." I called at the top of my voice. Within a minute a dog came bounding up, a medium-sized dog with black and brown hair, floppy ears, and an intelligent face. He wagged his tail and ran from man to man. I petted him and he stayed near me.

"Well," said Hildendorf. "We must be going now."

"What about my tent?"

"It's among the supplies. I'm sorry we came so late. But you can find something to sleep on tonight, I'm sure. In the morning, all will be there . . ."

I walked the men back to the helicopter. My packages were neatly stacked about a hundred feet away. I shook hands with them, the dog at my side.

Hildendorf handed me a large envelope. "Here are your

final instructions," he said. "And we'll see you in two years. God preserve you, and may this be a great adventure for us all."

"Thanks." I shook hands again. "Ralph," I said, "make sure about my family."

"Don't worry about a thing. You just write that book."

I moved back, and then ran back further, as the huge propellers of the helicopter started whirling. It was soon in the air. It circled the island once and then took off. I tried to follow its outbound direction, but it kept changing course, and I soon lost track of its lights.

It was growing dark rapidly. I petted the dog and sat down for a moment. The night was cool, but not uncomfortably cool. I was now irrevocably alone. I couldn't believe that I was here, and had volunteered to stay here for two years. It was still like a dream to me.

I pulled open the envelope in the darkness.

There was a letter inside addressed to me. I snapped on a Cricket lighter and read by its light, as my heart beat rapidly. Was the truth going to be in this letter, that it was all a trick and that I was stranded here forever? Jesus, I was nervous. I was holding the letter with a shaking hand.

Dear Mr. DeWinter,

You are embarking on a great adventure, and I admire your courage in this undertaking. I send you my best wishes, and know that you will produce a masterpiece, a classic comparable to *Robinson Crusoe*.

Two years from this date, we will meet again, and I will look forward to hearing about your stay, and particularly, will look forward to reading your book about your adventures here.

As to your supplies . . . although we discussed the subject thoroughly, and although I agreed to give you all you asked for, I felt that you could write a more forceful and exciting book if your supplies, like Robinson Crusoe's, were random in nature. This was my decision, and you can hold me alone responsible for it, but when you examine your supplies, you will find, rather than the food and equipment we went over so carefully in Los Angeles, a great many substitutes. However, they are more than sufficient, I assure you, for at least the two-year stay, and for much more time.

Again, may I wish you the very best of luck. I wish I could change places with you. Have faith in God and in yourself and all will turn out well. I look forward to our next meeting after the short span of two years is completed.

> Very sincerely yours,
> M. E. Hildendorf

What the hell did this letter mean? I groped my way in the dark toward the canvases covering the supplies. They were held down at the corners by large rocks. I got one of the corners loosened and saw all kinds of cans, stacked and piled in a hodgepodge arrangement. I pulled out one of the larger ones and snapped my lighter on. The can was slightly rusty and there was no label on it, just some kind of oriental markings. I shook the can. Whatever was inside was loose.

I felt a chill run through me and the strength went out of my body. I was really stuck now, and would have to live on whatever crap I found on this godforsaken island.

That bastard Hildendorf. Oh yes, a great adventure for me in this desolate place, on an island in the middle of nowhere, and he would be sitting comfortably on his fat ass thousands of miles away. He wanted to trade places with me. Bullshit, Hildendorf, just bullshit.

I sat on the ground and put my head in my hands. The dog was next to me, watching me anxiously. I petted him and his tail wagged. Thank God for a dog, for some kind of companion.

I looked up at the sky. It was inky black and a billion stars returned my gaze. Around me the vast waters of the ocean shimmered in the dim moonlight. Well, tomorrow there would be sunshine and light. It would be a new day. Tomorrow would be better, I hoped.

PART II

13

When I opened my eyes, the sun was mounting its attack over the eastern end of the island, its golden light shimmering on the vast bodies of water that surrounded the island. Those were the first things I saw, the sun, and then the water. All that water. I stood up and rubbed my eyes. There was sand in my hair, sand on my skin, and sand in my clothing.

I felt tired. I hadn't slept well, finding the sand an uncomfortable bed. I walked over to the pond with Sam at my side and bent over, throwing water on my face, and then drinking some in my cupped hands. As I drank, so did Sam, lapping it up quickly. He looked awfully thin and I wondered what he had been eating since he was here. Maybe nothing. Well, we'd see about food first, and then check out the island.

I went over to the canvas I had lifted slightly the night before. It was olive green in color and looked like army issue, but there were no markings on it. The canvas covered

a pile of metal cans about fifteen feet wide and ten feet
high. My two-year supply of food, I guessed, and Sam's also.
The dog was still at my side, sniffing and whimpering. I
guessed he was really hungry. Then I realized that if they
had left the correct amount of dog food for Sam, assuming
he ate two cans of it a day, it would amount to almost
fifteen hundred cans, which was far more than was under
this canvas. As for myself, I'd need tons of supplies, and
there weren't tons of food in front of me. I was really
screwed.

I managed, after a long struggle, to pull off part of the
canvas. The canvas itself was full of sand, which added to
its bulky weight. After I exposed most of the cans, I examined them. They were olive green in color, and none had
labels, but instead oriental markings stenciled on. It looked
like Japanese or Korean to me. How would I ever know
what was inside except by opening them, and right now I
didn't even have a can opener. I threw a few cans down in
disgust and rummaged around, picking up other cans and
shaking them. Some had loose contents, others were solidly
packed. A lot of good that knowledge did me right now.
And, if I managed to open one of the larger cans, how
would I preserve its contents? Right now the sun was moving up rapidly in the sky, and the air was heating up.

I pulled the canvas until all the cans were exposed, but
there were no surprises. All the cans were the same color,
though they were in different sizes, ranging from about a
half gallon to a half pint. Meanwhile the dog was still at my
side, whimpering louder. He was really hungry.

I kept lifting cans and shaking them, but what was the
use? I didn't have a knife or can opener, no implement to
open them with. Goddamn that son of a bitch Hildendorf.

I walked away from the pile of cans and sat down on the
ground. I wanted to cry, but instead laughed like a madman.
Bumble Bee tuna. Soup mixes. Heinz ketchup in cute little
packets. What a joke my requests must have been. How the

two fuckers must have chortled and rollicked, looking at the list they had copied down so carefully. What a joke. What a fool I must have been in their eyes. Oh, Jesus, one could kill for less. Bumble Bee tuna in oil. Dried pineapples with no added sugar, dried apricots with no sulphur dioxide added.

Right now I'd settle for a meal of sugar and sulphur dioxide. And right now this mound of cans was useless to me. I looked at them, piled high under the sun, some rotted, some dented, others leaking. What a joke this was on me.

Probably all war surplus stuff bought from some far off and long forgotten war. The Japanese war in China in the thirties or maybe the Sino-Russian war of 1905. With that cheap bastard Hildendorf anything was possible. Yes, anything was possible now, even that I should rot on this crap for two years, or worse, that I die of starvation trying to open these cans. Well, there must be a way.

I left the pile of rust and proceeded to the next canvas, which was about fifty feet away. This one was much smaller and covered an area about ten square feet. I had trouble with one end of the canvas, which was embedded in the sand, and with my hands sore and two fingers bleeding, I finally pulled it off the treasures below. Treasures all right. This was my clothing. Rolls of shirts and pants, fit for an army of dwarfs. I pulled out a pair of fatigues, olive green with a black stripe across. Probably not only war surplus but war rejects. I put it against my body; the pants came to about a foot above my ankle, and I would need a twenty-inch waist to get them on. Useless junk.

This was getting worse and worse. I found a few hats in the pile, floppy camouflage hats, but they fit on the top of my head, not around my head. I would have to be a pin-head to wear them. Again I had to laugh, thinking of my requests. Pith helmets, hats, optic gray sunglasses, what a goddamn joke, and here I was with stuff from an army of midgets that fought a hundred years ago.

I pulled and pulled and tried to come up with some use-

ful clothing. Most of it was damp, moldy, and mildewed
and stunk, having lain under the canvas for years in a pile
of sand. No wonder Hildendorf brought me here at night. I
never would have stayed otherwise. I would have fought
my way back onto that helicopter and left him here to rot
with this shit.

There was really nothing that I could wear in the whole
goddamn pile, nothing. And most of the stuff was crumbling
and rotted away. In disgust, I left this pile and went to the
third one.

I felt like a scared schoolboy taking a difficult exam.
Question after question eludes him, and he gets more panicky as he turns page after page, looking for one question he
can answer correctly. Then he is on the last question and on
the last page and still can't answer anything. He is sunk.

I still had pile number three to look at. My last question
on my last page. Otherwise . . . otherwise what? Would I
just sit here and weep? Eat the dog finally? I guess he
sensed my feeling, because he backed away; his tail fallen
between his legs. Or maybe the beast would end up eating
me. That was more likely.

This was the smallest pile of all. We had gone through
papa bear and mama bear and now it was baby bear's turn.
"Baby bear's turn," I said to Sam, just to hear my own voice.
He liked the words, and his tail wagged again. He could see
that I still had hopes of other meals besides him.

The canvas was deeply embedded in sand all the way
around. The pile was just a shade smaller than the previous
one, and after finding one end that extended three feet
down along a sandy ridge, I pulled and tugged until my
equipment was laid bare. The first things I saw weren't
promising at all, just piles of rust. Rusted utensils and
spoons. I tugged harder. There were bayonets and helmets
and cartons and boxes of all colors and sizes. One I recognized as an ammunition container. All right. Maybe some
weapons. The bayonet I pulled out was sheathed, and was

sharp and in good condition. An American bayonet. Now I could cut through tin and metal.

I turned over a couple of helmets, American army helmets, before I found what I wanted. Inside one was a helmet liner. I wasn't going to wear a metal helmet, but a helmet liner was detachable and lightweight. And it could be adjusted to any head size. I threw down the helmet and put on the helmet liner.

There was a use for the helmets as well. I could use them as pots. I put the two helmets to one side, and I looked around for more useful items. I found some utensils that were also in fairly good shape, with just a few rust spots on them. I put them to one side, inside the usable helmets. Then I rummaged some more. There was a real trove here. I found a few cans of sterno. Beautiful. I could cook now. I then found a container of waterproof matches. I also had three of my Cricket lighters in one of the packages that Hildendorf had wrapped. Thank God for the cigarette lighters, if they were there, if Hildendorf hadn't played the same game with the packages of supplies I had bought.

I ran to the area where the packages had been dumped the night before, Sam at my side. I took along the bayonet and cut through the wrapping paper. My books. My notebooks and paper. My drug supplies. A chess set, and here were the three multicolored lighters. Why didn't I buy a dozen, two dozen? How long would they last? I went back and got a can of sterno, two helmets, and a bayonet and walked to the can pile. I was about to have my first meal on the island.

I jabbed the bayonet into the metal of a smaller can, finally penetrating its surface. I jabbed a few times, till I got an edge opened, and then tried to pry it open, but cut my fingers on the jagged edges. Stupid. I didn't need an infection now. I didn't need a disease like tetanus, and realized I hadn't even taken a shot of any kind to protect myself. What an idiot I was.

Finally, I managed to pry enough of the can open to allow the contents to leak out slowly. I smelled it. Tomatoes, stewed tomatoes. Shit.

I put that can down and tried another one. It was an effort opening cans this way, plunging the bayonet against the top part of the metal till something gave. I went through four cans before I found one that contained meat. I didn't know what kind of meat it was. Maybe dog meat. It was partially ground and partially chopped and in a heavy soylike sauce. I put some into a helmet, with the dog running around me. I dished out half the can into the other helmet and propped it on the ground so that Sam could eat from this makeshift dish without knocking it over. He went right to it.

I got the sterno can opened and lit it. The flame wasn't that strong, but it was effective. I tried to hold the helmet over it, but that was a useless procedure. I found a few rocks and with some difficulty got the helmet propped up, with space below for the sterno to burn. In the meantime I went to the spring and rinsed off the spoons. I should have, I realized now, cleaned the helmets beforehand. Well, next time. If I was screwing up, at least I was screwing up in total privacy.

It took about fifteen minutes for the sauce in the helmet to boil. I stirred it continually and then tasted it. Not too bad. A little too salty but not bad at all. I didn't know what it was, but it was meat of some sort. My dog was more contented now, having finished his share. I had divided the can half and half. Half for his forty pounds and half for my hundred and eighty pounds. Such were the ways and mores of my new-found kingdom.

I ate all the meat and left the warm, salty soy sauce for Sam. He finished that off fast and followed me to the spring, where I drank some more water and got both helmets reasonably clean, then didn't remember which one was Sam's and which one was mine. Did it matter, really?

OK. I had eaten my first meal. There was going to be no kind of health food club here, I realized. I would eat what I could get. And so would Sam. Two hungry mouths to feed.

I now looked into the cans I had already opened. There was some kind of mushy vegetable in one that I couldn't make out. The other had more stewed tomatoes. I had dumped the first can ingloriously on the sand, where a wide red stain marred the surface. From now on I'd be more careful. The tomatoes and the yellowish beige mush would be my supper. I put them under canvas in a cool place, wondering if any animals or insects would get to them before I did.

Now I went back to the third pile to find more useful things. So far, I had a helmet liner, a bayonet, a couple of spoons, and helmets. And the sterno can. There must be more.

I dug around and found a carton half buried in the sand. It was hard to open, and then I found a rifle inside packed in heavy grease. I pulled it out, feeling the glop all over my hands. An M-1 rifle.

An M-1. I was overcome with joy. The standard rifle when I had been in the army was an M-16, but we had used these for drills. An M-1. In virginal condition.

I opened the ammunition container next. One hundred rounds of .30-.30 ammunition, neatly packed in. Still, I needed a cartridge holder or clip for the bullets, otherwise the weapon would be useless to me. I didn't quite know how to feed one bullet at a time into the chamber. There must be a cartridge holder.

I dug around, near the rifle carton, and then found an ammunition belt. All the pockets were empty. I dug and scraped till my hands were raw. A great many things were buried in the sand. I found more rusty spoons and then, just what I was looking for, two cartridge holders, caked with sand. They were made of brass and hadn't rusted. I went to the spring and cleaned them out immediately, then dried them on my shirt.

I put the clips to one side, among the useful equipment which now consisted of the ammunition belt and ammunition, plus my previous cooking gear. Then I found a couple of cleaning kits for the M-1. Serendipity. Oil and cloths and string to pull the cotton swabs through to clean the barrel.

Arms. And my dog. At least I'd have some kind of security on this godforsaken place. Yes, I felt much better now. Leaving this new-found treasure, I decided to go and explore my domain.

14

This island, this diamond set in the silver sea, yes, well, here I was on my island, the modern-day Robinson Crusoe. Only I wasn't really Robinson Crusoe, I was here of my own free will and accord, and that was the rub, as Hildendorf would have told me. That was the rub, Mr. DeWinter, you see, here you are on this deserted spot on the weary earth itself, with but a hound as a companion, not a soul to talk to or hear from, for that matter, but here you are nevertheless.

I walked with Sam at my side to the highest spot of earth on the island and gazed out over my sovereignty. All around me was the ocean, the blue sea sparkling in the sun. Ordinarily this sight would have sent me into raptures, but right now I was in a very pragmatic, almost prosaic mood, and the island was nothing more than a prison to me, and the seas around me the walls of that prison. There was nothing I could do right now but serve my time.

I looked out in all directions, scanning slowly, as if I was a camera panning the scene, but all I saw was water to the very edge of the horizon. No land, nothing on its surface. Just the sea. I shaded my eyes as I did so, for the sun was rising above me and the light was brutal. Where were my optic gray lenses? . . . Jesus, I had to laugh every time I thought of my lists. Telescopes, binoculars, and a magnifying glass. And don't forget the Jasmine tea, along with the Oolong, Orange Spice, and don't forget the Earl Grey for breakfast after I devour my meat and dried apricots, using a bit of salt, pepper, and of course those cute packets of Heinz ketchup. What an absurd joke this all was. A week ago I was coughing and choking in LA, with Santa Monica Boulevard as my main thoroughfare. Now I was here, a million miles from nowhere, alone, no telephone, no mail, no cars, nothing, nada, sans everything. Yes, I was getting literary in my exalted misery.

Sam looked on with me. He seemed like a good dog. I patted his head and his tail wagged. "Good Sam," I said, "good boy." His tail wagged more furiously. Patting Sam, I wondered how he had gotten to the island. When was he brought here? Not with the piles of junk rusting and rotting under the canvases. They must have been here for years, maybe for decades.

Then Sam must have been brought quite recently. He wasn't starved looking, just a little lean and hungry. A few days before, perhaps. But why just bring Sam over? They must have brought other things with him. They must have. A trip to bring a dog would be absurd, if I reckoned Hildendorf's cheapness correctly. All right, there must be other things on the island, other supplies. But where? The helicopter had landed in a flat area of the island, but there were other places for helicopters to land, all around the island. I started my tour.

"Sam," I said to the hound, "how'd you get here, boy?" No answer. "Sam, if you tell me, if you talk, I'll build a boat and we'll get off this dump and we'll make our fortune on the stage. I'll ask you questions and you'll answer. Just talk to me, boy. A few words. Any language will do. We'll get a spaniel to translate when we get back to the U.S.A."

Sam obediently wagged his tail and trotted a few feet ahead of me. I decided to test him.

"Here, Sam." The dog trotted over. "Now, heel." Damned if he didn't stay at my side. He started trotting ahead again and I said, "Heel," and back he came to my side. Good dog. I patted him and let him run ahead.

The island was very small, about a mile or a mile and a half long and about a half mile across. Or maybe I was exaggerating. I couldn't really tell. I could see both ends of the island from where I stood, the east and west ends. On the southwest side of the island there were rocky cliffs extending directly from the sea, and I couldn't tell what was beyond them, for the rocks obliterated my view. Sandy beaches were on either side, north and south. The beach ran almost the complete length of the north side, till it broke off at a small hill, and then resumed after an interval of about a hundred yards. The eastern tip of the island was made up of a forest thickly grown with trees full of heavy, flat green leaves. I had no idea what kind of trees they were.

Then the beach resumed beyond the trees at the eastern tip. I guessed the trees took up about seventy yards of space, maybe a little more. Looking south, I saw a narrower beach that ended in the sheer wall of rock I described before. I guessed that I was on the highest point of land by being on this hill, but I might be mistaken. The rocks might be higher still.

The highest points of all were the tops of palm and coconut trees growing above the hill. If I could get up there, another seventy-five feet or so up, I could really get a view of the surrounding water. Maybe see some land in the distance. I had heard that the horizon was approximately fifteen miles away at sea level, and from the height of the trees, which I guessed was another one hundred fifty feet above sea level, perhaps thirty miles away. I supposed all that could be worked out and calculated, but I didn't know the calculations, and about all I was coping with now was jabbing a bayonet into cans of stewed tomatoes.

However, those coconuts beckoned to me. Fresh food. I'd have to figure a way to get at them. Maybe climb the trees, but that was a scary thought, not that I wouldn't have tried to do it with another person around, but if I made one false move, one slip, that would be it. A broken leg, even a broken ankle, and I'd end up dead on this island. No need to risk that right now.

The other supply of fresh food was more obvious. There were all those fish in the ocean. Fish by the thousands surrounding the island. I'd have to figure a way to catch them, to find something I could use as a line, some way to get hooks, to string bait, perhaps even to lay nets. Fresh fish and coconuts, my new dream meal.

I continued my tour, walking along the elevated portion of the island. Underneath me was a sandy kind of dirt, with dry stalks growing in the soil. Weeds. Nothing looked edible. I knew the South Seas islanders cooked a root similar to the potato, but I had no idea what it was, or if I was in the South Seas. Goddamn. I should have found a book on desert island survival, if such a book was available. I could have given up my stupid anthology of modern poetry for such a book. Modern poetry. A lot of good it would do me here.

I walked all the way to the rocky cliffs, with Sam still nearby. I walked on the top of the rocks, and crept forward to the edge. I shooed Sam back and looked down. Underneath me the waves battered themselves into oblivion against the rocks. White spume flew up at least ten or fifteen feet. Marvelous sight, but dangerous as hell. I'd have to stay away from this place on the southwestern part of the island.

I backed up cautiously, testing the footing. I was still

wearing city boots, feeling uncomfortable in my outfit, which I had slept in and which was covered with sand. Maybe I'd find new things to wear among the supplies under canvas number two. Maybe deep down in the sand was buried the perfect outfit. Fatigue pants, and good army boots that fit, tank shirts. Yes, I might as well dream. And in each fatigue pocket a couple of Winchell doughnuts. Jesus.

I now headed down the slope of the hill toward the extreme western point of the island. The area was clean with drifts of sand and some overgrown weeds and stalks. Again, I had no idea of what this vegetation was, but it looked unappetizing and inedible. Still, I might boil it and see what happened. Feed it to Sam first. Shit, he might die from eating it, and I couldn't afford to lose him. No, I'd leave the weeds alone.

I slid down an embankment to the beach itself and walked on the firm sand. The water rushed to shore, breaking its progress with smallish waves. The water was a royal blue color close up. Absolutely clean. Nothing drifting on it, no sign of life, no sign of debris, nothing.

I walked along the beach, with Sam running at the water, getting his paws wet and running back to the dry sand. I walked now in an easterly direction, but the beach ended with a barrier of sloping ground from the elevated hill. I walked up the hill slowly, panting as I climbed. God, I was out of condition. But that would all change soon. Two years in this barren wilderness and I'd be like a rock itself.

I sat down halfway up the slope and caught my breath. Sam stayed near me. What a good dog. I petted him. He was really important to me. I should have asked for two dogs, or at least another pet, a cat. I loved animals, but in my city wanderings, I could never have them. I leaned back and closed my eyes, pushing the helmet liner forward, shielding my face from the sun. I dozed off before I knew it and woke with a start. I looked around. Sam was gone. How long had I slept?

The sun seemed not to have moved much. But where was Sam?

"Sam, Sam." I whistled and called, and then I heard the sound of his paws hitting the ground, and he came over the hill, jumping on me and licking my face.

"Where were you, boy? You shouldn't leave me, Sam."

More face licking. I got up, yawned and stretched, and walked up the hill, Sam leading the way. I decided to follow him, and went rapidly along the hill and then down near the far side of the north beach. Sam ran ahead and circled and there it was, several boxes and crates a few feet out of reach of the highest tide.

I ran down toward them.

The first things I noticed were two bagfuls of Purina dog chow, fifty-pound sizes, both unopened. Then a case of Purina dog food. Great. I set upon the other crates with wild abandon. A whole case of dog food. Another case of dog food. Another crate full of cans and packages of dog food. Nothing but dog food. Shit!

I went through all the boxes again, but there was nothing at all for me. Nothing. Still, food for the dog meant that I could keep my own supply of meat for myself, at least, until this food was used up. I spent the next few hours carrying the boxes and bags to the supply area. I realized, however, that this wasn't the best place for me to build a shelter of any kind. I needed someplace higher, with a better view of the beaches. And I'd have to figure out what to use for the shelter itself.

The night before, I slept on the sand, uncovered and freezing half the night on the damp, moist ground. Tonight I'd have to sleep on some kind of elevated surface, and put something between my body and the ground.

That afternoon I took some of the dwarflike clothing and laid it out in the open to dry. A great many of the things had become rotted and mildewed. I managed to dry a few things and packed them together to form a kind of makeshift mattress, and I rolled up a couple of shirts and made a pillow out of that. That would be my bed tonight.

That evening I opened the dog chow and gave Sam a half of a helmet full. He went right to work, gobbling it up. As for myself, I poured out stewed tomatoes, added some of the beige glop, and heated it up. I drank the mixture slowly. It tasted awful but it was nourishment. Then I washed out everything and turned the helmets upside down to dry. It was nighttime. There was nothing to do but sleep. I fell asleep soon afterward, Sam lying contentedly by my side.

15

One month had passed. I was marking each day carefully on a calendar, marking it upon waking in the morning. It was now September 23. In addition to the calendar, I kept a separate record of the remaining time. I would have to be on the island for 730 days, 104 weeks, or 24 months. Now the numbers were reduced to 700 days, 100 weeks, and 23 months. A slow progress, to be sure, but progress nevertheless. I figured that in that month I earned close to $5,000, if I counted my base pay and interest on the $100,000 deposited with Brundage.

If, in fact, any money had been deposited. If, in fact, they weren't just playing a game with me. If, in fact, they hadn't been killed in a crash on the way back to the United States. All these intangibles were creeping into my conscious thinking. All these ifs, and there were so many of them that, at night, I'd sometimes stay awake for hours brooding about my deal.

In that month, I'd done a great deal of work. The first

task I completed was uncovering all the canvases digging
into the sand, and examining all the supplies. I worked
every day on this till I had established some semblance of
order. After struggling through cans of glop, I now had a
method of examining them to know roughly what was inside. None of the cans, none of them whatsoever, had any
intelligible markings in the English language. All were stenciled with oriental figures. Every time I sat down to eat, I
had to think of Hildendorf and his cheap ways. If buying
American war surplus was cheap, what was it to buy
Korean war surplus? Probably the cans went for a penny
apiece, or perhaps some grafter in that unhappy land had
just dumped it all on Hildendorf for some political favor.
Well, I wouldn't know that for quite a while, and in the
meantime I had to eat.

The cans were in four basic sizes, with some variations.
One size held about half a gallon, the second size about a
quart, the third about a pint, and the fourth a half pint. A
pint can was one meal, a quart can two, and the half gallon
could make about five straight meals, that is, if I cared to
preserve the crap inside the larger cans, or cared to have
the same diet for five straight days. Because, what was in the
larger cans was unbelievably tasteless stuff. First, half the
cans held stewed tomatoes. I had by now recognized the
markings on these cans and put them, all eighty-four, to one
side, to whet my appetite for stewed tomatoes when the occasion should arise. One time I thought Sam might be in the
mood for some of these watery tomatoes, but he just sniffed
and sniffed, his tail drooping between his legs, then he gave
me a sorrowful look and walked away. I, the master,
spooned this shit into my system, while he crunched merrily
on the Purina dog chow.

There were eighty-five other large cans, of mixed breed.
A large group, twenty, had the same markings and contained the beige glop I had eaten my second night on the island. I still hadn't figured out what it was. What I knew

about it was that it was absolutely tasteless, was water-soaked, and slightly oily and coarse in texture. For all I knew, it could have been some kind of Korean antifreeze or formaldehyde in a solution of melted piston rings.

Thus, over a hundred of these large cans, in what I could laughingly refer to, using Hildendorf's words, as my "adequate supplies," contained shit. That left approximately seventy other large cans. There was a group, a dozen in all, with identical markings that I had set way in the back, because only desperation would force me to eat them, if in fact there was food inside. Floating in these cans was a dark scumlike creature, black and shiny, with white markings underneath. I tried to give some to Sam, but he wouldn't even go near his helmet. Perhaps it would be wise to just dump the dozen cans in the event I decided to try this foul stuff, but I kept them around just in case. Just in case what? I didn't know. Maybe if I had some unwelcome visitors, I could feed it to them. The gracious lord and sovereign liege of this miserable island would also show what a marvelous host he was. A scene perhaps out of *Titus Andronicus*.

Of the remaining fifty-eight cans, I had, I was sure, six cans of peas, six of something resembling rutabaga, and six of a pink vomity kind of vegetable. The other forty cans were random, and I had no idea what was inside until I opened them. But I had little hope that any of them would contain other than exotic vegetables or that slime that passed for seafood, black and unappealing.

The quart cans were a mixed breed. I hadn't opened too many of them, but I knew that of the 140 cans in this pile, thirty-eight still contained some kind of ground and chopped beef. An even larger number, forty-two, contained mandarin oranges in a sickly cloying syrup. The remaining sixty cans were of various markings, and I'd have to open them one at a time to find out just what was inside.

The pint and half pint cans were the best. Of the 200 or so cans in these exalted groupings, 123 contained a kind of beef stew, which was sustaining me in my craving for meat. Forty-seven other cans contained peaches in heavy syrup, and the others were of mixed contents, which again could only be ascertained by opening them.

Since there were 170 large cans and each could sustain five servings, that was 850 meals. The 140 medium-sized cans made an additional 280 meals, and the 200 pint and half pint cans a final 150 meals, a total of 1,280 meals in all. If I limited myself to two meals a day, that meant close to twenty-two months' supply of food, but that was if one figured on eating a helmet full of stewed tomatoes as a meal in itself. What had happened was that I was shortchanged, because there was no way this ungainly pile of rusted cans would serve my purposes. Of the cans already catalogued, these were the ones that weren't damaged or rusted beyond repair. I had already buried an additional pile of cans, about 100 I guess, which were rusted or leaky or in some way broken beyond repair. There were two other possibilities open to me for additional food, and that was the dozen or so coconuts on the trees and all the fish in the ocean. That was my main hope—the bountiful harvest of the sea.

The second pile containing clothing and what passed for clothing and bedding had taken a long time to sort out. I found twenty-six pairs of pants that would fit a midget, a number of shirts that would complement the pants, and some field jackets and miscellaneous clothing. All of the last items were rotted beyond any possible use. A sleeve or a flap would be unharmed, but most of the things were well gone from spending years moldering under canvas on wet sand. The camouflage hats were a separate pile of junk for which I could find no discernible use, since they were made for heads slightly larger than billiard balls. What army had used this stuff?

I dried out all the clothing that could still be salvaged and laid it out so that it formed a kind of rug under my feet, a place where I could rest and not touch sand or earth. I had found some string and rolled up a few of the shirts to make a pillow for myself. That was the main use I had for these items. There were also a couple of odd boots of various sizes, but no two that matched, and in any event, none that fit my feet or that I could even get my feet into. They were leather and I guessed I could have some future use for them, so they were put aside. In fact, the shoelaces had already been used as string to form my pillows.

The third and smallest pile was the key to my happiness and survival. Here were the items I found most useful. I had made use of the helmets as pots and the helmet liners as hats to shade me from the ever present sun. Digging around, I found some utensils, spoons, dull knives, and forks. Unlike the first pile, which was oriental in origin, and the second, which I could classify as indeterminate in origin, this third pile was definitely American war surplus. It was a motley grouping at best, but there were many things I could make good use of.

The most important was the M-1, which I had found at the bottom of a large carton, drowned in glop. I guessed that it was some kind of creosote, but whatever it was, it took days of careful cleaning, using precious alcohol, which I had bought in my drugstore excursion, to clean the rifle. It was a good weapon and contained a sling, so that I could carry it without using my hands. I had already tested the M-1 by putting five rounds in the clip, jamming it in, and firing. The gun fired beautifully. After the first round, which was aimed at the coconuts, I adjusted the sights. I fired two more rounds at the coconuts and two at a distant tree. No coconuts fell, but one was pierced to the heart, bleeding its white liquid down upon the sand. The tree's bark was shattered.

After firing the rifle, I cleaned it carefully with oil on a cotton swab, and used my hand mirrors to look up the metal barrel to make sure that the barrel itself was spotless. Take good care of your weapons, they had told me in the army, and the weapons would take good care of you. At that time, I thought it was all bullshit, but now I believed it. The M-1 was my guardian against any kind of danger.

I also found some old-fashioned army metal dishes, the kind that open up to hold a couple of food courses. In addition there were a few metallic GI cups. They were made of aluminum and hadn't rusted, but the plates were full of rust, as were the knives, forks, and spoons. I used sand to scrape off the rust, and it worked slowly but effectively. After cleaning off the rust spots, I washed all the utensils in the pond, using some of my precious Ivory soap. Then I dried them on a few of the small shirts, which I had previously washed out and used as dishtowels. Other shirts I used as a kind of makeshift tablecloth.

I found a trench tool, which was the army version of a combination pickax and shovel. It folded for easy carrying, and when rigid could dig quite well. In the army it was used for the ubiquitous foxholes. This was my main tool, for, when folded, it could be used as a kind of makeshift hammer as well.

In addition, I had two bayonets, one of which had a sheath. These attached to my garrison belt, and of course to the rifle, but there was no point in having the M-1 loaded with a bayonet. I didn't expect to meet anyone on my short journeys, and if I did, the rifle itself would be a formidable enough weapon. I didn't relish the idea of going to close quarters in a bayonet duel. The bayonet's main use was in opening cans. I'd hold the can rigidly between my knees as I knelt on the ground, and then, with a downward thrust, putting my full shoulder into it, I'd slam the bayonet point into the can, puncturing it. After a month's practice, I was pretty good at this, and could get a larger can open with about five of these thrusts, afterward forcing the edges open with the side of the bayonet. After my first attempt, which left a nasty gash on my thumb and index finger, I had no more mishaps, and both wounds had healed quickly and properly.

I found two canteens that were useful, and I'd carry one around with me, filled with water, at all times. There were three backpacks, one of which had broken straps, but the other two could be used in case I wanted to get off the island and load up with supplies. One of my best finds was a bowie knife in a leather sheath. I found it by digging about a foot into the sand, where it was buried along with some other things that had rotted. But the knife was sharp, and I stroked it against hard rocks to make it even sharper. It was my one cutting tool, because a bayonet was useful only for piercing. I always carried the knife around with me, along with the M-1, the ammunition belt, the cartridge holders, ammunition, canteen, and bayonet. It was like my old army days, except I walked around barefooted wearing my undershorts, which I washed out every night and hung to dry. I would be running out of clothing soon, which was going to be a problem, since it was just a matter of time before my boots split, my underwear was in tatters, and my shirt and pants fell to shreds.

I had slowly tanned myself, giving my body a little more sun each day, and although I have a light complexion and blue eyes and light brown, almost blondish hair, I had gotten a nice even tan, without any burning. I had also lost a great deal of weight, and my body was getting hard from the endless work and walking.

My shelter was still makeshift, and I was giving it further thought. I had taken the largest canvas and hung it to dry by stretching it tightly across piles of cans, while other cans held it down securely. Then after it dried thoroughly, I used the large cans containing the inedible black stuff as corners for my shelter, and hung the canvas so that it was about six and a half feet above the ground, with one end hanging over and touching the ground and the other end open.

Then I took two wooden racks that had held some of the

supplies off the ground and made them into supporting walls on two sides of the shelter, which I guess I could call my tent. It would be effective against the rain, since one end, the open end, had about seven additional feet of canvas doubled over on top and this could be lowered to make the tent entirely secure.

Inside this shelter, I had laid the shirts and pants that were salvageable, to make a kind of carpeted floor. It didn't fill up all the space inside, but it was two shirts deep and was my sleeping surface and also my pillow.

I had brought most of the important supplies inside this shelter. I had my writing materials in here, along with my medicines and drug supplies. My books were here, as were my lighters, the matches, and the candles. Thank God for the candles. I didn't have enough to last me two years, but what I had, if I used sparingly, would last a long time.

Generally, once darkness came, I sat in the dark with Sam alongside. I didn't build fires except for heating foods, and I hadn't used any of the candles except one night when part of the tent fell over.

This was my state of being after one month. I had done some journal keeping, noting the weather and my moods. The weather was invariably the same—cool, sometimes cold nights, warm mornings, and hot days. Rarely did I see a cloud in the sky, and there was always a late afternoon breeze blowing in from the west.

The only variations in the weather pattern were two cloudy days in which there was a light rainfall. I did see a couple of heavy storms at sea, however, and I could, from my vantage point, see lightning and thunderstorms about ten miles away. Seeing the lightning made me think of the hazards of a lightning storm. I wished I knew how to construct a lightning conductor. After all, I was surrounded by metal cans.

My reading was nil. I had started *Robinson Crusoe* but put it down after a couple of chapters. Living this life was more interesting than reading about it. I hadn't even opened my chess set or the chess book. I seemed to be busy all day long touring and planning and working. Time moved more rapidly this way.

16

The nights were becoming the most difficult time for me. As soon as darkness descended, there was nothing for me to do. I had a limited supply of candles, and didn't know how I would replenish them. Crusoe had used goat's fat for tallow, but I didn't know the process and anyway I didn't have any goats. I had begun the Defoe novel again after several false starts, but it held little interest for me. I would have been fascinated if Hildendorf had re-created the same conditions for me . . . an island full of goats, seeds for corn and rice, and a chance for both fresh meat and fresh grain. I had none of this.

Every morning, right after I marked off a calendar day, I took one of my vitamin pills. They were Thermagram-Ms, containing most of my needs for vitamins and minerals in a single capsule, but it was a poor substitute for the actual foods I should be eating. I had no fresh fruit, no fresh vegetables, no fresh meat, nothing fresh, in fact. The coconuts still beckoned to me. When the hell would they drop off the damn trees? Maybe a storm would do the trick, and I expected one any day. The winds were a little cooler, a little stronger, blowing from the north and west, and they were moist winds; though there were still few clouds to be seen.

The ocean was much choppier and I could see whitecaps way out in the sea. I had gone into the water a few times for a swim and to refresh myself, though I always stayed close to the shore. There could be sharks about . . . one bite and good-bye. When swimming, I stayed underwater as long as I could, holding my breath and keeping my eyes open. The water was crystal clear, and occasionally I could see schools of small fish about ten yards away from me, acting as though I didn't exist. If I had snorkel equipment I could spear a few of them, but of course, Hildendorf didn't give me any; neither had he given me any fishing gear.

I realized, in reading Defoe's novel, that Robinson Crusoe didn't do any fishing. He seemed content with his goats, for fresh food, even though he had a whole ocean of fish around him. Goats and birds. I hadn't seen a bird yet. I had gone down to the grove of trees on the east side of the island and stirred up the leaves, but no birds moved. Nothing moved except the flat, heavy leaves themselves. Maybe there was a season for birds; maybe they'd show up. Time would tell, and that I had plenty of, all the time in the world.

I had already gathered dead branches from the trees, those that had fallen on the ground or into the water, and dried them in the sun. The sun was great. It gave me unlimited heat and I put it to good use. I had already dried the second canvas, and that was set up as a miniature tent, holding most of my supplies now, except for things like the rifle and ammunition, which stayed close to me. Robinson Crusoe had a great deal of gunpowder, and had to keep that dry and buried all over his island, so that one storm or lightning strike wouldn't blow him and his powder sky high, or one downfall of rain ruin it.

I didn't have that trouble. The ammunition could get wet

and dry out. No problem there. But I wanted it at my side, and I was still fearful of a lightning storm. Where would it strike? Hit the palm trees most likely, but perhaps it would be directed at the metal in the cans. That thought always troubled me. I decided to have yet a third shelter, one for storms, where I would be perfectly safe from any lightning and rain. I looked around the island for just such a spot.

I thought seriously of moving my shelter to a different place altogether. In case someone did come to the island, I didn't want to be seen unless I cared to be, and I wanted to be in a position to observe whoever would arrive on these, my shores. I already figured it was my island, that I was the sovereign liege of this miserable terrain. I didn't take all this seriously, but as long as I was the sole occupant of island X, I wanted to have certain privileges, and one of them was to keep my privacy unless I wanted that privacy forfeited. Accordingly, I looked for areas where boats would anchor off the island, and where they would be most likely to send ashore smaller boats or rafts.

One thing I was sure of about this island—there was no place deep enough to permit a boat to sail directly to the shoreline, except near the sheer rocks on the southwest side. I had swum over there, and the water was rather deep, about twenty feet or more. But all around the island the water came to no more than a foot or two near the shore, and one could wade out about forty feet or so before the water had any appreciable depth. There was some depth of about four feet near the grove of trees, and that could be the docking area, but large rocks jutting from the water guarded that entranceway. I figured that anyone coming to the island by ship or boat would dock off either the north or west beaches, and then take a smaller boat in from there.

These two beaches, one on the north side and the other on the extreme west side, were the most attractive. The south beach was pebbly and not more than six feet wide, and at high tide there was hardly any sand discernible. I decided to place my shelter in a position where I could observe the long north beach, which ran almost the length of the island, and the west beach, which was much smaller but just as clean. Accordingly, I decided to move my things closer to the western part of the island. Right now I was in the eastern section, about three quarters of the way from the western tip.

I searched the terrain near the west beach, and thought of where the rains or winds would come from in case of a storm. I guessed they'd come from the north and west, and therefore it would be best to have a barrier between my shelter and the winds. Before moving my things I began a big digging project, moving a lot of sandy mush, packing it higher on the north and west side, till I had a barrier about six feet in height. I leveled the ground below it carefully, and then gathered what rocks I could find to reinforce this wall of sand.

It was a slow, painstaking job, and the sun was a difficult taskmaster, but I worked steadily. I had not smoked for almost two months now, and my wind had come back and I no longer panted after minor exertion. My skin was tanned, my fingers weren't tobacco stained, and my sputum was pure white.

I was getting into the best physical condition of my life, and I was thankful for that, since I had little else to be thankful for. I still kept up my journal but had done no real writing, and except for dipping into *Robinson Crusoe*, no reading whatsoever. My eyes were getting sharper, and my hearing was becoming more acute. I was aware of all the sounds around me, and those I couldn't hear, Sam did. We were a good team, walking our island, running along the beaches, playing together. The only thing Sam couldn't do was work, but he fulfilled my greatest need, that of companionship, and that was all I required of him.

After I had put up a solid earth barrier, I decided to place the canvas so that it would require no metal supports.

The wooden slats or racks, which were about three feet by four feet, were not quite high enough for side supports, and I had no nails to join them together, another item that I had asked for and missed sorely. I went back to the grove of trees and picked out two younger trees, which were ten or twelve feet in height. Not having a ruler, I tried to get a rough idea of sizes by using my belt, which was size 34. I wished it was a 36, for that would be three feet or a yard, but I divided the belt in half, and notched that portion, seventeen inches; then in quarters. Then I worked out a method of dividing the belt so that I could mark it by feet. After I got all through with this calculation, I realized how much simpler it would be to take some of the rope lying around, measure it against my belt, and then add what I considered two inches, about two thumb-joint lengths. This I did, then worked out the feet on the rope by marking each foot with blue ink. Then I marked out six inches, then three inches, then inch by inch.

Putting the rope around the first tree trunk at its widest part, I found that it came to nine inches. At last I had a way of measuring. I thought now of measuring the whole island by matching my stride to the three feet by continual practice and then pacing off the island, both in width and length, and then in smaller portions. I could mark off each one hundred yards with some kind of stone or wood. This could be my next project after my shelter was up.

I brought over my bayonet and knife and started hacking at the trunks of the two trees. I first had tried to topple them without cutting, but I could see that the trunk might crack in the center about five feet off the ground, and I wanted these trunks to be in one piece when I used them. Accordingly I started cutting with the bowie knife. It quickly dulled and had to be sharpened against rocks time and time again. The work was not only tiring but arduously uncomfortable, since I had to get into a squatting position with my back against a nearby tree to cut effectively. What

I wouldn't have given for an ax. I tried to use the pickax at the other end of my trench tool, but I had no space in which to freely swing it and it did little good, since it resembled a spade more than an ax and was about as sharp as an ordinary spade.

The one good thing was that the work was done in the shade. I cut and hacked and worked for three days on each tree and finally managed to topple them. Time was now working against me. The winds from the north were getting very cold, and in late afternoon they'd be joined by the west winds, which blew more fiercely every day, till the coconut trees swayed precariously. Still no coconuts fell.

After I got both trees down, I dragged them out of the groves, then put each one on my shoulder and carried them to the new shelter area. There I let them dry in the sun while I stripped the branches, which I put aside for firewood. I took off the broad green leaves, which looked like overgrown tobacco leaves except that they were a rich green, a deep shiny green. I'd find some uses for them and put them aside as well.

Then I dug holes and put each trunk into a hole six feet from one another, and pushed them into the ground until each trunk stood exactly seven feet in height. Having fixed this as the height of the shelter, I built up the sand barrier another foot higher, and then brought the large canvas over and placed it on the barrier so that about four feet overlapped. I took away earth and embedded the canvas into the barrier, and then added sand over the canvas so that the dirt itself rather than bulky cans formed the weight that held it firmly in place. Accomplishing this, I stretched out the canvas to make contact with both ends of the freshly fallen trunks so that the canvas fell over to the ground, resting on the trunks. There was a sag in the middle, the shelter had no opening, and I had to figure out a way to support the front portion of the canvas.

I wasn't going to use the cans at all. That left the wooden slats. I dug a trench in front and placed the slats in, and then placed the canvas on them. It still wasn't very steady, but it would do till I got more material. I decided to knock down another couple of trees to finish this shelter.

But it was too late for that. Instead I brought all my perishable supplies over to the new shelter, and laid them on the carpet of shirts and pants I had previously used. Already the sky was turning a deep gray, and lightning was flashing in the sky, followed by the rumble of thunder. I counted the interval. Twelve seconds. Then eleven seconds. It was moving closer.

The wind had picked up in velocity so that when I ran to get my remaining supplies, I was unable to make much headway against its force. The coconut trees were bent at odd angles, and one was almost parallel to the ground. The cans were toppling over, and the sand blew in huge, gusty sprays. I crawled into the shelter. The wind was hitting the sand barrier I had built so carefully with no effect. Lightning flashed. I could see it through the canvas, which I now lowered so that I was in complete darkness. Sam was in with me, shivering and whimpering in the dark.

The storm hit in early afternoon. Thunder now was one second away from the lightning, and then the rains came down with torrential force. They smashed against the shelter and, using my trench tool, I pushed at the canvas top continually to clear the water that was forming and weighting down the center of the canvas.

I tried to peer out of the shelter by raising it a little but a thick cloud of sand flew into my face. My eyes stung, and my face was soaked with rainwater. I closed the canvas and sat there in the dark, then lit a candle, and pulled Sam over to me to hold him. I could feel his body heaving and his heart beating rapidly.

"Easy, Sam," I said. "We're safe here." I had my helmets,

the canned food, two canteens full of water, the dog food, plus all my weapons, books, and perishable things surrounding me. The candle cast an eerie glow. It was strawberry scented and its aroma seemed strange and alien.

The rain poured down. I kept clearing the top of the canvas, but then there was an ominous sound as some of the trunks cracked and the whole side of the tent collapsed on us. Sam jumped up and the candle was extinguished. The wind lifted up the canvas and blew in sand followed by rain. I struggled to keep some semblance of order, tugging at the canvas, praying that the other trunk would hold. I pulled till my arms were weary, as the rain now came directly on us, with the canvas around my head, with my arms instead of the tree trunk holding it up.

I cursed the trunk that had fallen and cursed myself for building such an inadequate tent, but I couldn't give up now. I was soaked to the skin with perspiration, and my eyes stung with sweat, and the rains had soaked the carefully dried shirts and pants that formed our carpet. The books were getting wet, everything was getting soaked, and there was no way to work with any kind of light, since the canvas was collapsed around us.

The second trunk fell a short time later, but didn't crack. It simply uprooted. Now I was being smothered by the heavy canvas, and water was seeping in in all directions. I stood up, using my head as a support for the canvas, but the front of the shelter was now losing the battle to the winds and rain. Only the earth barrier was holding up, and I wondered if that too would fall.

Lightning hit nearby with a tremendous roar and flash. Sam whimpered and howled and cringed in the furthest corner near the earth barrier. I was scared out of my wits. I could smell smoke and fire but what was burning? Was it the canvas? No. Then the smell disappeared as more rain thudded down. I didn't even know if it was night yet, but all was pitch black. I stood there with the canvas pressing and weighing against my head, groping for the fallen trunk to possibly set it aright, but every time I moved, I dragged down another piece of canvas.

Oh yes, free room and board for two years. I had to laugh despite my misery. And I was miserable. I was soaking wet and sneezing, and I was bone weary, but if I let go of the canvas, everything would collapse around me, possibly including the earth barrier. My support took most of the pressure away from the sand wall. I didn't know how much longer I could keep standing like this. My clothes were sopping wet and I was freezing cold and shivering. The storm was still picking up force, the wind howled with increasing ferocity. Sam whimpered in the corner, and I girded my final strength to keep the canvas up. My shoulders were sore, my back hurt, and my head pained. Weariness and fatigue were defeating me, but I held out as long as I could, feeling that, if I let go, it would be the end of everything.

17

The storm raged on all night. After a while, completely exhausted, I gave up and dropped the canvas and lay on the wet clothing, shivering with cold. I managed later to get back on my feet and prop up the canvas somewhat, closing down both ends so that the flooding was kept at a minimum, but it was a losing effort. The dog and I huddled against the earth barrier, trying to keep warm as best we could. There was no chance to light a candle or to get any heat against the raging of the wind and the continual sprays of water soaking us.

I didn't sleep all night, and the next morning the rain had reduced itself to a fine drizzle. I staggered out of the broken-down shelter and surveyed the damage around me. The tent was finished. I'd have to start all over again, using canvas and new tree trunks. I went back inside and lit a candle. Everything in the tent was sopping wet, and that included the notebooks and the books I had so carefully placed in the shelter. Nothing had escaped the rain.

Outside, the island looked weary and crestfallen. The coconut trees were still standing, although a couple were bent
over precariously, but I guessed as soon as their trunks
dried they'd contract and straighten out again.

Most of the cans were still at the other side of the island
and I didn't care to walk in the rain right now. What
difference would it make if some glop spilled out anyway?
No difference at all to me in my present condition. Right
now the most important thing was to get dry and warm. I
was shivering, and occasionally my whole body would shake
with cold. What I wouldn't have given for a fresh change of
clothes, for a dry blanket to wrap around myself.

The wind had abated considerably, and I used this respite to pull the canvas as tightly as I could, stretching it
and trying to shake off the water that had formed in huge
puddles on its surface. The canvas seemed ten times heavier
than it had been before the rain, and it was thoroughly
water soaked. If I had been clever, I would have put it up
as a tent, with a sloping front instead of a flat top, to dis-
courage water from forming and weighing it down. Also, I
would have extended the earth barrier, which was the only
thing that held throughout the storm, to the west as well as
the north, so that both sides of the shelter would be permanent.

It was too late now for all this. The storm was still going,
but was in its last gasps and there was nothing to do but
make myself as comfortable as possible, and try to dry out.

I picked up both tree-trunk poles. One had split in two,
but the other was still in perfect shape. I cleared out some
of the wet rags underneath my feet and dug a hole with the
trenching shovel, working as best I could in the cramped
and wet interior of the shelter, with the heavy canvas pressing against my back. I was crouched down, working by
flickering candlelight, squatting on my haunches. Since
there was no inside support for the tent, my back was the
replacement, and I could feel my skin rubbing against the

canvas, rubbing itself raw. But I had to get something going here, in case another storm hit now. I couldn't go through one more night of that agony.

However, if another night or a week of storms occurred, what would be my alternative? There was nothing I could do but endure. I'd be in great discomfort, probably catch pneumonia, but what could I do but make the most of it? I couldn't get away from the island, I couldn't improve my position here, I was stuck with my fate.

After working for about a half hour, I got the hole dug and placed the undamaged pole in, and sufficiently enclosed it so that it stood by itself. With the pole in place, I was able to prop the canvas on it, and the water began draining off the sides. I then dug one more hole and placed the smaller, broken pole in the ground, near the front of the shelter. After this was done, I had a sort of bastardized tent, with the canvas flat in the back and tentlike from the middle section to the front. I removed the slats from the entrance and propped them up on the sides, to keep the canvas from falling inward. This was easier said than done, and finally I just left the slats slanting outward, hoping that the wind wouldn't pick up and knock them over.

Having done all this, I was exhausted. I drank some water from the canteen and poured out some in a helmet for Sam. I gave him some dried dog food, which was now soaking wet, and he halfheartedly ate a little, sniffed, and retreated back to the far corner against the barrier to lie down and shiver.

I removed all my wet clothes and stood there like a naked bird, flapping my arms to keep warm. I had no alternative clothing to wear, and no way to build a fire, since all the firewood was soaked, and only a can of sterno could be used. I lit the sterno, smashed into a small can which I knew contained meat, and cooked it over the sterno in the can itself. I didn't have the patience to wait for a helmet to heat up, which took forever. I held the tin can with a makeshift glove made up of a couple of shirtsleeves which I picked up off the sand. The meat heated up and I ate it slowly, feeling my insides warm up. This was my only hope to stay warm. I had both the candle and the sterno going, and I tried to dry my clothing over the two flames, but they didn't give off that much heat. There was nothing I could do now but wait for the sun to reemerge, though when that would happen, I had no idea. I didn't know how long these storms lasted. It might be for another few hours or another week, and what I'd have to do now would be to cope. Endure.

I heated up a can of dog food and gave it to Sam. He ate it slowly but surely and that perked up his spirits. It was our first meal in many hours. His shivering stopped, and he made some effort to walk around the shelter. So we waited out the rain. I shook the notebooks and the books, to get the excess water off them, but it did little good. I would have to wait for the sun to dry out everything.

I sat naked, as close to the sterno and candle as I could, then I tried to lie down and sleep. I was too cold to sleep and opened my eyes every few minutes, as chills shook my body. The rain hit the shelter steadily but little was seeping in. I sat and shivered, Sam whimpered in the corner, as we waited out the storm. It rained all day, all that night, and the next day. We sat in the shelter and waited. I used up one can of sterno on heat and meals, and then blew out the candle as we waited in the dark. Finally the rain stopped. It stopped so suddenly that I awoke from a dozing sleep. I stepped outside. It was nighttime. Clouds raced in front of a full moon. It was cool out, but for once I could stand without being rain pelted. Sam came out and stood with me. Then we went back inside. I again tried to sleep, but couldn't because of the cold. I waited for morning, for sun. The sun would rouse me again, bring me back to life. It was a long, long night, but dawn broke brightly. For the first time in three days the sun was shining. I stepped out with

Sam and raised my arms to the sky. To heaven. To my god, the sun.

I spent the day sleeping outdoors, surrounded by the soaking clothing that made up the floor of my tent, besides my own clothing, the books, and notebooks. The sun was bright, but not as bright as before the storm, and the air was definitely cooler, but one day's sunlight was sufficient to dry out most of the clothing.

I also spread out the canvas, but it was still damp the following night and I couldn't use it till it dried again. Thus I spent the night under the open sky, covered by the cotton war-surplus clothing. I huddled in the dark and slept somewhat, waking more refreshed the next day. The first thing I did was add the three days I spent trapped in the shelter to my calendar, keeping it up to date. October had slipped by and this was now the third of November, the month of Thanksgiving. I circled Thanksgiving Day.

"No turkey this year," I told Sam, who wagged his tail and went bounding off ahead of me.

"No turkey," I told myself aloud, "just stewed tomatoes this year."

My work was now cut out for me. I had to build an adequate shelter and build it fast. I didn't know when the next storm would strike. The weather had definitely changed for the worse, with cooler days and colder nights. Perhaps a storm was brewing somewhere over the horizon, and if it struck I wanted to be prepared. No more makeshift shelters. I had been deluded by the fair and calm weather that had prevailed for the first two months. I had been indolent and lazy. No more. I needed a good strong, solid shelter, and I needed it fast.

I took my tools and went to the small forest, surveying the trees. I wouldn't be satisfied with two trunks. I needed something quite substantial.

I began hacking and sawing that morning. When I grew too exhausted from this work, I returned to the canvas, turning it in the sun, getting it dry. I also surveyed the cans, which the storm had strewn around a half acre area. Lightning had hit a few of the cans, which were charred. That's what I had smelled that night, that sudden smoking sensation. God, I was lucky I hadn't been using them for the support. One lightning strike and that would be good-bye. I never thought of lightning back in the United States, and storms had meant nothing but discomfort previously, but I was growing respectful of electrical storms. Very wary of them. I wished I had more knowledge of electricity and what precautions to take. If only I had chosen useful books instead of the junk I had brought. A lot of good T. S. Eliot's poems were now, when I needed information about life and death situations.

Yes, the sky above was naked and I was naked as well, defenseless against the elements. I would have to be very careful and take nothing for granted, nothing. If I had lolled around that old shelter, I would have probably been dead today. I would be super cautious about my new shelter.

All week long I hacked down trees till I had cleared six fine poles, of unequal length, but all were over eight feet in height. I carried them to my new shelter area and decided how I would build the new tent. The earth barrier was still there, and had held up well against the wind's pounding. It blocked off the north. I wanted the west blocked off as well, and dug out earth and sand, piling it up on the west side till it ran perpendicular to the northern barrier. It was eight feet in length, while the northern barrier was six feet in width. The canvas was twelve by fifteen feet. Armed with all these figures, I decided to put two poles in the center, so that the canvas would slope and not be flat on top. I then hacked two eight-foot poles in half and placed them in a position to hold the eastern edge of the tent in place.

It was a peculiar-looking shelter all right. The canvas was secured on the north and west by earth, holding it tightly in place. In the center, the two poles raised its height to seven feet, a foot higher than both barriers, allowing the rain to slope off. The problem here was that the rain would run off easily on the east side, but would gather and form on the north and west sides, trapped by the earth. To solve this dilemma, I dug troughs, two on each side, in the earth barriers so that the rain would run out and away from the shelter.

On the north and west sides, the height inside the tent was six feet, in the center, seven feet, and on the east side it sloped down to three feet, which was the length of the poles showing above the ground, each pole having been buried for one foot. I now took the remaining poles and buried them on the south side, at a height of five feet, so that there was a slope there, and thus I could enter and leave lowering my head, since my only method of egress and ingress through the tent was at the south side. I placed two poles there, and now I had a secure structure, one that I felt could withstand a severe storm.

I folded back the canvas so that the south opening was always open, but in the event of a storm I could close it down. I folded the canvas and placed it on top of the structure, using the extra canvas on the south side this way. My vision was hampered, since I only had a view of the south side of the island from my tent, but it served a purpose in case of storms. This was going to be my main structure.

Now I'd need an alternate structure for nonstorm use, where I'd have an unobstructed view of the two good beaches, on the north and west sides, which were, unfortunately, the two sides naked to the prevailing winds.

Since I had already built a barrier on the north side, I decided to use this as the back wall of my other structure. I began digging and built up another wall on the east side, which left the north and west sides free of obstructions. In the event of a storm, this structure could easily fall, so I decided to use the smallest canvas here, which would serve as a sleeping tent, and I went to work cutting more poles for this structure. Before I could finish, however, the winds began to rise and were full of moisture, and I prepared for another storm.

It hit that night. I was in my new shelter, and stayed there, my candles nearby, all my ammunition and supplies inside with me. Again the rains pelted down, and the winds blew fiercely till they screamed above my head. Again Sam whimpered and cringed. The storm lasted all night and part of the next day, but other than one of the side poles falling down, there was no damage, and the structure held up beautifully. There was some leaking on the west side, and I realized that two troughs weren't enough to drain out the water running off the western slope of canvas. Having learned this, I then built a third trough on both sides.

Some damage was done to the barrier I had built for the temporary tent, but not anything I couldn't repair quickly. I set to work again after the storm abated. I also began to camouflage the tent from the beaches, so that while I would have an unobstructed view, unwelcome visitors wouldn't be able to see it. I built up sand barriers and dunes on all sides, and I was able to lie in this new tent, my rifle at my side, secure in the knowledge that I could follow any activity on the north and western beaches while remaining hidden from view.

There I was, impervious to all kinds of imagined enemies, none of whom had set foot or shown themselves yet. But who knew when they would come? Or when anyone would come to the beaches of my stronghold island, my fortress.

I worked through November in this way. Thanksgiving Day came and went. Instead of stewed tomatoes, I opened a new can and found corn. This was a little more tasty, but how much corn could one eat? I mixed it with the meat and

gave thanks to God for being alive and for Sam's being alive
and being such a good companion. I even read aloud from
the Bible, from Ecclesiastes.

"Cast thy bread upon the waters: for thou shalt find it
after many days.

"Give a portion to seven, and also to eight; for thou knowest
not what evil shall be upon the earth.

"If the clouds be full of rain, they empty themselves upon
the earth: and if the tree fall toward the south, or toward the
north, in the place where the tree falleth, there it shall be.

"He that observeth the wind shall not sow; and he that
regardeth the clouds shall not reap."

"Isn't that so," I said to Sam. "Isn't that the living truth,
Sam?"

Sam wagged his tail.

18

My beard was a luxuriant reddish blond color. Looking at it in a small hand mirror, and never having had a beard before, I realized that some unknown ancestors of mine had been redheads. Perhaps they had been inhabitants of similar islands.

I didn't know much about my ancestry, and my attempts at questioning my father about his family had usually ended up with his complaining about me some way or other. All conversations with my father, as far as I could remember, seemed to end up in arguments or cold indifference on his part. He was an unhappy man and a drinker, and he took out his unhappiness on the family. His idea of a good time was to mingle with his cronies in some bar downtown till closing time, then stagger back to the house and sleep it off. When my mother tried to wake him the next morning for work, he flailed at her, and then would get up cursing and screaming. To this day, I've been turned off by the bar scene, by that vision of lights and glasses and bottles and bleary-faced people gulping down their liquor.

Having had enough of my father's bouts, I could now take or leave alcohol. When I was a kid in college, I did some serious drinking, and got sick and hung over and went through the usual disgraceful things, throwing up at parties, and so on. Then, once my college days were over, so were my drinking days. My brother, who is seven years older, is a big drinker, the martini drinker, who invites you to his house and plies you with what he calls "highballs." He drinks a lot with his wife, who is a rummy, and they hide this vice under the canopy of good parenthood, with all their stupid Christmas cards showing the family at the Yuletide tree, and an accompanying letter telling of all their accomplishments during the year.

"Phil was given a nice promotion, and we are setting out for a new place, Iran, which we all look forward to with great eagerness. The children are particularly thrilled; imagine being in an Arabian [sic] wonderland!!!! And little Betty had the tooth fairy visit . . ." and on and on with this bullshit. I don't even know what I have in common with my brother. The same blood must course through our veins, but I might, like the red streaks in my beard, have additional blood of some ancestor which permitted me to deviate from the path of holy uprightness, of middle-class valuedom.

My mother was the sufferer throughout her life, and I suppose, as I have reflected many times in the past, that was the life she wanted, the life of a martyr. Or maybe she didn't know any better, or now, as I think of my own plight here, maybe that's all she could get out of life. There probably is an ideal life, which to me would be a life filled with joy, love, and happiness. I thought about this more and more during the long nights here, while I sat alone and stared out at the sea and the starry sky.

If I had been in love with a good woman in LA, then no money in the world would have dragged me out here. It hadn't been the money, after all, that had seduced me into this insane idea. It had been my own emptiness, my own vacant life, figuring that the money would buy me something called happiness, that the money would somehow give me a satisfied life. But that was really middle-class bullshit thinking. I remembered Freud's remark that man hungers after the satisfactions of childhood, and money wasn't one of those satisfactions. Therefore he seeks substitutes.

What were the satisfactions of childhood? To be loved and comforted and supported despite your faults . . . and to have Mama there when you needed her, no matter how badly you had acted. Mama was there to love you, not to judge you. You were her flesh and blood, and her womb had brought you forth.

But even as I thought these thoughts, I realized that I could not look back upon my childhood with any degree of nostalgia. My mother had tried to supply these comforts, but she was too weak to overcome my father. Just too weak. When she was harassed by him she often took it out on me. Later she'd be sorry, and rock me in her arms, holding and kissing me when I was a little boy. I lived for these moments of tenderness, not the hours of frustrated anger. Oh yes, my childhood. I thought of the schools I had gone to. The teachers wanted order and they wanted standardization and normalcy, and I was an alien among the stalks of robots the schools were turning out. Any deviation from this norm, any sign of creativity or nonconformity, was severely punished, and when reports of my "bad behavior" were sent to my father, he whipped me. "Don't cause trouble, boy," he'd shout. That was his battle cry: "Don't cause trouble." To him, reeling around the streets wasn't trouble, but any desire to do something different was.

My father reeled once too often and was hit by a car on his forty-fourth birthday. I was ten at the time. He had been celebrating his birthday, with his gang of drinkers. The car hit him and threw him about fifty feet, so I was told, and his head and back were crushed. He didn't die on the street, and came to only long enough to mumble something in the hospital before expiring. The nurse told my mother the words: "It's beautiful, it's beautiful."

"He must have been a fine man," said the nurse. "I'm sure he was describing you, Mrs. DeWinter."

My mother stood stony eyed, because she knew as well as I did that he was probably describing the last bottle of scotch he had hauled down, or perhaps a cheap cake some crony had brought to the bar, for him to ignite with his whiskey breath. My brother, who was seventeen, was at the University of Texas when my father died. He was studying petroleum engineering and wanted to be as far away from us as possible. So I stayed home with my mother. She had a job in a department store, wrapping gift boxes, which forced her to be on her feet all day. But she gave people some pleasure, and sometimes a particular gift that she wrapped brought her joy, especially if a poor person had purchased it and it was going to be a wonderful surprise.

Sometimes I went down to the department store to speak to her, or on Saturdays to have lunch with her. On Saturdays I'd pack a lunch for both of us. I already knew something about taking care of myself, and would boil eggs and make egg and tomato sandwiches on whole wheat bread. I'd put in a piece of lettuce and some pickles and if it was a nice day we'd sit on the lawn near the store and eat the sandwiches. My mother would buy me a malted milk sometimes as a treat, while she drank coffee.

Those were pleasant afternoons, as I remember. I didn't care whether or not I was out playing ball on those days. I didn't often go to the store on Saturdays, but I went at least once a month. The rest of my spare time I read books, for already I was a loner, separate, with separate dreams. Thus passed my childhood. My brother, on the other hand, joined

fraternities, and my mother sent him what she could out of
the pittance she earned, to keep up his social life. She found
extra work in part-time jobs, helping rich women with their
private social parties. I was invited to one of these children's birthday parties by some magnanimous rich bitch,
and remembered how awkward I felt, knowing no one and
wearing my inferior clothes. A girl asked me who I was, and
the hostess's son said, "Oh, he's with that lady there," pointing to my mother and frowning. What he really said was
that I didn't belong, that I was an intruder, and he was so
right. It was the last party I ever went to like that.

By the time my brother graduated from engineering
school he was engaged, but he wouldn't bring his girl to our
filthy neighborhood. Instead, he stayed with her family the
summer after graduation, and then told us to come to Dallas
to meet his future in-laws. My mother couldn't afford the
trip, but she borrowed some money and we took a Grey-
hound bus there. It was a long, dismal ride. I was fourteen
then, and I remembered the hours spent doing nothing but
looking at fleeting landscapes through the window. We
seemed to do most of the traveling at night.

When we got to Dallas, my brother inspected my
mother's clothing and makeup as if prodding a chicken he
was about to slaughter. He was ashamed of her and of me.
We met the family, who were full of false heartiness and
good spirit, and "Well, what do you think about Texas,
young man?" I thought it sucked. When the future father-
in-law heard we had come down by bus, he put two and
two together, and knew his daughter was marrying into a
nondescript family, and told us that we should fly down for
the wedding, which was scheduled for the following May.
In the meantime, my brother was going to be working for
the same firm his father-in-law was vice-president of and
which he still works for, by the way. The plane tickets were
going to be paid for in advance and mailed to us, but when

the envelope arrived, there was only one ticket, so my
mother took the flight herself. I didn't care to go anyway.

I roused myself from these fond memories and got up and
called Sam over. We walked over to where my notebooks
were, and I sat down and wrote something in the journal for
that day. This was December, with Christmas but a week
off, but I planned something spectacular for Christmas Day.
I would shoot off the rifle or masturbate three times that
day, or something unusual like that, but what was the point
of celebrating? It was a time more for reflection than anything else, and it amazed me that I was reading the Bible
rather than the other books.

I had played with my chess set and gone over a few of
Fischer's games, but they held no real interest for me, and I
put the book of chess games away, knowing that I wouldn't
care if I never opened it again. Games. They were for the
birds. . . . My game was life itself, and it was far more interesting than playing out Fischer's moves on a chessboard,
abstract and artificial as it was. I wondered how long he
could spend on this island by himself, with no one to complain to about seating or lighting or money arrangements.
Another of my private jokes.

I wrote a page and a half in the journal, trying to get
down my feelings as well as the weather, the scenery, and
what else I could think of. But the journal writing was es-
sentially boring to me, as were all the other vestiges of
civilized life. I didn't care to read or write or be involved in
what I had been involved in before. I had now been on the
island for close to four months, and it was as though I had
been here for years. This was my life now, here was my future.

Time was different on the island. Nights were times of
sleep and thought; days, times for work and walking. I kept
myself as busy as I could. When I wasn't working, I inspected the island, continually checking it out. One of my
projects had been to measure the island, but I gave that up.

It was too civilized. What difference would it make? It was all an artificial measurement anyway. When I measured the canvas or the trees I was chopping down, that was important, that meant survival, but the size of the island, that was something that went into books, and I wasn't interested in books. I had two immediate projects in mind, both of which I was working on simultaneously, but by different methods. One was to get the coconuts off the trees, and the other was to do some fishing. My eating habits had slackened, but I craved fresh food. The canned glop was getting to my mind and intestines, and I could hardly retain some of the things I was finding in the cans, liquid swills of unknown origins.

In order to get to the coconuts, I'd have to climb the trees. I guessed I could do it, but still I didn't want to take the chance of a fall, of a possible broken leg. So I experimented with a harness. I got some rope and tied it around my waist and around the palm tree trunk and then inched my way up barefoot, holding on to the rope and the trunk simultaneously. I had already made some progress over the bent tree, climbing about fifteen feet in the air, testing it. I would soon make the big climb.

Christmas Day dawned as all other recent days here, sunny and cloudless. But my spectacular effort was going to begin. Today I had decided to climb the tree. I had worked on the rope arrangement carefully, tying one end of the rope around my waist and around my thighs, so that it formed a harness. The other part of the rope was tied around the tree trunk, with a slack of about a foot. If the rope broke, I was a goner, and would fall on my back and probably break it. But, on the other hand, if the rope held, I could get up the tree and, in the event of a slip, I'd only go down a few feet. And since the topmost part of the tree was bent by the previous storms, I'd have to climb out to the coconuts with my back almost parallel to the ground about sixty feet in the air, a scary proposition.

My mind was made up, however. This was the day. I got

up early and decided not to eat anything before the climb. I drank some water and went to the tree. The palm trees hung over the slope of the land, so that the coconuts, when they had previously fallen off, would have rolled down into the water and have been swept away. When climbing, I would find myself over the same slope, but wouldn't land in the water if I fell, but on the land itself.

I tested the rope one last time. I had tested and retested it till I was sure it wouldn't give. It was a heavy, coiled rope. I wore my undershorts and my regular belt, tightened to the last hole, which I had recently made because of the shrinking of my waistline. I also carried my knife, shoved between the belt and my flesh.

I stood at the base of the tree and looked up. It seemed so much higher from this spot, but whatever the height, it would be climbed today. I attached the rope carefully around both myself and the trunk, so that we were bound by one continuous loop, and then I tied the rope around my belt and around my thighs, but not tight enough to stop any circulation. I put my bare feet on the trunk, pressed myself against it, and started climbing, using my hands and feet. I paused every few feet to lift the rope with me.

The rope was definitely a hindrance, because I had to pause and keep lifting it up with me. I climbed about half-way up the tree, and looked down at Sam watching me with consternation. I decided not to look down again because it was a little frightening and dizzying, so I continued my climb looking at the trunk itself. I inched my way up, feeling an ache in my shoulders and arms. Now I paused, not so much to bring the rope up, but to rest my arms, which were getting weary. Up to this point I held on nicely, because the trunk became narrower the further up I climbed. My arms were getting very, very tired, however.

I now was at the section of trunk that sloped and bent almost parallel with the ground. To get to the coconuts, I'd

have to climb with my arms and legs wrapped around the
trunk and my back parallel to the ground itself. I held on
tightly to the trunk and thought of going down again, for
this was my last chance to go down the tree in safety. Once
I climbed out further I was committed, and if the rope or
trunk gave way, God help me.

I held on and sweated, sorry I hadn't brought a shirt so
that I could wipe off my hands and face. I rubbed my hands
against the rough bark of the tree, thinking that it would
have been so much easier to chop down the palm tree, but I
didn't want to destroy one of these trees just to get at some
of its fruit. That would be sacrilege. No, this was my test,
and I would know very soon whether or not I failed it.

I took a deep breath. Then, with my arms and legs securely around the swaying trunk, I moved forward. The
trunk bent about two feet, and for a moment I thought it
would break off. Sweat rolled into my eyes. But the tree
held. I inched across, staring directly at the blue sky. How
blue it was! I wanted to wipe my face but didn't dare loosen
my grip. I kept moving, closer and closer to the palm leaves
and the coconuts themselves. My arms felt like lead, and it
was all I could do to keep them around the tree, and at last
I could hold on no longer. I hesitated, hesitated again for
what seemed an hour but was perhaps five seconds, and let
go. My upper torso went pitching down to the ground, but
the rope held me. I dangled there, my head pointing to the
earth, my legs wrapped around the trunk, the rope creaking
along with the tree trunk. Blood rushed to my head. With
my free hands I wiped off my face, rubbed the muscles of
my arms and relaxed them. I counted for sixty seconds, then
with an effort, got my hands back around the trunk and
pulled the upper part of my body to its rough texture.

The rest had done wonders, though I felt a strong pain in
my lower back, where the pressure of falling had been
stayed by the rope. It really hurt. I was perhaps ten feet

from the palm leaves and the coconuts, and I moved toward them. Finally, the leaves were scratching at my arms and face. My next maneuver was to turn myself around on the trunk, so that I was on top rather than below it. I used the power of my legs to begin the motion, and felt my bare skin getting scraped badly as I turned. Then I pressed my chest against the trunk and turned slowly. I was now on top, and the effort made me dizzy. I closed my eyes to regain my balance and for a moment I was really frightened. Everything was spinning. I had momentarily lost my equilibrium with the turn, and I hung on for dear life, my whole body pressed tightly to the trunk. I was facing down, but was afraid to open my eyes, afraid that I would fall from dizziness.

I kept my eyes tightly shut for a long time, then opened them. Nothing had changed. I was a few feet away from the coconuts and crawled on my belly toward the palms. The coconuts dangled beneath them. I stopped and got my knife out of the sheath. I was among the palm leaves now, brushing them aside with the same hand that held the knife.

I got to the first coconut and dislodged it by cutting through the stem holding it. It fell to the slope below and rolled toward the water, but stopped on the sand. I got to the second. I cut five coconuts off the tree before my work was over. Then I replaced the knife and rested for about five minutes before turning myself upside down. I began my downward climb with my hands and feet. This was easier except for one mishap. I lost my concentration at one point and slipped. The rope caught on the trunk and stopped my fall. I scraped both arms in my momentary panic, but soon righted myself and made my way down to the ground without further trouble. Sam was waiting for me, wagging his tail.

I untied the rope with shaking and tired hands, and then

went and gathered up the five coconuts. Then I lay on the sand, utterly fatigued. My whole body ached, but I had accomplished what was for me the highlight of my stay on the island. I had gotten those coconuts down by conquering my fear. I had won this battle by myself.

19

Christmas came and went; the New Year glided by. I kept writing in the journal and wondered what kind of book I would produce. The more I thought of the whole project the more I felt I was deluding myself into thinking that Hildendorf was serious. It was just too insane. Perhaps there were other motives involved. Perhaps it was a plan engineered by my wife to put me away for good.

That thought entered my mind from time to time. Could it be that somehow Brundage and my wife were conspiring for my demise? That Brundage had hired a Hollywood character actor to portray Hildendorf, given him a couple of thousand dollars to play this part, and then had me shipped out here, to be discarded and forgotten? Anything was possible in the realms of the unconscious when naked fear took over.

My imagination seemed at times more insane than the idea. Still, I couldn't believe that my stay here was anything more serious than a lark or a dream, and although I was

spinning it out, in the end it would all disappear into fluff
and I would be my own victim.

The plots seemed to evaporate when I thought of how
simple it would have been to dispose of me at several times
during this madcap spree. After all, I was blindfolded and
helpless from the moment I left the hotel till I arrived on
this island. At any point I could have been put away or
disposed of. So, I guess that was not the plan. Perhaps they
really thought I'd turn out a kind of modern *Robinson
Crusoe,* but the circumstances were too dissimilar. I was a
volunteer; I was doing it for money; I knew just how long
I'd be staying here. Completely different circumstances. My
present life was like a prison term for embezzlement. You
stole so much and you figured you'd plead guilty and do
your time and the time would be worth the money you'd
have when you got out. In my case, $100,000 for two years.

Every now and then I'd get into this mood and regret it
later. It was all nonsensical conjecture and drained my energy, which could be used for more important things.

January crawled on its merry way. The new year was the
same as the old year. Things were timeless on this island.
No change occurred unless I instigated it, unless I rear-
ranged cans or did some work on the shelter, or knocked
down another tree or two. By the time February 23 came,
my life had become one of indolence. I celebrated my six
months' stay by eating the last of the coconuts and marking
another landmark on the calendar. Now I had only 546
days, seventy-eight weeks, and eighteen months to go. Time
had passed rather quickly, I realized that morning. Already
I had served one quarter of my time. I took stock of things.
I had finished both shelters. My permanent shelter had been
further improved by cutting holes in the canvas so that the
side poles fit in them securely, thus making the tent twice as
sturdy as before. In addition, I had added another center
pole.

The smaller shelter suited my everyday needs perfectly,

and was tightly built, with as many poles holding it up as the larger tent, because I had done a prodigious amount of woodcutting. I had also moved the cans closer to my shelters and had them placed in orderly rows. My meat supply, and thus my protein supply, was fast diminishing since most of the cans contained vegetables.

Sam's dog food was near an end, which was my main concern now. I didn't mind sharing my meat with him, but there was little enough of that left, and I knew, unless I got more protein in his diet, he would really suffer. After all, as a human I was omnivorous, while he was carnivorous. A great gulf lay between the eating habits signified by those two words.

With this in mind, I decided to find some way to catch fresh fish. I had already tried various crude methods, using just my hands or a knapsack, trying to scoop fish out of the water, but none of these worked. I whittled branches till they had a sharp point and went underwater, trying to spear fish, but without the opportunity to shoot the spears at them, I couldn't hit anything, and my spear would float harmlessly to the surface time and time again. I even waded out to my neck, holding the spear, ready to strike it into a fish. A few times a fish would come near, but up to now I was unsuccessful, with several near misses.

I determined to build a fishing rod and to use bait and hook to catch the fish. I wasn't much of a fisherman, and had only gone out a few times in my life on fishing boats in the East because I never really cared to find a fish struggling at the end of my line, his life expiring quickly in terrible pain. But this was different. This was survival.

I needed, above all, a workable hook. Accordingly, I examined the cans I was continually chomping into with my bayonet. The edges I produced were ragged and sharp, and I finally found a few that I could shape into a semblance of a hook. They had to be thin, very thin and pointed, about the size of a paper clip. And then, to my surprise, I remem-

bered that I had a box of paper clips with me. I had bought
them in a stationery store that last week in LA, along with a
lot of other nonsense, like erasers and manila folding enve-
lopes. I shook out a few paper clips, and then, using both
my bayonet and whatever hard rocks I could find, I filed a
few of them to a fine point. The trouble with these clips was
that they were made of very soft metal and had little rigid-
ity. Still I decided to try and fashion them into useful
fishing hooks.

I bent the clip so that it resembled a hook, and sharpened
its edge till it could penetrate and cut. Then I tied a shoe-
lace to it, and tied the lace to the rope I had used for my
tree-climbing expedition. I then tied the other end of the
rope to a branch of a tree I had whittled clean. The branch
was strong and supple, perfect for a fishing rod. I tested it
by penetrating a batch of leaves with the makeshift hook
and then lifting them. My main problem was not with the
rope or the branch, but with the clip. It tended to open up
under pressure of any weight whatsoever and would not
stay bent. I didn't know how to solve this problem but
hoped that a fish would get caught long enough for me to
bring it to the surface. In any event, I decided to try out my
fishing rod, if I could call this amalgam of parts such an object.

My next requirement was bait. I immediately thought of
the black stuff that filled several cans and that I had no use
for, yet smelled fishlike. I'd put that crap to use. I took a
handful and diced it into small pieces, so that I could bait
the clip. I put the rest in one knapsack which I carried on
my back. I carried another knapsack on my shoulder and
jabbed holes in the shoulder bag so that, if I got a fish in,
the excess water would run out through the holes.

I put on my fishing outfit, which consisted of the two
knapsacks, a belt, and my knife. I wore a helmet liner to
keep the sun away from my head, and waded naked out
into the water near the middle of the north beach. I waded

out to a point where the water was against my chest, and dropped in the line. The pole was about five feet in length, and the rope hung from the pole, so there was no casting possible. I stood as still as I could and waited for results.

I stood in the water for a long time, and nothing happened. Then I moved to a different spot, and then to several others. I traversed the whole of the beach front that day, without even a nibble. As I was about to give up, the rope jerked and the branch bent. I lifted up the rod slowly but the clip was empty of bait. Well, at least that meant that this bait might be acceptable. I resolved to try again the following day.

It's remarkable how patient a man can be when he is on the quest of basic food. I now understood the solitary patience of the hunter and the fisherman. I was in the water all the next day, from early morning until sunset, fishing. There were several nibbles but no real bites. I lost the bait five times.

By the third day, I had intertwined two paper clips to give the hook more strength, and to allow it to hold a larger piece of bait. Not only that, but it had a more rigid bearing and didn't easily straighten out when weight was produced on the metal. Again, I awoke at dawn and began my fishing. I stayed out in the water till the sun was above my head, then gave up till dusk, since I didn't think the fish would be around when the water was heated during midday. I started again at sunset, and then stayed in the water most of the night. Finally the rope jerked, the branch bent, and a fish jumped out of the water, hooked on the clips. I quickly pulled the rope toward me and grabbed the fish, a silver beauty shimmering in the moonlight. He seemed to be about a foot in length and to weigh a couple of pounds.

I pulled the rope so that the fish was forced into my knapsack opening. By the time he was in, the clip was out of his mouth. I had grabbed him just in time. He thrashed around but I had a good grip on the knapsack pocket and began to leave the water in a hurry. I walked up the beach to a large, flat rock that stood near the slope of the hill. There I laid the fish out, looking him over. Sam was right there, watching with hungry eyes. The fish was a beauty all right, and he was tiring rapidly with lack of oxygen.

Not having had supper, I decided that this would be an ideal meal. I shoved him back in the knapsack, not trusting him there alone with Sam, and went back to my shelter, where I had stacked wood, and brought some firewood to the rock area, along with some broad leaves from the trees I had torn down. I built a fire, placed rocks in the fire, and then pulled out the fish, cut into his belly with my knife, and emptied him out. Then I hacked till I had his head off. I didn't quite know how to filet him, so instead I scaled him as best I could. It was a tough process with a knife not meant for such work. Finally I removed practically all of the scales and wrapped the fish in the broad leaves, placing them on the hot rocks. Every few moments I'd open the leaves and examine my meal. Within a short while the fish was done. The aroma was maddening to someone who hadn't eaten fresh food, other than five coconuts, in the last six months. I brought the leaves back to the flat rock and cut up the flesh of the fish. I gave one third to Sam, and took the rest for myself. Sam destroyed his food in two or three short gulps. I lingered with mine. Cooked fish. It was a treat. It had been worth three days of fishing to get this one meal.

After eating, I went back to the disemboweled remains and threw them and the head into the water. I splashed sea water on the rock and returned to my smaller shelter, where I lit a candle and turned to the Bible, opening it at random. I read "The wicked flee when no man pursueth: but the righteous are bold as a lion." I closed the book and thought about that line. "The wicked flee, the righteous are bold as a lion." I had fled to this island . . . hadn't I?

I blew out the candle and thought about that. The moon

was almost full; its silver light was pale on the dark waters. I stared at the moon and reflected on those lines. "The wicked flee . . ."

The next day I went fishing again and caught two good sized fish. I cooked one for myself and one for Sam. The sea was bountiful and held an endless supply of food for us. The sea was good to us. God was good to us.

Now that I had completed most of my work on the island, having built my shelters and gotten my goods in order, I found that time dragged. I walked around the island every day, inspecting it, armed with my M-1 and with Sam loping at my side. But time was slowing down for me. I still kept up the journal, but I never reread what had been written, nor did I know if it would be a worthwhile story. My agent had told me to write at my usual level, but it was one thing to write a novel of human conflict and another to just write of solitary pursuit.

Still, I was content in the way time was passing by. I had fresh fish and was planning another assault on the coconut trees. I thought of how I missed other human company, but not having it for so long, I didn't really crave it. I had erotic dreams and masturbated, but less and less frequently. My new life was a celibate one and it was no problem being celibate when there were no temptations to be otherwise. February slipped by and March came and went, and April moved in one sunny morning, and with it, to my stunned surprise, a sail on the horizon. I ran up to my shelter and stood there, peering out at the north. The sail was coming closer and closer.

"Sam," I commanded. "Heel, boy. Stay here."

The sail moved ever closer. There were in fact two sails, one green and white, the other yellow striped, all on one vessel. I got some rope and tied Sam to a pole in the larger shelter, out of sight.

"Be quiet," I commanded. "Quiet." The dog had never

been tied down by me before, and he looked soulfully into my eyes. "Quiet. Be still," I commanded again. I went to my other shelter and hidden from view looked out to sea.

The boat was coming closer and closer. I could now see figures on the vessel but couldn't tell if they were men or women. I slung the M-1 on my shoulder, put on my torn and ragged trousers, my ammunition belt, my knife, and waited and waited.

Would they land? Or just sail by? They seemed to be heading for the island directly, and as I watched, the boat put down anchor about a hundred yards off the shore.

I wished I had binoculars or a telescope. Damn, what I would have given for a strong pair of field glasses. Listening carefully, I could hear human voices. Men's voices. Women's voices. I couldn't make out the words or the language, but they were human voices. A shiver went through me. I crouched in my shelter, behind the barriers of sand, and waited to see what would happen.

20

The boat remained anchored off the island all morning, while I watched. As afternoon came on slowly, I heard music, electronic music, blasting from the boat, a heavy rock sound, a sound that had already escaped my consciousness in the eight months I'd been on the island.

I took a short break from my surveillance and went back to the main shelter, where Sam was lying down, looking aggrieved. I petted him and gave him some water and dried food, petted and spoke to him some more, but left him tied up. Then I went back to my outpost to observe any further proceedings.

A small boat of some kind had been launched from the larger boat and was heading for the north beach. I wondered for a moment whether it was Hildendorf and his party coming to check on my progress, but dismissed that thought rapidly. Hildendorf would fly in by helicopter, make a quick landing, and leave me another note. Yachts weren't his style at all. Neither were lingering visits.

The smaller vessel came closer and I saw that it was a rubber raft, with one person paddling while four other people were sitting and pointing to the shore, jabbering excitedly. Had they spotted me? I ducked down involuntarily, but realized they were pointing to an area several hundred feet west of my station. The raft moved steadily inward, and I could make out the figures a little clearer. There were two men and two women in the boat, with a third man paddling. The man with the paddle was in a white uniform, while the others were dressed more casually. Two women in the boat. Women. God, what a beautiful sight for me. And they were coming closer. The boat came up to within ten feet of shore, then the men jumped out and helped out the women, while their servant backpaddled, trying to steady the raft. A hamper basket was passed over to the men, then something was said to the servant, and he turned the raft around and headed back to the yacht, while the others splashed through the shallow water onto the beach. I couldn't keep my eyes off the women. I couldn't see their faces clearly, but one was blonde and the other a brunette and both were tall and slim.

One of the men was tall and had dark hair, slightly bald in front. The other man was shorter, more robust, stocky rather than fat, with a full head of dark hair. That was about all I could make out except for their clothing. Both women wore sarongs or kimonos of some sort, loose open garments, while the men were dressed in shorts and sports shirts. I glanced at the retreating raft, which was well away from the island by this time, heading for the yacht.

With the men holding the picnic basket between them, the two couples walked along the beach in my direction, looking for a place to have their early dinner. They stopped about two hundred feet from where I was, and the women took off their sarongs and laid them side by side as a beach blanket, and then the men put down the hamper, and they all sat down.

Bottles of wine, small roasted birds, meats, salads, and condiments came out of the hamper in profusion. I licked my lips looking at the food, and swallowed hard. Wine was poured into glasses, and I heard words like "*salud,*" and "cheers." The conversation was animated during this time, and words flew back and forth, punctuated by shrieking laughter. They were having a good time on my island.

At one point, one of the women pointed to the anchored yacht, and the shorter man stood up and put a pair of field glasses to his eyes, focusing toward the sea. Binoculars. I couldn't keep my eyes off them. What I wouldn't have given at that moment for those glasses, something to extend my vision. And I couldn't stop looking at the women, sleek and tall and good looking. The women looked to be in their middle twenties, while the men were older, in their early forties, I guessed, though the taller one could have been about my age.

From my hidden spot on the hill I sat and watched the two couples. What could I do? Go down and introduce myself? That might be good for kicks, but I didn't want to blow three hundred grand on some impulsive gesture. If they found me, there was nothing I could do about it, but it would be foolish for me to announce myself. At least that's the way I was thinking at the time. So I stared at my visitors. I removed the rifle from my shoulder and laid it down, together with my ammunition belt, carrying only my knife at my side. If they did stumble upon me, I didn't want them to be frightened by my arms. I was in a peaceful and observant mood.

After eating, they put away the dishes and utensils, and the women stretched and lay in the sun, while the men sat and talked. I couldn't make out the conversation, except to catch an odd word here and there, spoken in English. Then the stocky man stood up and walked to the edge of the beach, stuck his foot in, and shook the water with his toes, then walked a little ways away from the others. Now and then he picked up a small stone or shell and threw it into the water. He was a loner . . . I could tell the type, having been one all my life. I surmised that he was bored with the company and wanted some moments of reflection alone. One of the women called to him . . . his name was Carlo . . . but he shrugged and continued walking away from the group. Then the dark-haired woman ran to him, and they talked, but he continued to walk toward the eastern part of the island, staying close to the waterline.

The woman returned to her companions, shrugged with an expansive gesture, then turned and watched Carlo's solitary ramble. She shrugged again, turned, and extended her hand to the other man, who got to his feet. Then the man who had just gotten up shouted to Carlo that he was going to take a stroll with Andrea, that they were going to look over the island. He picked up the binoculars that Carlo had used before and put them around his neck. The couple began walking in the opposite or westerly direction, leaving the other woman alone on her kimono. She unfastened her bathing top, turned over, and lay on her stomach.

The couple was coming toward me, walking away from the beach itself. I moved back, retreating behind the sand dunes I had built as camouflage for my shelter. I watched them walk toward the west beach, then turned and saw that Carlo was still walking in the opposite direction, and the woman was still sunbathing.

Now the couple was no more than fifty feet from me. I prayed that Sam wouldn't bark, but no sound came from the shelter. They were silent, then the man looked around, looked directly at me in fact, but saw nothing, since, I guess, he wasn't looking for anything. If he had been seeking another human being, he would have spotted me, I'm sure of that. He turned away, and took the glasses and scanned the sea with them, then let them dangle from his neck.

He extended his hand to the woman once they were beyond sight of the people on the beach, and both, walking hand and hand, went down to the western tip of the island. By this time the afternoon sun was sinking slowly in the west, and the air had a translucent quality about it, as the reddish sky was filled with magenta clouds. The couple kept walking down to the glistening west beach, the jewel of the island. When they were out of sight, I moved myself, crouching and running slowly to get a better view of them. From my position I could be seen if the sunbathing woman looked up or the other man turned toward my direction, but nothing stirred down on the beach.

I caught sight of the couple again. They had found a place to sit and talk, near some massive rocks that guarded the approach to the west beach. I moved as close as I dared, and stopped. Their backs were to me, and they were below me. The man took out a pack of cigarettes, offered one to the woman, lit it with his gold lighter, then lit his own. They dragged in smoke and sat in silence. Finally, the man spoke.

"Well, what do you think?"

He had an American accent, but the woman, when she answered, had a distinctly Italian one.

"He knows, I'm sure," she said.

"What's he going to do about it?"

"Carlo?" She shrugged, in the same effusive manner as on the beach. "Carlo," she repeated, "he's going to keep building his automobiles."

"I mean, about us?"

"Oh, nothing. Don't worry. You're so . . . so American. Nothing will happen. You think too much of stories about us Italians . . . so hot blooded. We're very civilized, you know. We're from the north; we're not Sicilians. Carlo is civilized and you're civilized and I'm civilized, and it will all work out."

"What will work out?"

"Oh, John . . . don't ask so many questions."

"But I have to know."

"Know what?"

"What will happen . . . with us."

She shrugged. It was a magnificent gesture. "I'm married, a married woman, you see . . . and I have three children. And Carlo is a man of responsibility. We'll stay married, and life will go on."

"Are you serious?"

"Of course I'm serious."

"How can you say that?"

"What do you want me to say?"

"Andrea . . ." He brushed out his cigarette in the sand, and paused and lit another, cupping his hands against the mild wind that was starting to blow from the west. "Andrea, I love you."

She put her fingers to his lips. "Don't say that. Just don't talk."

"But I do."

"What has love to do with all this?"

"What are you talking about? Are you serious?"

"Yes, John, I'm serious. I'm very serious. I have a family, I have responsibilities. What do you want me to do, move to America with you?"

"Yes. Yes, that's what I want."

"And then what? What if it does not . . . happen . . . I mean, work out?"

"It will. I love you. You love me, don't you. Don't you?"

"Of course I do, darling."

"Let's walk further down the beach."

They got up and with their arms around each other walked along the beach. Then they stopped and hugged and kissed savagely. I could see their bodies straining, pressed against each other, and my own heart ached for such a moment, for the touch of a woman again pressed against me. God, my whole body ached for such a moment.

They began taking off each other's clothing. Her naked

body was tanned except for a bikini whiteness around her pubic hair and the tips of her breasts. She was lithe, slim, breathtaking. Her pubic hair was dark and shiny. It was all I could do not to run out, stab him, and ravage her. He took her by the hand, and they moved away from the clothing, around the bend of rock that guarded the beach, so that they were out of my sight, and out of sight of anyone else who might come this way. As an afterthought, he returned and took his shorts and her bathing suit with him, leaving his shirt and binoculars on the sand. I moved closer to their trysting place, knowing it was just around the rock. Moving as quietly and stealthily as I could, I went down to the rock itself and peered around the side. He was on top of her, and they seemed to be struggling in the sand, but her eyes were closed and her head shoved back.

"Give it to me, John, give it to me," she said.

He was on her, his bare body naked to the sky, pumping into her, his head to one side, panting loudly.

"Oh, my God," she said, "oh, God."

She had one orgasm after another as the man continued to screw her. I was transfixed watching, and if either had turned they would have had the shock of their lives, a bearded wild man with crazed eyes watching their act of love. I got my senses together, however, and started backing off, still unable to keep my eyes off them. On the way back to my shelter, I picked up the binoculars and, cradling them in my right arm, retreated quickly to my tent.

After stowing them safely, I went out again. The sun was setting. The woman on the beach was now sitting wrapped in her sarong, smoking and talking to Carlo. I couldn't catch their muted conversation, but Carlo kept glancing at his watch. Finally, as the island became dark, he got up. He started up the hill toward me. "Andrea," he called. "Andrea."

Then I heard Andrea's voice calling back. "Carlo," she shouted. "Carlo, we're coming." Then both figures came out of the darkness, running toward Carlo. "We were watching the sunset," said Andrea, a little breathless. "It was so beautiful. Beautiful."

"Good," said her husband, in a flat tone of voice. "We should be heading back. I'll signal for the raft."

They went down to the beach, and Carlo flashed a light at the boat. A beam flashed back from the yacht, which was ablaze with light now.

"This is such a lovely island," said the other woman. "Have you ever been here before?" she asked Carlo.

"No, my dear." Their voices were carrying in the night air, and I could distinctly hear each word.

"I see the raft," said the same woman.

"Where?" said Carlo. "John, give me the field glasses."

"Uh . . ." Then he realized for the first time that he didn't have them. "Uh . . . Jesus, I must have left them on the sand."

"Where?"

"Over there . . ." He pointed in the direction of the west beach.

"Well, get them," said Carlo.

"Right. Excuse me." He ran up the hill, panting as he did, a replica of my condition when I first arrived here. He went to the rock, looked around, then went out of sight down to the beach, came back, scratched his head, looked around, kicked sand, looked all around the rocks. The raft was now close to the shore, about thirty feet out.

"I can't seem to find them," said John, yelling to the group on the beach.

"Never mind, then," yelled Carlo. "The raft is here."

"I'm sorry," said John, rejoining the others on the beach. The raft was bobbing up and down on small waves about ten feet out.

"No matter," said Carlo.

"I'm really sorry," said John.

"I said, no matter."

"It was so stupid of me . . ."

"Just shut up," said Carlo. "Would you please just shut up for once."

And they waded into the water, moving toward the raft, carrying away their hamper and their women. I watched the raft head back to the yacht. When it came near to the larger boat, a strong beam of light illuminated the nearby water, then in a few minutes the light was turned off. The yacht began to move away, and its lights slowly grew dimmer and dimmer as it retreated to the horizon. Night's darkness took over and the boat disappeared.

21

After the boat was out of sight, I went back to the shelter and released Sam from the leash. He nuzzled up to me as I petted him, but never having been tied up by me, he was still uncertain of my faith in him. I continued to pet him, and then lit a candle and sat with my back to the barrier, stared at the flickering flame, and wondered about myself.

Having seen a woman for the first time in eight months, I felt a disheartening intensity possess me. I was of the human race, and yet I had purposely put myself away on this island. For what reason? For money? Was that the only reason? I tried to think about my motives, but my mind felt muddled by a hundred different emotions. Suddenly I was sick of this island and the self-imposed imprisonment. It was only because of my inferior situation that I was here; if I had been rich like those people on the boat I would never have allowed myself to be in this position.

Why was I selected? Why did I choose this life? I was a victim and yet I knew that the victim selects himself as well as being selected. I had not only been picked by Hildendorf but had picked myself, and for what? For mere money? What would the money buy, if, in fact, it ever was paid to me? It wouldn't buy me one thing worthwhile. What was worthwhile I knew, from my short experience on this wretched planet, was love, happiness, and satisfaction with one's life. I had none of these things. In fact, up to this moment, I had been more content here alone than I had been for the last several years among mobs of people. What did it all mean? Was it all stupidity or vanity, or both?

"Vanity of vanities, saith the preacher, all is vanity." I was zeroing in lately on Ecclesiastes in the Bible. I read and reread that book over and over again. "Vanity of vanities . . ." What did it all mean? What did my existence mean?

I blew out the candle and lay in the dark. The only sounds were Sam's breathing and the distant pulsation of the waves breaking on the shore. I had heard the sounds of this water, of this endless rhythm, for so long, I considered it part of my own rhythm, but tonight I listened with different ears. The waves never ceased, the rhythm was not man's but God's, and His time wasn't man's time. It was endless and man was nothing, and I was nothing. I was a fleck in the universe, and by chance or fate or time alone, I could be wiped out and few would moan my loss. Few would even know I was gone. My mother would miss me, and maybe even my brother, but then time would pass, and one day someone would ask about me, and they'd say, "He went away and no one ever heard from him again. He was a writer, and he said he was going on a writing assignment or something like that."

Yes, dismissed in two sentences. In twenty-five words or less, one's life is summed up, and then put away for good. Just like that. I sat in the dark, feeling a small breeze blowing in, feeling the heat of Sam near me, feeling my own heat, my heart beating, my regular breathing. My body, my very existence, all shut up in the temple of my being, all so mortal, all so quickly capable of being snuffed out.

I rolled up my pillow and put my head on it, staring at the dark canvas above me, at the poles, at this little shelter I had built. My inner palace, and the island my outer kingdom. So strange to be here alone, to live with what I had, in this makeshift existence.

I was restless and got up a little later and walked outside. Sam obediently trotted along with me. The moonlight played upon the ocean, a silver stabbing of the water. The white foam of the waves looked translucent against the beach. I was all alone, without a soul within miles of my voice. I walked a little ways and sat on the sand, looking out at the sea. I stared at the great ocean, this eye of God that never blinked. It saw me and was weighing me even then, and I knew it found me wanting, as God found me wanting. As mankind found me wanting.

I thought of that woman, naked, writhing under her lover. Possessed by him, open to him, wanting him. Wanting him . . . when she pushed herself against his body, I knew that feeling of possessiveness, of wanting. Of desire. I had blotted it from my consciousness for so long, and now I was in its power. It took possession of me, of my mind, body, and spirit. I wanted a woman to love, I needed someone so badly, yet there was no one and there was nothing I could do about it. I was an outcast from life's feast, I was excluded from life's joys. My heart felt heavy. I went back into my shelter and lay down, and called Sam over. I stroked his head.

"Sam, I'm so alone," I told the dog. "I'm so alone."

The next day I slept late, and when I awoke I still felt heavy and plodding, filled with a kind of apathetic fatigue. I went out and took my new prize, the binoculars, with me. I stood on the hill and looked around. Everything came into focus. I looked out into the surrounding seas. No sign of land or boats or anything but water. I walked around the island wearing my M-1 and the usual equipment. Sam walked alongside and now and then ran into the water playfully.

I thought of new ways to catch fish. Perhaps try to spear them again in shallow water, at night. Perhaps dig some kind of inlet so that they'd swim into my artificial pond and then be easy prey. I decided that these were worthwhile projects, but I had no energy for them that day. I felt tired and dragged out. I retreated to the shelter and lay down.

I slept that afternoon, then fed Sam and myself, and got some water and filled up my canteens. I drank a lot of water. I was exceedingly thirsty that day. That night I slept fitfully. I touched my head, for I felt feverish, but my forehead was cool. I didn't know what was the matter with me except that I was continually thirsty. I drank and urinated constantly.

This lethargy continued for almost a week. I tried fishing but caught nothing, having neither energy nor patience to stand waist deep in the sea. I drank more and more fresh water, and sometimes, when I urinated, I felt uncomfortable. It was a very peculiar sensation. Nothing hurt and yet something was different.

April moved along slowly. On the tenth of the month, I awoke earlier than usual and saw that the sun was just breaking over the horizon. I had a strange feeling in my penis, as if I needed to urinate, as if the urine was at the tip of my penis. But when I tried to piss, nothing happened. It got more and more uncomfortable. I walked around feeling dizzy and sick. I couldn't quite understand what was happening. I drank a canteenful of water, feeling very thirsty, but somehow, even though I constantly felt I must piss, nothing came out except a random drop or two.

Then the uncomfortable feeling went away. It was a relief for a few moments, but suddenly I was aware of another, more painful feeling in the left side of my back, in my kidney region.

The pressure increased and turned into pain. It felt as if I had cramps, severe cramps, located in the kidney, but there was no relief. I drank more water, and still couldn't manage more than a drop or two when I tried to piss. The thing I had dreaded before the trip, that was always in the back of my mind, was happening. I was very sick and in great pain, and I was helpless, not having anything more than aspirin. I opened my chest of medicines and took four aspirins with water. The pain got worse moment by moment, and I broke into a cold sweat because of its intensity.

I finished off a canteen of water and still couldn't urinate. What was wrong? Then I remembered a film director in LA telling me about a kidney stone attack he had had. It sounded like the thing I was going through. That's what I was having, a kidney stone attack. What was supposed to happen? I tried to think of what he had told me. Either you were able to pass the stone or they had to operate on you as a last resort, and until you passed it, the pain was unbearable.

Unbearable seemed a mild word to me. It was excruciating. It was devastating. I was used to pain, having endured a lot of it on the island, with scraped skin, the wrench in my back climbing the tree, the cuts and bruises, the normal aches and pains of the body. But this was something horrible. It gripped my kidney region with a ferocity that I never had experienced before. I was writhing now, running around on the sand, with Sam watching me quizzically, my back bent almost parallel to the ground, my legs bent. I must have looked like a bearded Groucho Marx, but it was no laughing matter. I was desperate. I didn't know what to do. If I only had some pain killer, some morphine or codeine or Demerol, something. That bastard Hildendorf was supposed to get me pain killers, along with penicillin, but gave me dog food instead. I cursed him, but curses were useless.

I just couldn't take it anymore. I didn't know what to do,

whether to cry or scream. I fell to the ground and hugged my knees to my chest and rolled around, trying to find a comfortable position, but nothing helped. I was in the grip of a demon, and the sweat was cold all over my body. I took off everything and rolled around naked. Any pressure on my flesh, even undershorts, was too much.

"Oh, God, God, please help me," I cried aloud. "Please help me, I can't stand this. I'm going crazy." I got up and fell down again, weakened by pain. I didn't know what to do. I reached around with my left hand and pressed the kidney region. It didn't diminish the pain, which was getting steadily worse by the minute. I rolled around, trying to do something to stop it, but nothing helped. I got up and staggered back to the shelter and drank more water and took four more aspirins. Then I took four more. Nothing. Not a dent in the pain. I rubbed the sweat away from my face. My whole face was cold and soaked with perspiration. I grabbed a hand mirror and looked at my reflection. My normally tanned face was gray, and my lips looked blue.

"I'm dying," I said aloud. "Oh, God, help me. Help me, I beg you. Help me, please, dear God, do something to help me."

I staggered around and came to the rock that had hidden the screwing couple. I banged my head against the rock, banging it till a cut opened, but I couldn't knock myself out. I thought of cutting my wrists, for death would relieve the pain. I would have gladly put a bullet through my head at the moment. Maybe I should just end everything, I thought, just end everything.

The pain increased. I was doubled over and drooling from the mouth. I tried to urinate. Still nothing. If I could only piss, I felt all would be well. I fell to the ground and turned and twisted and moaned. I was in a lather. My body was sweating profusely, and sand stuck to my skin, to my face and hair. I rolled in the sand, trying to relieve the pain. It got worse and I was getting weaker. My heart was pounding and my pulse was racing, faster than I had ever felt it run. I was dying. I would die of pain. I couldn't stand it.

"Save me, God, save me," I muttered. I didn't recognize my voice. There was nothing but a whisper left. I bit my lips and gritted my teeth and prayed for deliverance, but none came. The sun was burning brighter now, and the pain was voracious. I wondered at what point I'd pass out, and if I did, whether or not I'd die. I didn't care about dying; it didn't scare me. If it stopped the pain, it would be worthwhile. I lay on my back and arched it, pressing my kidneys with my hands, but that didn't help. I drooled and muttered and cried aloud for God to do something.

And then I must have passed out. When I awoke, it was afternoon, and the pain was still throbbing. I couldn't move. I was cold and shivering, and Sam wasn't around. I staggered to my feet and walked around and tried to urinate. Nothing came out. It must have been twelve hours since I had last pissed. The pain shook my body. I crawled and walked and called weakly for Sam.

I found him in the shelter, in the corner, his head on the ground, looking up at me. I drank water from the canteen and thought of taking more aspirin, but what could that accomplish? I was cold, and sweat stood out over my face in heavy drops. I left the shelter and staggered around with my back arched, holding on to my kidneys. I must have staggered in this manner for over two hours, crying for mercy, for God to help me somehow.

And meanwhile I couldn't urinate. God knows what was happening to my body, with the urine backed up, contaminating and poisoning my blood. I wandered around like a madman. Drool drenched my beard. My hair was matted with cold sweat. I sank to my knees.

"Please have mercy on your servant," I prayed. "Please help me. Don't leave me like this to suffer."

It was getting dark. I crawled around and went to the

slope leading to the north beach. I fell in the sand and began rolling downhill. The pain was unbearable. I got up and tried to piss once more, standing over the water, my feet in the ocean.

And then, a miracle. I urinated. I felt a sharp pain in my penis, a really sharp, overwhelming pain that knocked me off my feet, but I was still urinating as I fell to my knees. I looked down, and blood was pouring out of my penis. I pissed and pissed. Finally I was finished. The tip of my penis was red with blood and blood was oozing from the opening. But the pain was gone. It had suddenly disappeared. I wanted to go back to the shelter and lie down, but I wondered if I could make it up the slope again.

I did, climbing step by weary step. By the time I got back to the tent, I was worn out. I lay down and fell into a dark, dreamless sleep. When I awoke, Sam was gone and the sun was high in the sky. And my head burned with a harsh, frightening fever.

22

I lay in a stupor, sleeping most of the time, having wild dreams where my ex-wife dragged me to Hell, put me into deep fires. Other times I addressed parliaments and gave marvelous speeches about my philosophy. Still, in other dreams, I was in the winter cold of some unknown small town, huddled among angry strangers, fearful for my life.

I'd awake from the dreams, my body burning, sweat running down my face, my hair soaked with my own perspiration. I'd reach for a canteen and drink some water, and look around for Sam. Sometimes he'd be in the shelter with me; at other times he'd be gone.

Time had lost its meaning. I didn't know, except by the light outside, just what part of the day it was, and sometimes I was unsure whether the sun was rising or sinking, whether it was dawn or nightfall. Days may have slipped by in this way; I wasn't certain of anything. I lay on the abandoned clothing of some previous wartime army, and turned and twisted in the agony of my fever, afraid that at any

time I would die. Once my sleep descended to deeper re-
gions than ever before, and I felt Death pulling me down
into that land from which there is no recourse. I struggled
in my sleep, I fought and pushed and held on, clawing with
my hands, intent on surviving, holding on to life itself as if
it were an animate object. When I opened my eyes after
this fierce struggle, my hands were covered with blood from
my damaged fingers, scraped raw from digging into the
clothing and dirt. But I was still alive. I was weak and my
whole body was like a sponge freshly dipped into tepid
water. No part of me was dry. I slowly took off my clothes
and put them aside, and then tried to keep my eyes open. I
didn't want to go back into that fearful sleep, and I thought
that, if I did close my eyes, it would be for the final time,
for the inexorable and irrevocable journey from which no
man returns.

That was the crisis point of my illness. From then on, I
recovered slowly. Soon I was able to crawl across the shelter
for some more water, dribbling it out of the last canteen. I
was fearfully thirsty and still needed more. I got out of the
tent and slowly dragged myself with two canteens to the
freshwater pond. It was early afternoon, and the sun glowed
orange against the backdrop of a deep blue sky and turquoise water. I dipped the canteens into the pond, filled
them, and slaked my thirst, then refilled them and brought
them back to the shelter. Sam was nowhere to be seen, but I
was too weak to call out his name.

I drank water all evening till I emptied out the canteens,
and then went back and refilled them again. The next time I
did this, it was morning, but whether or not it was the following morning I didn't know. In any event, I went back to
the tent and felt my forehead. It was warm but not hot. I
slept soundly, and woke and felt my head again. It was
cool. I sat up and yawned. I was hungry. I drank some more
water, and got out of the shelter and whistled for Sam.
Soon, I heard him loping up to the tent. He looked haggard

and thin, and probably had had nothing to eat during the
time I was ill. I opened a can of meat and shared it with
him. He ate voraciously, licking the helmet dry. Then he
wagged his tail and came near me and licked my face. I petted him. Good old Sam. His nose was dry, a bad sign, but it
was probably just hunger. Later, I fed him again, and then
putting on my belt and knife, strolled out of the tent.

The sunset was incredibly beautiful. Colors lit up the sky
in various shades of pinks and yellows. I stood transfixed,
glad to be back among the living, among the mobile of the
earth. What a lovely planet, what beauty unfolded before
our eyes. I felt my own eyes tearing, sorry that I was so
alone and had no other human to share this magic moment
with. I stood and cried, and then the melancholy mood
passed.

It took two days before my strength returned to the point
where I could think of work. I looked at the calendar I had
so carefully kept. The last marking had been April 16, but I
had no idea what day it was. How long had I been under
the spell of fever? I estimated that it was five days, and so I
marked down April 21. It was a rough guess, but I figured
that it couldn't be that far from the truth, perhaps one or
two days in either direction. Sam, now that he was eating
regularly, had returned to his former activity. I also felt
stronger and began fishing again, this time with a hand-cut
wooden spear.

I was more patient and worked only in the very early
morning or in the cool late afternoon. Finally, after two
days, I speared my first fish. I drove the wooden point into
it as one would drive a stake through Dracula's heart. It
twisted fiercely, but to no avail. I raised it out of the water,
its blood dripping through the wound.

That night, Sam and I feasted on fresh fish. I mixed mine
with water chestnuts and the always available tomatoes. By
now, my meat supply was at a critical ebb, and I decided to

save it for Sam, and to eat only vegetables and what I could
get from the sea. There were only thirty or so cans of meat
left, and if I rationed them out to Sam at a can a day, that
would hold him for the next month. Plus whatever fish I
could catch. Now, whenever I caught fish, I shared them
with the dog, and I dragged out the supply of meat for
three months before stabbing the last can open. By the time
the first anniversary of my stay on the island rolled around
on August 23, there was no more meat left, unless there was
still some in unlabeled and unopened cans of the larger size
that I hadn't yet looked into. But so far, none of the larger
cans had yielded anything but vegetables and the sickly
black floating stuff that I had used as bait.

I was now using my spear instead of the rod for fishing.
I'd swim underwater with my eyes open, looking for a
school of fish or an occasional stray. By this time I was in
rhythm with the fish that surrounded my little atoll. There
was a great variety, many of which were rather exotic. Occasionally I would spot a small shark, the only kind of fish I
could positively identify. Once a huge white shark was in
the water, not more than thirty feet away, but luckily I was
in very shallow water, and I stood up and quickly ran back
to shore, expecting to feel its powerful jaws snapping at me.
But nothing happened. That was my only encounter with a
shark, and although I was momentarily terrified, there really
had been no danger.

My prowess with my spears was considerable. By now I
had fashioned three very good ones, which I used alternately. I was catching at least two fish a day. My endless ex-
cursions in the water were hardening my muscles. I had
practically no fat on my body, and my thigh muscles stood
out in bulges. I hadn't been in this condition since basic
training in the army. My body was tanned, my skin was
smooth, and my breathing regular. I sometimes ran around
the island barefooted, up the hills and down slopes and
across the huge rock that guarded the southwest corner,

without drawing a deep breath. I ran four times around the island one day just to see if I could do it, and it was no problem, but at the end I was very tired and my left kidney area throbbed.

All traces of the infection and the debilitating pain of passing the kidney stone had long since passed except that, when I felt exceedingly tired or weak, I'd sometimes feel a pressure in my left kidney, a discomfort more than pain. I drank as much water as I could, saturating my kidneys constantly, and with time, the pressure ceased. My body was getting rock hard. I was amazed at the thinness of my waistline, at the muscles bulging from all parts of my body. If for no other reason, it was worthwhile coming out here to get into such fine condition.

It made me think of the real reason for being here, and that was to write a book about my experiences on the island. I had not made an entry in the journal in over a month, and I thought that, once I returned to civilization, I would fake the journal and write some kind of adventure story. At the moment, I had little inclination for either writing or reading. My books, other than the Bible, lay in deep sand getting ruined. I hadn't touched the chess set in months. It was all vain, purposeless nonsense as far as I was concerned.

What was there really to write about? The whole act of writing seemed to me a useless idea. Why should I want to write, to fill a page with aimless scribblings? What was important was to be alive, to breathe the fine crystal air of this planet Earth, to set foot in waters of turquoise loveliness, to see the sky turn a molten blue at sunrise, and then diffuse into brilliant magenta and purples at sunset. What was important was to have the companionship of a good dog, a friend who asked little, and thus I provided all, giving him my meat and always the equal part of any fish I caught. All this meant more than the dry, dusty books moldering in my shelter.

One night I burned the chess book to start my fire. I watched the flames lick up the pages and then work slowly on the cover, and I was glad. In the future, I'd burn up the other books, and the Bible if necessary, keeping only the book of Ecclesiastes intact. That was enough reading for me. I next fed the chess set and chessboard to the fire. Little by little the remnants of the civilized world were being removed from my sight, fed to the sky and the great god of fire.

Two weeks after the anniversary of my first year on the island, I decided to celebrate by once more going after coconuts. Again I made the rope harness, and, in addition to the knife, I took along my binoculars. I climbed up the tree with much more ease this time. It seemed no problem, and halfway up I cut the rope which only hampered my ascent. I watched it land on the ground and then continued carefully up the trunk of the tree, confident of my body's strength, which had increased tremendously. Neither my arms nor legs were tired. After I cut off the coconuts, I put the binoculars to my eyes and scanned my seaward dominion. I could see nothing but endless ocean in all directions except in the north. There was land there! A rocklike apparition greeted my eyes. Either it was a rock or a large body of land, its tip the only thing I could focus on. I rubbed my eyes and looked again. Sure enough, from this height and with the use of the glasses, I found land within my sight.

I scampered down the tree to Sam's waiting greeting. I was too excited by what I had seen to pay much attention to him, and the ritual of picking up fallen coconuts, which had given me so much pleasure a few months before (or was it longer?) now took second place to my new discovery. My heart was beating fast. Why was I so excited? I couldn't understand the thrill that surged through me. I didn't even know what to think. So there was land nearby. Obviously it was uninhabited or its occupants would have been here

many times, would have populated this island and made use
of its resources.

I gathered up my coconuts and brought them to my big
tent and began to break the outside cover on one of them.
Then I punctured it and drank out of the sweet milk. Ah,
what a taste. What could compare to coconut milk, after
months of only having water as an alternative drink. What a
sweet taste must come from fresh fruit . . . a taste long
buried within me, like the feel and smell and, yes, even the
taste of a woman. That pungent, lemony taste of an excited
woman. I closed my eyes and shuddered, thinking about
that.

It was surprising how long I could keep things under control, and then the sight of that woman on this island, or
viewing another island nearby, or the taste of coconut milk
would set me off, taking and breaking away my self-control
as if I were some fresh fruit myself, peeled of my outer skin.
I cut into the coconut with my bayonet, and the white meat
inside stood firm and solid against the brown covering of
the inner shell. I put the knife under the skin carefully, as if
I were a surgeon, and cut out a chunk of coconut and
chewed on it slowly. I put another chunk in my mouth, and
then stopped. I was glutton enough.

If only there were other fruits here—pineapples or man-
goes or papayas—if only Hildendorf . . . how that name
stayed like a craw in my conscious strivings . . . had given
me the dried fruit I had asked for. What a pleasure now to
taste a slice of dried pineapple. Thinking about this set off a
whole row of sensations, taste treats I had buried for the
last twelve months. What a fine treat chocolate would be.
Some good Lindt imported chocolate with nuts, or any do-
mestic kind. A Nestle's bar . . . or See's chocolates, milk
chocolate filled with buttercream or chocolate butter or
cherries. God, my mouth was watering. I craved it all, all
the sweetness I had been deprived of for so long. Ice cream.

I thought of Clancy Muldoon's on La Brea (was it on La Brea?) or Baskin-Robbins, or any ice cream, creamy or chocolaty, or filled with fruits and nuts. Damn. I stood up and had to leave the tent, thinking about these sweets. Ice cream, hot fudge sundaes, chocolate, nuts, fresh fruits, dried fruits, mounds and mounds I could mix together in one giant jumble of sugary delights, then down like a pig. Gobble it all up, stick my face in it, till my beard was soaked with chocolate and dripping with ice cream. Sheer ecstasy.

I had to stop thinking like this. The taste of the coconut was with me, in fact one piece was stuck between two teeth and I worked it around with my tongue and then my fingers. The taste of the coconut lingered, and then I thought of meats . . . of veal cooking in a buttery sauce, of steaks being charcoal grilled, of hot corned beef sandwiches, of a frankfurter on a roll with mustard . . . all the ordinary foods of the city, and here I was starved of them all. I had my fresh fish, but what a delight to have it with a butter sauce and with lemon. God, my mouth was watering, I was actually drooling. Not even sex had such a powerful meaning now. When I had seen that naked woman, I was restless but not this way. I was going crazy with thoughts of food. A fresh bowl of fruit, then a good hot soup, a really thick creamy clam chowder . . . enough, enough.

I began to run. I ran along the crest of my hill and then down to the beach, with Sam right near me, sometimes scampering ahead, sometimes lingering behind. I ran along the beach, keeping my feet just beyond the reach of the foam, running faster and harder. I ran up the slope and down to the west beach and around and around and up again and over the hard, dark rocks that guarded the coast of my island from the southwest, and down to the south beach. I was sovereign liege of this kingdom, I told myself, King Tom of . . . whatever, and I ran even harder. I was literally streaking across the sand, heading east, to the groves of trees that supplied my firewood and spears and poles and whose fellows I had decimated in my forest, the King's Forest. I ran to the edge of the forest and touched the nearest tree, and then turned away, and ran toward the northern side of the island, back down to the beach and once more around it and up the slope to my tent, my smaller tent, where I dropped, panting. I sat, catching my breath, feeling my pulse, which was hardly racing. Resting, I thought about the island I had seen that morning. I could plan to visit it, but what would I find there? Perhaps fresh fruit trees . . . that was reason enough. How far could it be? Thirty miles perhaps . . . maybe a little less, a little more. But not much more. What would thirty miles mean on a raft with a sail? Three hours, four hours, or five hours with a backing wind and then the return. A day's journey both ways, or I could stay on that island overnight and then return here, loaded with fruits. . . .

Crazy, insane, I'd hope to find a fruit tree or two there, but nothing more. I needed fresh fruits and vegetables, but why should that island, which looked darker and rockier than this one, provide them? Well, it was something to think about.

I got up later and fished with my spear. I caught two lovely fish and cooked them in the big leaves of my forest trees. Their succulence seemed supreme that night, and Sam and I feasted like gourmets.

23

In September a big storm kept me in the tent for three days until it subsided. There was little damage to the shelter, but some of my cans were blown into the sea by the winds, which blew with hurricane force. All I could do was endure and hold on in that kind of weather, hearing the whistle and whining of the wind, the waves breaking high on the shore, the rain falling in sheets. After it was all over, a calm came over the sea. A deathly calm. I wondered what it foretold. I had never seen the ocean so placid during my stay, nor the air so dead. Everything seemed to hang in suspension. Nothing moved or stirred. I could find no fish near the island.

My main concern was the weather, and I reinforced my shelter, adding more poles and buttressing those that were standing, tying them with rope and with strips of bark I had cut away from the trees. My candles had held up well, since I used them so sparingly, and I found myself with an abundance of firewood. The Cricket lighters I had bought in LA

on a lark were priceless, since they provided me with fire
when I needed it. I thought of that day in Los Angeles, and
it seemed ages ago. It seemed as if I had been a different
person, someone far removed from the present Tom De-
Winter. I thought of my previous life there, of the days in
that smog-encrusted hell, where I spun out tales of fantasy
and misery, and found in the end that it was my own life.

I tested and retested the shelter which had, by now, become a rather permanent structure rather than a tent. My
other, smaller tent also had been repaired and improved,
and I used it in calm weather because of the view it
afforded of the two beaches, the northern and western ones.
It was my summer house; my vacation house. The other was
my home.

The calm seemed to last day after day, while I was very
aware of the threat of another storm. Then the weather
turned. I could feel it; feel the moisture in the wind, see the
whitecaps on the sea. Then the storm struck. I saw the gray
sky come like an ominous curtain blotting out the blueness
of the horizon blown forward by fierce winds. I brought in
all my supplies and covered them as best I could, and put in
a supply of firewood and extra clothing.

The winds increased, and the air was full of cold spray.
The waves rose and the tide moved higher on the island.
The trees sagged, and the coconut trees bent. The rains
came, and thunder and lightning charged over the sea. I
could see it flashing on the water; an eerie sight; the sky
split by jagged lines of white fire. It was awesome and very
frightening, for it was moving closer to the island. The
whole sky was lit up at times; the air was charged with electricity. Sam huddled in the shelter, shaking. I groped
around inside the shelter putting the provisions in place,
making certain I had available food and water for a big
blow.

The rains fell steadily, then the wind picked up, and the
rains poured down, sagging the canvas. The winds then rose

and struck with tremendous power. The poles guarding the south side of the shelter gave way first, but by this time I had so many poles supporting the tent that I was able to work and repair the damage by candlelight. However, as soon as I got the poles back in place, they came down again, and then the whole east side of the shelter bent against the wind's power. The wind outside seemed to be swirling and changing directions by the minute. I was vulnerable to the south and east, and the howling brute force of the air shook the tent to the foundations. Poles cracked and gave way. The tent collapsed in half, and I pushed Sam and myself against the earth barriers, trying to hold on. I pulled the provisions in with me, but rain was coming in under the tent and from a gaping hole in the canvas.

This storm was awesome. It blew harder by the minute, and the winds picked up everything loose in the tent and carried them away. Cans, my books and notebooks, the clothing on the floor, all were blown away. I was becoming desperate as item after item was lost to the storm. Then the earth barriers started to crumble as the wind blew the sand apart, crumbling the north and west walls.

Sam whimpered and I clutched our water and food. Candles rolled out and disappeared. All my essential provisions were going fast. I shouldered the M-1 and put the binoculars around my neck. I buried the ammunition box in a hole I dug inside the shelter. The ammunition belt was around my waist, and tied to it were the bayonet, knife, and canteens. I couldn't lose those valuable items. The winds picked up yet more speed. Torrents of water inundated me now, breaking apart the canvas, and for the second time since my stay on the island, I was open to the elements, finding them whipping me at will. At one point I was nearly blown clear of the tent. It was now impossible to stand up. I kept my body flat and pressed against the earth barriers, which were now half their original size. The canvas, which had been so carefully tied down by sand and poles, now flapped loose and was ripped apart. It was in danger of blowing away completely.

And lightning struck closer and closer. Once more I smelled that burning odor, and it scared the hell out of me. Twice everything in the tent lit up from a nearby bolt. Sam whimpered and I almost screamed when the lightning and thunder hit simultaneously, right over us. Everything smelled differently for a few minutes, as if a fuse was lit and smoking, and I frantically looked around for signs of flames. Then the smell vanished as fast as it had arrived.

By this time I was thoroughly soaked, and everything around me was filled with water, so that I had no chance to warm myself. Most of my candles and wood had been blown away, and practically all the clothing that made up the carpeting on the ground had gone to the wind's lair.

The canvas was now in shreds. The holes I had cut in it so that I could put support poles through was its undoing. It was still holding together in a couple of places, but large chunks had ripped away completely. I had to use most of my strength pulling and heaving the remaining sections to keep it over our heads. This was becoming a more and more difficult task, since the canvas was waterlogged and very heavy. Only my sweating efforts kept us under some kind of shelter.

I was now flat on my back, clutching at the canvas with bare and bleeding hands. I held on grimly. Meanwhile the winds were blowing us and the canvas away from the shelter, for the earth walls had been almost decimated and no longer protected us from the wind on any side. Sand and dirt blew over me, till my whole body felt weighted down with earth. My eyes burned from the sand, and my mouth was full of it. Worse, I was wet and cold, and losing all my remaining strength.

Finally the canvas itself was blown away from my grasp. I was now naked to the sky and the elements, helpless in the face of its brute power. I picked Sam up and staggered to the second shelter, hoping to find something there, some respite from the wind and rain. My eyes were narrow slits, filled with dirt and tears, and I chewed on earth. The wind continued to howl like a madman on the loose, subject to no one's control.

Miraculously, the second shelter's canvas had been blown into a corner of the remaining earth barrier, which by this time was no more than two feet high, and there it lay, crumpled and watersoaked and covered by sand. I lifted it and pulled Sam in with me, wrapping it around our bodies, hoping that it would hold this way.

The wind was now blowing directly from the north, then it abruptly changed directions, forcing us and the canvas into the corner of the small sand pile. I rolled around, wrapping the canvas about us in this manner, so that we'd all blow away together, the canvas, Sam, and myself. The M-1 pressed into my back, for I still had it slung over a shoulder; I also had the binoculars, ammunition belt, bayonet, knife, and canteens. Everything else was gone.

For three days and three nights the storm relentlessly raged. Then slowly it abated. A fine rain fell for another day and a cool breeze blew, but once more we had survived the worst. When I emerged finally from the dark recesses of the canvas, my body was raw with sores, my beard and hair were a mass of sand, my clothing was torn to pieces. Sam was in the same shape. His legs were badly bruised, and he had an open wound on the side of his head, near his right eye. But we were alive, thank God. We were still functioning.

The loss from this storm was tremendous. All the books and notebooks and stationery supplies had been lost and all but one candle was gone. Most of the clothing had disappeared, and all my medical supplies had blown away into the far reaches of the vast sea.

When the sun finally came out, six days after the onset of the storm, I began my search for missing supplies. I could .

find very little except some tattered shirts wrapped against trees in the forest on the eastern side of the island. Many of the food cans had been blown away, never to be found again, and from time to time I'd stumble on one, broken open in its shallow watery grave.

I caught a bad cold from the storm, and sat and shivered for a few days, until the sun finally dried me out. I got into awful coughing and sneezing fits. When I finally assessed the damage, I realized it would now be a battle just to survive. Everything had been lost—my medical supplies, candles, books, writing supplies, everything. The vitamin pills were nowhere to be seen. That was a frightening loss, because I depended so much upon them with my inadequate diet. Now I had little food and no supplemental vitamins. And I had nothing to write with and no record of my stay on the island.

The main canvas was gone. I found bits and pieces of it during the next two weeks, but no segment was larger than a foot square. The other canvas that I had placed on the supplies had also blown away, and that left only the small canvas that covered my secondary shelter. I looked over the paltry few cans that were left, half buried in the sand. That was all, except for what I had on my person. The ropes were missing, nothing was left. For several days my moods alternated between fatigue and depression. I had lost so much, and all of it was irreplaceable.

Yet, Sam and I were still alive. We were flesh and bone, and soul and spirit, and we had survived. The losses had all been material. Let them go. I patted Sam and examined his head wound. It was healing nicely. I heated a bowl of fish soup for the both of us, and we ate in silence, while I looked out at the wreckage of my island empire.

24

The next few weeks found me working harder than ever, rebuilding what had been destroyed by the storm and salvaging what had been blown away. The final material count was dismal. I had my binoculars, miraculously unharmed though slightly scratched by sand, my M-1, the ammunition, my bayonet, knife, ammunition belt, two canteens, and a cracked helmet liner. I also found one helmet and the trenching tool, both embedded in the sand on the south beach.

As for clothing, my present outfit was but one step away from disintegration. I feared that if I gave one tug to what I was wearing, it would all fall apart, as it seemed to be held together by loose threads. The boots were impossible to wear, having split open and become so waterlogged that I could no longer get my feet into them. I therefore walked around the island barefoot.

As for my reserves, there was none in the way of clothing. I found a few tattered shirts and pants, but they couldn't be worn. My food supplies had also taken a fearsome beating, for many of the cans had simply been blown away and several had been broken open so that their contents were suspect. I had enough food from cans to last a few more months, and I still had, as December approached, nine more months to go.

I didn't know what I'd do when my food supplies ran out. I suppose I could live from the sea, perhaps boil seaweed as soup, eat fish, eat some coconuts, but there was little else I could find. I thought more and more of the island I had seen from the treetop, and thought I might go over there when the food shortage became critical, in the hope of finding more provisions. But, in my heart, I knew the likelihood of finding anything but some coconuts was remote. I made one more trip to the top of the trees and found six more coconuts. I ate them sparingly.

I went to work on a new shelter. I decided to build one entirely of mud and sand, using three sides for walls and only one side as an opening. It had to be considerably smaller than the original one, almost an oversize pup tent at best, for I was down to one canvas, and it was the smallest of the three I had started with. I also had to cut more trees for firewood, support poles, and spears for fishing. The first thing I did was make two new spears so I could catch fish daily. I had become quite adept at this, and had begun drying out fish for future use in case I should become sick or otherwise unable to go into the water. I laid up a supply of these dried staples, as well as my coconuts. That was my fresh food in its entirety. The cans that were salvaged were mostly unknown in content, and now and then I found one completely useless, containing some kind of powder or filler that I couldn't stomach at all.

This was the state of affairs that presented itself to me as another Christmas approached. For this holiday I didn't even have a Bible available, and so I tried to recall the story of the Jesus child, and thought to myself of his mes-

sage to the world. Peace and good will . . . I could understand it better here because my heart was more at peace
than it had been in the last dozen years. I thanked God for
that, and for providing me with good health again, and for
allowing me to escape death as a result of the kidney attack.
And I thanked Him for providing me with such a good companion in the way of my dog, Sam.

As for Christmas gifts, I declared that I would share all I
had with my dog. I would give him my loyalty and my love
as long as he lived. Christmas seemed to have a special message here on the island. In previous years this season had always been depressing for me. For one thing, Christmas is a
time when one is supposed to be joyful and happy; and
when you are supposed to be happy and are not, it is dreadful. It is terribly dreadful. I hadn't been able to spend any
of the previous five holiday seasons with my mother, since I
was always in financial trouble and couldn't afford to get on
a plane . . . and on top of that, I had been in that most
alien of places to spend Christmas, Los Angeles. Sunshine
and smoggy Christmas mornings, with the traffic backing up
outside my windows—that was my usual overview of Christmas.

I knew in my heart that much of my unhappiness, if not
all of it, in past years had been my own fault. I had purposely isolated myself from human contact, had done inap-
propriate things, had filled my heart with anger and greed,
and for all of these things, I suffered. I prayed that I would
cleanse myself of these bad habits and learn once again that
life is to be lived in joy and hope and in giving. If I could
learn all of these things because of my exile here, then it
would have been worth the stay a thousand times over.

The storm season seemed to have passed. I found the
days getting longer and warmer. A new year came and
found me in good health, and my dog Sam had a shiny coat
and a black wet nose, both good signs of his health. I had
been growing progressively thinner, since my eating habits

had deteriorated to one or two meals a day, usually some kind of vegetable at midday and fish at night, with an occasional piece of coconut thrown in. My waistline had grown so thin I could almost enclose it by spreading both hands out. My body was now just bone and muscle. My ribs protruded, and my muscles were rock hard and sleek. I ran and swam every day and did heavy physical work, and I was in the best shape of my entire life.

I had no more books or notebooks to write in, as all my stationery supplies had been lost, but instead of this concerning me, I felt a kind of relief at the fact that I no longer had to worry about writing a book. I felt very free, realizing that I didn't have to force myself to fill in a journal with idle scribblings, or put down on paper what I was thinking and living. I simply thought and lived. And I didn't miss reading. My eyes were clear and sharp, and I could easily see myself spending the rest of my life as a physical man rather than as an intellectual one. When I thought of my previous life in LA, of the misery and drudgery I had fashioned there and had called my existence, it was as if I was looking at another human being, a stranger far away in both time and spirit.

My new shelter faced north by west, so that I had a good view of the two beaches, and often I'd sit outside my tent late at night watching the moon shining on the water with a silvery effervescence. It was a sight I never tired of, just as, as a child, I could spend hours looking into a fire burning in a fireplace. There was calm in fire and water, and the great beating heart of the ocean seemed to be in tune with mine. Often Sam would sit by me, or go exploring alone on the beaches, returning in response to my call or whistle. Then we'd go inside and sleep. Sometimes he'd leave in the middle of the night and prowl around the island, and then return before morning.

I was in the middle of an involved dream one night when sounds of barking awakened me. I opened my eyes, unsure of what I had heard. Sam never barked at night. Then I heard the barking again. I sat up and listened. More barking. I crawled out of the tent, carrying my binoculars with me. By the time I got out, there was the sound of a gun being fired; I heard a loud howl and then silence. Jesus, what was this? I saw a fire going on the north beach, and I trained the binoculars on the fire. Two men were sitting around it, and a third was about ten feet away, bent over. I put the binoculars on the third man. He was standing over Sam, examining him, a pistol in his hand. The bastard had shot Sam. Had killed my dog. For a moment I was frozen. I couldn't believe what was happening right before my eyes. My dog dead, men on the island . . .

Then, rousing myself, I went back into the tent and got my M-1 and put my ammunition belt on, attaching my bowie knife. I groped around in the dark, removed a clip, and put it into the M-1, carefully releasing the bolt. The safety was on, but I now had eight bullets in the rifle. I crawled out again, and moved stealthily away from the shelter, crouching as I moved, till I had a closer view of the men and the fire. I put the field glasses on them again. Now all three were around the fire, while not more than ten feet away, the lifeless form of Sam lay in the sand. My dog, my only companion, and he was dead. I was shaking with anger, but I didn't make any move. I focused the glasses around the area. There was a raft of some kind near the men, beached on the sand. I scanned the nearby waters and saw a boat docked about one hundred yards away, its lights on. These men were probably not alone. I focused on them again, meanwhile moving closer and closer, till I was within hearing range.

"You think he belonged to anyone?" one of the men asked.

"That mutt? I don't know. Maybe we should check this place out, but who the fuck would be on this island. This is in the middle of nowhere."

"Should we look around?" the original questioner asked.

"Nah, if anyone's here, we'd know. He'd be down on us already."

"I don't know," said the third voice. "I'm bugged by this dog and shit. Let's get the fuck off of here."

"Not till we work this out. We got to figure it all out," said the first voice. It came from the man who had shot Sam.

"OK," said the third man, "you tell us, Johnny."

"Here's how I figure it," said Johnny. "We got six keys, right?"

"Right. We got it here, six keys."

"And there's three of us, right? And the two dudes on the boat, right?"

"Yeah," said voice number two. "Three of us and two of them."

"And Billy. Don't forget Billy," said Johnny.

"Billy don't get a full share nohow," said the third voice.

"Yeah?" said Johnny belligerently. "But he's on the boat now, keeping an eye on those dudes. We don't want them to take off or we wind up here playing with ourselves for the next year."

"OK," said the third voice. "Billy gets his share out of your end, Johnny."

"Fair enough. We'll give the dudes two shares, two keys. Four for us. I take two for myself and give Billy from my share."

"Hey, what is this?" said voice number two. "Two for you? No way, man."

"All right, so you asked me to tell you. That's what I'm telling you."

"No way. You take . . . you take one and a half, and give Larry and me two and a half. What do you say, Larry?"

"It's OK with me. Two and a half is OK."

They lit cigarettes or joints . . . I couldn't quite tell, and then I saw it was a joint because they passed around a smoke. I could do nothing but watch. I was tempted to blast them to bits, but if one or two surrendered, what was I supposed to do? Could I kill unarmed men? Take prisoners? I didn't want prisoners. I didn't know what I wanted, but I didn't want prisoners. I lay on the sand, listening.

"You hold the stuff," Johnny told Larry. "And we'll go back to the boat and tell them the deal."

"You're coming back, aren't you?" Larry asked.

"Sure. That's why you're holding the stuff."

"What if they don't go for it?"

"Well, we got the guns."

"They got guns also."

"Like shit they do," said Johnny. "Their guns are on the bottom of the ocean somewheres . . ."

"OK, but be back fast. This place gives me the creeps."

"Well, take my knife. Here."

I could see a knife transferred, then the other men got in the raft and began paddling back to the boat. I focused on Larry, sitting by his fire, smoking. He wasn't the one who had killed Sam, but he was part of this bunch of bastards. I tightened my lips, thinking of my next move. Punishment was called for, but to shoot from here would attract attention, and then they'd be back, all of them. Five more of them, from their talking. Still, revenge was called for. I wouldn't be a man if I let them kill my dog on my island and not exact payment.

I slowly crawled down toward the beach, my knife in my hand. Larry was watching the progress of the raft, and he had his back to me. I was now within fifty feet of him, in full view if he turned around. I crawled closer.

Larry stood up and stretched. His sudden movement startled me. Now I could see Sam's body clearly, close by, the water lapping at it. Those bastards. There was blood in my eyes, but I tried to compose myself. Larry's back was to me, and I couldn't kill him, not like this. What good would his death do? No, there must be another way. But I had to make a quick decision before he turned around. I removed the rifle and held it in my right hand, and then sprinted toward him, my bare feet silent on the soft sand. I swung the rifle butt against the side of his head and he went down like a rock. He was out cold.

I looked around the ground near the fire till I found the six bags, large plastic bags filled with white powder. I took out my knife and cut each bag open, dumping the contents in the water, and then let the empty bags float on the incoming tide. Then I ran to Sam. He lay still. I turned him slightly, but he was lifeless. Dead. Forever gone. Tears welled in my eyes, but I couldn't take him with me right now. I ran back up the hill and took a position about one hundred yards away from the fire. I was on my stomach, with the rifle loaded, another clip nearby for use. If they came for me, they'd all die. I could fire off sixteen bullets before they knew what hit them, and I had more bullets in reserve in the ammunition belt. Let them try something now.

I waited on the hill, my heart beating savagely, whether through tension or anger, I couldn't tell. Every now and then I'd scan the beach with the glasses, looking at the inert figure of Sam. Those motherfucking bastards.

Then the raft reappeared in the shallow water. Three men were in it, and all three waded toward shore. They called Larry's name.

"Hey, Larry, what happened, man?" I heard Johnny ask. He bent down near the fallen man, and then noticed the bags of dope gone.

"Jesus Christ," he screamed. "Hey, where's the stuff?"

One of the other men was holding an empty plastic bag in his hands. They became frantic, thrashing around in the water, picking up all the empty bags.

"Hey, Larry, what happened, man?" Johnny was slapping

his companion's face but the man was still out. Maybe I had killed him, I thought, but I saw his head move. "What happened, man?"

"I dunno."

"What happened to the stuff?"

"What?"

Now all four were looking around, shining flashlights in all directions. I lay still, my rifle ready.

"What happened? Who the fuck did this?"

Larry couldn't tell them anything. They kept the flashlights shining, aiming them at random. Then they started shooting in all directions. The guns blazed and bullets poured out, none even coming close to where I was.

"What are we going to do?" someone asked Johnny.

"I don't know. It must have been the dog we killed."

"What?"

"The fucking dog. That dog there. There must be guys on this island."

"Where?"

"You're asking me? I don't know."

"What the fuck we going to do, Johnny?"

"We could go get them."

"Yeah . . ."

I tensed, waiting for their charge up the hill.

Then they got together and whispered to each other. I couldn't make out their words. They shined the flashlights again, but I was well hidden.

"There might be too many of them," said one of the men.

"Who the fuck knows?" said Johnny. "Let's get off this place."

"What about the stuff?"

"What stuff? The fucking stuff is gone. . . ."

"You fuckers," one of the men yelled, "we'll be back. We'll bury you fuckers."

They waded out to the raft, and I watched them paddle back to the boat. I didn't move for a long time, until they reached the boat and it pulled away, out of sight. Still I waited, unsure. They might be coming back. But after about an hour, there was no sign of the boat from any direction and I went down to the beach to get Sam.

He was much heavier dead than alive. I carried him on my shoulders back to the shelter area and put him down gently. There was a bullet wound right through his head, and dried blood covered one eye. Those bastards . . .

I carried him down toward the eastern end of the island, and dug a large hole with the trenching tool. I worked steadily, sweating in the moonlight. Then I put him in and covered the hole with dirt and sand.

I knelt by the grave, tears filling my eyes. I didn't know what to say.

"You were a good dog and a good friend," I said, my voice breaking. "I'll miss you and remember you for the rest of my life. Good-bye, Sam."

I crossed myself and remained on my knees. I looked up at the black sky above. "Oh God, be good to Sam," I cried aloud. "And forgive me. I'm so alone now, God. God, have mercy on me. I'm so alone."

And I began to weep. I loved that dog. I missed him terribly. I cried till there were no more tears; then, picking up my tool, I went back to the shelter.

PART III

25

Bits of songs floated through my head, and often, in my solitary walks, I would sing aloud, from old ballads . . .

> "Ye Highlands and Ye Lowlands,
> Now wherefore hae you been?
> They ha' slain the Earl of Murray
> And laid him i' the green.
> He was a bra gallant
> And he rade at the ring.
> Ah, the bonnie Earl of Murray
> He might have been a king."

Yes, he might have been a king, as I was of this domain, this ragged isle set in the ragged sea. I looked out at the water, at the waves lapping the shore with quiet but firm intent, and felt that I was a prisoner of myself more than of the island. I was now alone, inexorably alone, without any animal or human contact. Oh, how I missed Sam! Sometimes I'd go to his grave, which I had since marked with a ring of stones, and sit and contemplate our life together, short-lived though it was.

I thought of the men who had invaded my realm that night, who had committed murder. It would have been so easy to wipe them all out, obliterate them with the M-1 I carried about at all times. They had left with curses and threats. I didn't take their threats lightly, but armed and prepared myself. This was not the mainland of America, where, if things got too heavy in one place, I could flee to another state, another city, another town. Here was where I was destined to be and where I'd fight it out if necessary.

I checked my rifle daily, making sure it was clean and in proper working order. Luckily, all the ammunition was intact, and the cleaning equipment had been stored in the ammunition box, which I had buried during the storm. I oiled the barrel and checked it out with my little hand mirror. It could have passed any army inspection. I set and reset my sights, using up a clip of bullets in the process, aiming at distant shrubs and rocks. The sound of the rifle going off was fearsome, and the smell of the burning powder was a potent odor. I adjusted the sights until they were perfectly aligned, for my eyesight had improved considerably here. In my ammunition belt, I carried not only two clips, but twenty-four extra bullets, giving me a firepower capability of forty bullets, more than enough, I figured, to meet any attack. I also carried a small bottle of cleaning oil and a cloth to clean the barrel with, kept in one of the ammunition belt's pockets. In addition, my bayonet was at my side, as was my hunting knife and a canteen of water. And the binoculars were always around my neck. When I went fishing, I kept the equipment near at hand, not more than twenty feet from shore, and constantly turned to make certain no one was coming at me from the shore. In other words, not only was I armed against any actions engendered by the threats, but I was alert to any attack, and slightly paranoid about the whole thing. But here,

I felt, paranoia was useful. This was a matter of life and death to me. I couldn't call the police, I couldn't complain to authorities. I was the police and the authority here, and to ensure my own survival, I had to be armed.

> *As I was walking all alone*
> *I heard twa corbies makin' a mane,*
> *And the thane unto the other he say*
> *Where shall we gang and dine today?*
>
> *In behint yon old fail dike*
> *I wot there lies a new slain knight*
> *And nane ken that he lies there,*
> *But his hawk, his hound and lady fair.*

I recited these and other lines of old ballads, walking around near the grove of trees, examining my woods. I came here every morning, because I had also lost my calendars in the storm, and only notches on a tree told me what day it was. It was now March 19, and that meant that five months and four days would have to elapse before I'd be rescued. If that was the right term to use. Perhaps I should say returned to civilization or flown back and reprieved. . . .

If I had had Sam with me, I believe I could have stayed here indefinitely, but being utterly alone, I became restless for companionship. Thoughts of animals gave way to thoughts of people, and then of women. I dreamed erotic, fantasizing dreams of women smothering me with their breasts, with their flesh open to me, with their smells and aches and moans. I would wake in the middle of the night and, gasping, look around my little shelter, my night world, and realize that I was still alone, that not only were no women here, but there would never be any. My dreams and my waking hours became filled with thoughts of sex, debauchery, orgies, wilder and wilder erotic imaginings. I thought of the woman I had seen getting fucked, and wondered why I hadn't revealed myself. Why hadn't I gone further and screwed her? Fantasies of holding the men at gunpoint while screwing her dominated my thinking for a few days; then they were replaced with wild thoughts of killing those two decadent rich men and holding the women as slaves on the island, keeping them only for my pleasure. Crazy, it was all crazy.

Then I thought of my past life, of the women I had known. Of the women before my wife, and my wife, and our times together, and the women I had met in LA, of a woman named Lorraine who had taken me out to Tarzana in the Valley to a sex party, where bodies were piled up on one another, where everywhere you turned a cunt was open and waiting. I thought of Lorraine, big hipped and big breasted and young, with flashing white teeth and the softest lips, and of her moans. . . . God, I was going crazy with my thoughts.

I thought of a woman who had told me all her fantasies, about being fucked in front of a bunch of men, of being sucked off by another woman, and I closed my eyes, visualizing myself watching those scenes. . . .

All useless thoughts, as I could only clutch the air and nothing else, no other flesh but mine. I masturbated often, spending most of my days drowned in erotic thoughts, while my body grew indolent and weak. I needed a woman desperately. If only those women returned to the island now with those rich arrogant men, oh yes, if they returned now, they'd be in for a real surprise. Let's see how the men would react facing the muzzle of my M-1, while I screwed both their women. Oh yes, that would be a sight . . . women, their smells, their flesh, more clawing at the air. . . .

The blue sky and its eye, the sun, blinked not at all at my mad meanderings. I roamed the island like a bereft soul shouting words at the ocean, hearing only my own voice above the constant sounds of the surf. I was sick of the surf and my own voice. I needed someone. I didn't even have

walls to climb, I had no way to get my frustrations out except in solitary pursuits. Running, sweating, masturbating,
they were all the same to me, all ways to drive the excess
sexual energy out of myself, and all were unsuccessful, all
poor substitutes for what I really needed.

Oh God, I cried, send me a woman. Drop her from the
sky, if necessary, wash her up on shore, make her visit me
somehow, in a boat, a seaplane, somehow . . . any way . . .
but give me a woman, God. I need a woman. The sky
remained constant, the sun stared down at me and did not
blink. The waves beat relentlessly to the shore. Nothing
changed. I was going crazy but nothing else changed.

As April came in, the thoughts of women slowly left my
mind. I was spent with frustration, and began worrying
about my food supply. It was diminishing fast, and all I had
left were a few random cans, none of which I knew by
markings. Each time I plunged my bayonet into one, I was
surprised and usually disappointed by the contents. Now I
ate everything they contained. If the contents were pasty, I
ate the paste. I needed whatever nourishment I could get.
Four and a half months to go. I could probably survive on
my coconuts and fish. I now cooked seaweed, boiling it and
drinking the soup. I figured there was nourishment there. I
cut various vegetation, boiled it, and drank the liquid that
resulted. Much of it was sickening or tasteless, but I knew
there was nourishment. If only I had my vitamins, if only
Hildendorf had given me . . . if only . . . but I couldn't
think in that way. I had to cope as best I could, and I continued to fish daily and to dry fish, to mix fish with seaweed
and grasses in thickened soups. Somehow I was surviving.
Occasionally I felt a little dizzy, and I was sure that I was
missing valuable essential vitamins and minerals, but there
was nothing I could do about it. I moved from my erotic period to my food period, thinking of ideal menus, of meals I
had eaten in the past, of delicious pastries for dessert, of
chocolate, of meat sandwiches, and charcoaled steaks and

lamb chops, marinated meats, of endless varieties of food. I couldn't stop my thoughts anymore. I couldn't channel them into constructive paths, but was subject to their incessant demands. Food, women . . . craziness.

Sometimes I'd go into a trance, trying to imagine that my mind was a blank wall, a gray wall, with nothing on the wall, a blank slate as it were, and in this state I could sit and be content for a long time, but then the slate would open up into the world of dreams and thoughts, and once more visions of meat or flesh or pastries or women would flood into it. What I wouldn't have given for just one fine meal, followed by coffee, a chocolaty dessert, and then the company of a woman afterward. My soul, God. Take my living and immortal soul, for just one day and one night of pure pleasure. At these times I missed the Bible, I missed what could be a rock in my life, holding down these cravings.

March and April had fled before my wild demands, my incessant wishes, my unbearable longings. I ran more and more. I cut down trees with a vengeance. I built fires at night so that I could stare into their depths and calm myself, but always the thoughts would flood away everything else, and visions of women would dance before me, amidst the fires. My dreams became so vivid that I found myself sleeping when I could, trying to dream again of some female body, some face, someone out of my past, some person I could hold and who would hold and kiss me, who would fulfill my needs. Dreams and sleep, the visions of the unconscious, the world where man drowns in desire. . . .

These thoughts came to an abrupt end one morning while fishing off the west beach. I was holding my spear and looking into the water, which here was of a greenish, almost emerald tinge, when I heard a sound I hadn't heard in almost two years. A motor, an airplane engine. I looked up, and then saw the plane, a speck approaching from the west. It was a small one-engined plane, and it came directly for the

island, then began circling around, as if exploring the land-
scape. I scampered out of the water and put on my ammunition belt and M-1, but there was no shelter here, so I ran
up the slope toward the rocks and watched the plane circle
about. I was fearful that the pilot and passengers might be
the same men who had invaded the island and killed Sam,
and were back for revenge and would shoot me from the
plane. I loaded the M-1, prepared for battle, but after flying
around for a while, the plane turned about and headed west
again. I went back to my shelter and lay down. I brooded
about the plane. I couldn't know who was in it, but the way
it circled without dipping its wings or in any way recog-
nizing my presence caused me great anxiety.

I could only think that these were the same vicious men
reconnoitering the island before coming back to seek their
revenge. That seemed the most logical explanation, for anyone else would have flown low enough to shout something
to me, to ask if I needed any supplies. No, the men in that
plane weren't interested in my needs, but in revenge. They
could have fired from the plane, but that might not have
been possible. They might have simply rented both the
plane and the pilot, and were just scouting.

Yes, it all seemed clear to me. They'd be returning to this
island soon. When? I couldn't be sure, but from now on, no
more indolence, no more idle dreaming and sleeping away
the hot afternoons. I'd be constantly alert.

I awoke several times during the next few nights, sorry
more than ever that I didn't have Sam with me for his ears
were so much better than mine; he would have given me an
early warning. But now I had to depend solely on my per-
ceptions and my senses, and I had to trust them all. A couple of times I awoke in a sweat, having dreamed that the
men were in my shelter, with drawn knives, about to kill
me. But all was quiet and peaceful. I wondered when they
would attack. Would it be night or day? They now knew
that I was alone on this island, and they could come from

several directions at once, but in the daylight I could pick
them off with my rifle. No, it would be a night attack. I'd
have to get my sleep during the day and stay awake at
night.

I tried this for about a week, but then the whole structure
of my life became unbalanced, and night was so barren. I
couldn't do anything but sit in the dark. I went back to my
old habits. I moved my extra ammunition to the forest of
trees and hid it there, figuring that this was the ideal place
to make my final stand, if it became necessary. The rocks
guarding the eastern shore were formidable. A boat
wouldn't come in from that side, but from either the west or
the north. Still, they might come in from the south by raft.
That was possible. Or through the forest itself, if they
wanted to venture among the rocks. They might launch two
rafts and come in from two different directions.

I brooded about the possible attack most of the time,
wondering if I really was going off the deep end. Perhaps
the plane was sent by some foreign company just to look
over an abandoned island, or Hildendorf had sent it to
make sure I was still alive. Those were possibilities, but in
my heart I felt that the plane meant imminent danger. That
was my feeling, and if I couldn't trust my feelings here,
abandoned and isolated as I was, then I couldn't survive.

26

On May 4, I counted out the last five cans of vegetables, and realized that somehow I'd have to find some additional food to survive. I scoured the island, picking and tearing at all types of vegetation, which I took back to my shelter and tried to boil up as food. Nothing was any good. I found something that tasted like wild onions when cooked sufficiently, and I drank it as a thin soup, but had trouble digesting it. I suffered severe stomach cramps and had to remove that substance from my diet.

I had by now depleted all the coconuts, and had to wait for another season before they'd reach full eatable size, and that was way in the future. What would I do till then? I again climbed the tallest palm tree and looked out toward the north. The rock island was still there in my sight. I'd have to launch a raft and go there. I'd be in serious trouble if that island was barren, for I didn't know how long I could survive on my two staples, fish and seaweed.

To build the raft I examined what I had in the way of

wooden equipment. I still had a couple of the slats that had been on the island originally. If I could bind them together, they'd make a raft about four feet wide and six feet long. If I covered them with poles and bound the poles with rope and vines, I'd have a raft that would float on water, but its seamanship was another matter. If I installed a sail by using my canvas, it might help. I realized I needed a rudder of some sort, but I could use a pole as a makeshift one. I started working on it with my limited tools. I still had the trenching tool and my knife, but the work was slow as usual, and torturous. What I wouldn't have given for some planks of wood and nails and a hammer! But wishes were out of the question out here; reality was all.

I cut up some trees and spread the poles crosswise on the slats of wood, and then tied them carefully. First I tried each separate section, which measured about three by four feet. I launched one on a calm morning off the north shore and paddled around with my hands, and it held up well. I wondered whether or not to tie the other section to this one, or whether it would be best to go out in this small raft. If I tied the two of them together, there were possible problems. First, there was the danger that they'd split apart in rough water. Secondly, there was the added problem of handling a larger raft with the inadequate tools at my disposal. I didn't have any paddles and I was spending a great deal of time turning the trunk of a couple of trees into makeshift ones by slowly shaving away the wood until I could get a flat surface. The work was tedious, to say the least, and a whole day spent with my dull tools produced little in the way of progress. I was getting very discouraged.

After a particularly fruitless day, I went back to the shelter and ate some dried fish and drank some water, watching the night come on. The moon was but a slice in the sky, and a few clouds raced high over the island. I leaned back and closed my eyes, and my thoughts were of my mother. I wondered how she was getting along; if she was still alive.

Then I thought of Katy, my ex-wife, and when I had first met her.

It was at a party given by mutual friends, and we were purposely introduced since we were supposed to have something in common. She wrote poetry, and a couple of her poems had been published while she was at college. Katy and I didn't really get along at first, and it took some insistent calling on my part to arrange a date. We went to a movie, and then out for a drink, but the evening wasn't that exciting, and nothing at all happened between us.

I had almost forgotten about her when, one night, out of the blue, she called me up. She was troubled and wanted someone to speak to, and she had thought of me. I went to her apartment. It seemed Katy had just broken up with someone else, and was feeling very low. So I comforted her. She asked me to spend the night with her, but we didn't make love, just slept together. Then we saw more of each other and became lovers, but always the specter of her previous relationship haunted me.

Katy was very pretty and intelligent, and it was nice to have a woman who kept in touch with me every day. After a while, I was dependent on her attention and her calls, and when she told me her former lover had called again and wanted her to go back to him, I became panicky. In a crazy moment, which I have since long regretted, I asked her to marry me. She cried and said she couldn't, and would have to think things out, but after a few days, she suggested we run off and get married in a hurry. Which we did. It was a fatal mistake, for I married her, not out of any love for her, but out of my own weakness. Later on, when I did fall in love with another woman, I realized what I had been missing all those years with Katy.

I opened my eyes. Thinking of my past mistakes, of my humiliations and defeats, was depressing me, making me feel very lonely and sad. Then I heard an unusual noise. I bent forward. Nothing. Then the noise again.

What was it? I got to my feet and went to the edge of the shelter. I looked down at the north beach, but nothing was different. From what I could see of the west beach, all was still and just as before. Yet again I heard an unfamiliar sound. I walked over to the crest of the hill and stared down at the south beach, and became almost paralyzed with surprise. There was a rubber raft there, beached on the sand.

Someone else was on this island. I went back to my shelter and with trembling hands put on the ammunition belt. I had difficulty fastening it, and I silently cursed both the belt and my shaking hands. I finally got it in place with the bayonet and knife attached and then I picked up an extra canteen, along with my binoculars. I put the field-glass strap around my neck, got my M-1, and slung it over my shoulders. I stuck a few pieces of dried fish into my shirt and left the shelter. I crouched as I moved along, heading directly for the forest. I still hadn't heard any human voices, and every ten steps or so, I'd stop and cock my head. Still nothing. Had the raft been empty when it was stranded on the shore? Impossible. Or was it possible? I moved toward the southern part of the ridge and adjusted my glasses so that I could bring the raft into focus. It was still there, high and dry, but no one was around. Then I focused on the ocean. A boat was offshore, its lights out. It was bobbing about two or three miles away, and its engines, I gathered, were shut off. Not a sound from there either.

It was fairly dark outside, but the white sands always picked up whatever light was in the sky, and even the thin moon gave off illumination which bounced off the ground.

I moved closer to the woods, stopped, turned, and looked at the island through the glasses. Then I saw a shadow, a figure of a person, man or woman, I knew not, still as a mouse when it sees a cat. I kept the glasses on the figure, then it moved slowly. It was a man, and he held something in his hand. It looked like a revolver, but I wasn't sure from this distance. Then the man waved his hand and I moved the glasses in the direction of the signal. Nothing was to be seen, then another figure came up slowly and joined the first one. He was carrying what appeared to be a carbine or rifle.

Suddenly I was in great fear. I swiveled around, imagining that I heard someone behind me, but there was no one there. Was it just nerves? I was now unsure of everything, because I didn't know how many strangers were on the island. Right now it appeared as if my worst fears were being realized; I was being hunted down. I crouched and, running lightly, headed even closer to the woods. They were now no more than three or four hundred yards away, but I was in the open.

Then a shot rang out. I fell to the ground immediately and the bullet whizzed by me. Jesus, it was true. I was the target and they had found me. The shot came from the west somewhere, but I wasn't sure if it had come from the two men. Then I saw the fire of another weapon, and this was from a different direction, from my shelter.

I heard the thud as the bullet harmlessly crashed into the sand. I got up and ran in a zigzag fashion toward the woods. More fire. I fell down. Their aim was getting better, as the bullet split a rock not more than ten feet away. I got up once more and ran, and there was a hail of gunfire this time, from at least three weapons. I fell again, with the trees nearby. My heart was pumping fast and I seemed to have flying power in my legs, and made another quick dash and fell just before another hail of bullets flew against the trees themselves, smashing into trunks and bark. Now the trees were but a sprint away. I looked back. Two of the men were kneeling to take better aim. I ran, fell, twisted the rifle off my shoulder, and then ran again, afraid to pause too long to load it. A bullet grazed my calf. I could feel its searing bite as I bolted for the trees. At last I was safe within their shadows. I quickly worked my way through till I had about five trees between me and my assailants.

I paused and caught my breath. I got out a clip and loaded the weapon. I searched for my other clip. That was in another pocket of the belt, as was some loose ammunition. I guessed I had about forty rounds with me, and the rest of the ammunition was buried nearby. I stayed in one spot as long as I could, for it had been a long, hard run of about a mile from my shelter to these trees, and most of it done in a crouch, under fire. My heart was still pounding, but now, in this safe terrain, I wasn't as afraid as I had been in the open. I moved forward, the rifle in one hand, the binoculars in the other. I got to the front of the trees and bent down in their shadows, scanning the western area. I saw nobody. Moving back, I climbed a tree in the second rank, forcing myself up slowly, as I once more slung the rifle over my shoulder. I climbed about twenty or twenty-five feet above the ground and there I dug in, carefully placing my rifle on a nearby branch, while focusing the binoculars.

I kept my eyes on the cupped lenses till they were sore and wet with tears. I carefully scanned the entire area in front of me. The men had to be there and still others might be behind me. Anything was possible now. The main thing was to make sure that I wasn't outflanked. Then I realized that blood was dripping down my leg. I looked down at my right calf, which was bleeding profusely. I put my hand there and it came up coated with oozy blood. Damn. I wiped my hand on a broad leaf and then pulled off another leaf and wiped the blood, keeping a lookout at the same time for my enemies. Feeling the cut with my fingers, I could tell that it was a nasty one, for the bullet had not only grazed my calf but gouged out a piece of my flesh. It didn't seem that serious, but it was more than a flesh wound, and in the excitement of my flight, I hadn't really noticed either the blood or the pain, which was quite severe now.

There was nothing for me to do but play a waiting game. I figured that there were at least three of them, for I was sure that at one time I heard three guns firing. Of course, one man might have held two weapons and fired them off. It was all conjecture, and being alone this way, hunted down like an animal, I could probably spend all my time in random guesses. However, I had to protect myself, and the only way was to make some definite decision about the danger and where it would present itself. At the moment I was facing an attacking force from the front, and possibly from the rear, if they could land on the eastern shore at my back, behind the grove of trees. There were dangers present for them in that case, for the water was filled with large cutting rocks extending out at least fifty feet into the sea, and any craft as small or as soft as a rubber raft would be vulnerable. However, there might be some way for them to get there in safety. There was a small beach, perhaps six feet in width, running for a short distance near the grove of trees. The beach itself wasn't more than one hundred feet in length, for it was cut off by the trees from the rest of the shoreline on both sides.

If they did land there, they'd have to come through the forest, and I was certain that I'd hear their progress. If they outflanked me by moving to the forest on either side, the north or south, which was respectively now my right and left flanks, I'd probably hear them as well, for it would be difficult to come through the trees, overgrown vines, and leaves without stirring up something. I decided, therefore, to stay put in my present situation on the branch, and watch the action directly in front of me. I realized that sleep was impossible, for these men, whoever they were, meant deadly business, and if I was caught unawares, I'd be wiped out in a hurry.

By this time I guessed that the men were the same ones who had been on the island before, whose drugs I had so angrily destroyed. They had probably been the ones who had sent the airplane for scouting purposes, and they knew now that there was only one man to contend with, namely me. Why they wanted revenge was beyond me. What was to be gained on their part but bloodshed? Nothing more. But again, to give motives to angry men was a waste of time. I had done many stupid and unaccountable things in my life under its trance.

In addition to the three men, there would be one or more men on the boat itself. It seemed inconceivable that they'd leave the boat unattended, for if I shot away their rubber raft, they'd be just as stranded as I was, unless one of them was an extraordinary swimmer and wished to move through a bloodbath of sharks. So, there must be at least four adversaries against me, three on the island and one in reserve.

In a short while I saw flames shooting up from the north central part of the island. They were probably burning up my shelter and the canvas, for the smoke seemed thick and black. They were also probably destroying the last of my food supplies. Well, there was nothing I could do, and the paltry few things that were left were not worth dying for. If now, having their revenge by fire, they left the island, I'd be satisfied. I wouldn't even attempt to harass them. Live and let live would be my motto in that case. I hoped they'd depart now, but I couldn't go out in the open and check this out. All I could do was sit in the tree, my weapons at the ready, waiting to see what happened. A waiting game. Well, I had been playing that game for close to two years now, and could easily spin it out for whatever time it would take.

27

During the night I dozed off a couple of times, but each time I snapped myself awake to see that it was still dark and no one was near. The men must have decided to pursue me in the morning, or perhaps they had already left by raft after burning and destroying my possessions. The day would reveal all. Finally, dawn broke behind me, over the eastern tip of the island, and sunlight filtered through the trees.

Then I saw them. There were only three men, and they were spread apart, about fifty feet from each other, slowly advancing toward the trees. I didn't move. When they got within two hundred yards of me, one of them began shouting. I recognized the voice as Johnny's.

"Hey you. Hey you, can you hear me?"

I didn't answer. They hadn't spotted me yet, and I didn't dare move. I held the rifle ready to fire. Already I had Johnny in sight.

"Hey you, listen. Come on out. We just want to talk to you."

I sat still.

"Come on out. Nothing to be afraid of. We need your help here."

I watched Johnny looking around, trying to find me. He still hadn't spotted my hiding place.

"Listen, about the shots. We thought you were someone else. Come on out. We just want to talk."

I unfastened the safety on the M-1.

I saw Johnny walk over and talk to another man, then all three got together and were talking. Johnny shouted again.

"Listen, are you Japanese? We friends. We good guys. Good friends. Come to help."

I kept quiet.

"You son of a bitch," shouted another man. "You fucking son of a bitch. We're gonna wipe you off the face of the earth."

The third man had a carbine with which he was scanning the trees. I knew he had me in sight when it stopped moving, directly facing me. I could see him pointing and gesturing at the tree I was in.

"Twang." The bullet ripped through the tree next to me. I jumped out of the tree as a barrage of bullets smashed the spot I had just been sitting at. I fell to my knees, recovered my balance, and took aim with my rifle. But now all three had dropped to the ground, and I didn't have a target.

I scampered through the thick underbrush, being careful to stay out of sight. I moved toward the south, so that the sun would remain at my back, and went to the edge of the trees. I stayed there all day long. Nothing else happened. It was a standoff. They disappeared beyond the hill and I remained in the trees. I didn't know what they'd do next, and when evening came, I still didn't know if they had left the island or not. I scanned the water for the boat, but it had vanished out of sight. Where was it?

I ate some dried fish and drank water. I was getting very sleepy, but fought the impulse to close my eyes. I crawled deeper into the forest and climbed another tree, and it was there I napped for a little while. When I opened my eyes it was very dark outside. The moon was not to be seen. Nothing stirred. I looked in all directions with the glasses, focusing through branches and leaves, but could see little. Then I heard voices. They were very close, and possibly at the edge of the trees.

"Listen," Johnny shouted. "Don't force us to come in there. Give up or we're gonna burn you out."

I held the rifle in my hands.

"Come on out, you bastard."

They hadn't yet heard my voice.

A barrage of gunfire flew through the trees, some hitting near me. Another barrage followed. Then I heard them talking among themselves.

"You think we got the fucker?"

"I don't know. What do you think?"

"There's just one, right?"

"Just one, yeah."

"Let's give him one more chance to come out."

"We've given him too many chances."

"Maybe he don't speak English."

"That's probably it. He's probably a Jap, left over from the war."

"Hey, Jap, come on out."

"Maybe we should leave the fucker."

"Maybe."

Another burst of gunfire flew through the trees. I held my ground, not daring to move or give away my position. That was the last gunfire or sounds from them that night. The next morning, I scanned the frontal area but didn't see them. When I focused the glasses on the sea behind me, I came in for a shock. The boat was circling slowly near the shore. I could even see a man behind the wheel. No one else was on the boat. They were surrounding me slowly. I heard rustling now in the woods to my right. I put the glasses to that area but could see nothing. There were too many branches and leaves in the way. I didn't dare move. I figured if I couldn't see them, they couldn't see me. Another standoff. Then I saw something white moving not more than sixty feet away. It was a man all right, moving slowly, chopping the underbrush with a broad bladed knife.

I raised the rifle and sighted the blade. I put the glasses on again and zeroed in. There was a glimpse of a face. Then the blade moved in a wide arc. I aimed. The safety was on. I put it off safety and aimed again. I lost him for a moment; then the silver blade, then the white face came into sight. I aimed carefully and squeezed the trigger.

The sound of the shot reverberated through the forest. I heard a scream.

"Jesus, Jesus, he got me."

Activity was rampant in the forest. I heard men moving the leaves, and underbrush thrashed about. There was heavy gunfire, as bullets whizzed in my general direction, but far from target. I dropped to the ground again, clutching the rifle.

Behind me the boat was still circling. I moved toward the south side, keeping distance between myself and my enemies, who fired from my right, or the north. I got to the edge of the trees and looked over, finally getting a clear view. A man was bent over, not more than two hundred feet away, in the trees. A leg was extended, probably that of the wounded man. I raised my rifle and took aim at a crouching figure nearby.

"He's there, there," one of the men shouted, but I fired. Another scream pierced the silence. A horrible, dying scream. Then silence.

Moving back into the woods, I retreated to the edge of the forest, to the spot where the woods ended in sea. I saw the boat circling still, but now it was moving in a northerly direction, away from the island.

Here was my chance. I pushed my way through the woods, to the southern tip. Between me and the rubber raft was nothing but barren distance. The men were on my right still. I was closest to the raft now, and if I could outrun some bullets for about fifty yards, I could get out of sight down the slope, then run for the beach. I could get to the raft.

Still, I had to make a run for it. I listened for sounds. I heard loud moans from the woods. One dead, one wounded. One whole. One in the boat. I aimed at the woods, in the direction of the moans, and fired off six shots, emptying the clip.

Gunfire was returned in my direction. I put in another clip and then loaded up the ejected one. I fired another round at the woods. More gunfire back from one weapon this time. I ran for the open space. I ran and dropped, then got up and ran again, zigzagging. Gunfire exploded from the woods. But it came from too deep in the woods now to be effective. I ran down the slope out of sight and went straight for the raft. It was going to be a long, long run. They'd have to come out of the woods to sight me, and shoot with accuracy, and I was now safe provided no one else was in front of me or on top of the hill. I was a dead pigeon if they had a fourth man with them.

But no one fired. I ran and fell, got up, looked around, and kept running. I ran all the way to the raft, which was still beached on the sand. By the time I got there I was burned out and panting. My lungs felt on fire, and I was sick to my stomach. I dry heaved a few times, then took possession of the raft and jumped in, examining it, while still watching the beach to the east. There were provisions which I dragged out . . . beverages and food. Sandwiches! I couldn't believe my eyes. Cans of beer in a cooler. Bottles of pineapple juice on ice. I grabbed a couple of sandwiches and a bottle of juice and ran from the raft, running up the hill with one final effort. I made the top of the hill and dropped down, expecting a hail of fire. There was no fire and no one was near. But I saw the boat coming around the island from the west, moving into the south.

I worked my way back to my old shelter slowly, and saw that it was a mass of burnt and charred ruins. They had destroyed everything. Those bastards. I waited there, with the earth barrier in front of me, blocking me as a target to the east, where they were dug in. I sat down and ate a sandwich. It was ham and butter on white bread. I chewed the sandwich slowly, savoring each bite. Then I drank some juice. It had a sweet and yet tart taste . . . I had forgotten this taste. I drank out the remaining water from one canteen and filled it carefully with juice, trying not to spill too much. When it was filled, I drained off the rest of the juice out of the bottle and wiped my mouth.

The sun was at midday when I finished this meal. Then it dipped and afternoon approached, then evening. When it was dark, I moved out of the area, toward the woods, for it would now be my turn to attack.

I moved slowly, thinking of a way to surprise my adversaries. I moved cautiously, keeping near the north beach, staying on the hill. I waited for gunfire to announce my presence, but none came. I moved slower now, waiting for the bullets to come. Still nothing. Was I being set up?

I had one clip in the rifle, the other ready. I had used up about nine bullets and had twenty-nine left. Plenty of firepower left.

It was pitch dark now, the middle of the night. No moon out. Nothing was moving. Then I heard a cry, a moan. It came from the woods, but not from the northern end. They had moved away from there, and were in the deep woods to the south. I ran along the crest, then down toward the north beach, waiting for the gunfire. Still nothing. I ran to the edge of the woods and slipped in. Nothing yet. I moved slowly, careful with my bare feet not to disturb anything, not to create any noise. I stopped every few feet, cocking my head, waiting for another sound. Then I heard a moan, another, almost a scream.

"I can't stand the pain. Help me."

No other sound. Maybe Johnny was somewhere else, away from the wounded man. Maybe it was a trap for me to go into. I stopped and didn't move. My safety on the rifle was on. In case I slipped, I didn't want the M-1 to go off accidentally, giving away my position. I stayed this way, in silence for about ten minutes. Then I heard definite movement. I moved to the edge of the wood, facing toward the south, and peered out. Nothing. I put the glasses on the area I had heard sounds from. Then I saw one man holding another up. Both were armed. One man's arm was around the other's shoulder. They were slowly trying to get out of the woods, down to the beach, to the raft. I stayed back in the woods, keeping watch on their movement. They were going to try and get off now. I could tell just what was in their minds as if I were inside their brains. Escape from the island. Come back another day, or send men here to kill me.

I still didn't move. No sound, nothing. I could hear my breathing. Regular breaths. Nothing out of the ordinary. I felt my pulse. Slow beating. Then they moved out of the woods. I moved forward slowly, ever so slowly. I raised my rifle and aimed.

The sound of my fire blasted the stillness of the night. The lead man fell over, raising his rifle to the sky. The other man dropped and started firing at me. I ducked down and slowly moved along the woods. He was firing fifty feet behind me now.

"You son of a bitch," he cried. "Come out here, you son of a bitch."

I stood still. He fired again, then there was a loud click.

He cursed, and started crawling to his fallen friend, to get his rifle. I aimed carefully. When he had the rifle, I fired in rapid succession. I saw the ground kick from the bullets, then they hit him with dull thuds. I emptied the clip.

No sounds now. Only my breathing. I waited. Still nothing. I reloaded the rifle. Ready for more action. Now I moved cautiously around the edge of the wood, still staying inside the forest. Then stopped. In front of me was a body. I almost screamed, then saw the face of one of the men, his eyes open, his mouth gaped open. I gulped and bent down. He was dead, all right. I got up and stepped over him, and kept moving. I went to within fifty feet of the two fallen men, who were very still. I came at them running, my rifle aimed at them, but there was no movement.

Both were goners. I turned the first one over, and he fell back like a limp rag. The other one was on his back, his head tilted, a huge stain around his heart. His eyes were closed. He was very dead.

Three men dead. The boat still out there. I had to get it in. There had to be a way. It was still night, dark sky and no moon, and the sand was glowing white under my feet. I started undressing the man on his back, the one called Johnny, the one who had killed my dog. I took off his captain's hat and untied his shirt and pants and sneakers. His skin was turning cold. I worked as fast as I could, and for the first time in three days I was able to turn my back on the island without fear. When I had stripped him down to his underwear, I left him there and went down toward the raft. The boat was out at sea, its lights off. I would be patient and wait for the boat. In the darkness I dressed in the dead man's clothing. They were about my size, but the sneakers and hat were too big. Nevertheless it would do for my plan. I waited for daybreak.

28

When the first rays of the sun hit the water, I was prepared. I had my rifle loaded and my binoculars focused on the boat. I saw a man walk about, then look toward shore. I raised my rifle and waved. It was a few minutes before I caught his attention, then I heard the engine fire up. The boat stayed stationary for a couple of minutes, then turned and headed for shore, coming directly for me. I stood by the raft, holding my old shirt in my hands so that it would partially cover my beard and make me unrecognizable. The boat came closer.

With my captain's hat, white shirt and ducks, and the sneakers, I looked exactly like the man I had killed the night before, and from this distance there was no way of telling that I was an imposter. Not yet. The boat moved forward, as the sun came on more strongly. It was going to be a clear, hot day. I had the safety off the M-1, and another clip at the ready. The boat was coming right at me, its wake a bubbly froth of white water. When the vessel was about fifty yards away, it turned slowly to the right, or east, and slowed down. The man operating it came to the side of the boat. He shouted at me but I couldn't understand the words, and I shouted back something unintelligible, and waved him further in. I could see him peering at me, trying to see exactly who I was. He then disappeared from sight, and came back to the side with a pair of field glasses. I was holding the rifle casually, and waving it, but then I suddenly took aim. He saw the muzzle aimed right at him, and for a couple of seconds he was frozen, as I snapped off two shots. They missed him but smashed into the side of the boat, only a few feet away, kicking away pieces of the hull.

He ran for the wheel and gunned the motor. I fired rapidly, unloading the clip of bullets at the boat. It was heading east, trying to cut around the island. Jamming in another clip, I fired. Wham. Wham. Wham. Wham. Wham.

The fifth shot did the trick. I saw the driver twist, still holding onto the wheel, but now the boat started moving in a crazy pattern, heading inland, and for a moment I thought it would beach itself as it moved toward the shore. Then it twisted away, and zoomed for the far corner of the island, past the forest. Somehow it missed land because it vanished out of my sight, but there were big rocks ahead in its path. Then I heard a deafening crash, followed by an explosion, then another explosion, and huge billows of black smoke fed by orange flame shot beyond the height of the trees, then quickly died down. I ran along the edge of the beach, back toward the trees, then stopped, quickly out of breath. I slowed down to a walk, then trotted along, then walked. It seemed to take forever to get to the trees, past the bodies of the two dead men. I went through the trees as fast as I could, and walked down to the eastern beach. Other than a few pieces of debris floating in the water and an oil slick, there was no trace of the boat. It had vanished into the sea, perhaps no more than fifty feet out, but the water was deep enough there to bury anything. And it had quickly buried the boat. Nothing remained but loose scraps of plastic and wood, floating out with the tide. All gone. And all the provisions in that boat lost to me.

I sat down exhausted. I still had work to do before I could go to sleep, important work. I had to bury the dead rather than leave them exposed to the brutal sun. So I dragged myself away and walked once more back to the shelter in the middle of the island. My trenching tool was still there, among the charred ruins. The handle had been burnt a little, but otherwise it was in good shape. I put it on my shoulder and walked once more to the forest.

I began to dig a big hole. Digging is brutal business, especially with inadequate tools, and especially when one is exhausted. I dug up earth and threw it over to one side, and kept going. The sand was loose and continually caved in. The sun burned down on me. Luckily I had the captain's hat on my head or I would have passed out. I limited myself to water doing this work, because I sweated profusely, and could have gone through all the juice and beer in one afternoon. Water would do. It had sustained me and would sustain me again. I refilled the canteen time and time again, pausing in my work to walk to the freshwater pond. Had these idiots taken control of the pond, they could have brought me to my knees in a few days. But they were out for vengeance. Vengeance is mine, saith the Lord. Yes revenge is a dish that many eat, some hot and some cold, but in the end the meal destroys them. It is a bitter meal indeed.

Why couldn't they have just left me alone? They killed my dog, my one companion, and then invaded my island to kill me. It was my island, didn't they realize that? They were on my territory, land I knew intimately and would defend to my last breath. My one burst of nationalism. I wouldn't lift a finger if LA or North Orange Grove Street were invaded, but this was my land. It was the one thing I had ever possessed fully and had to myself. My little island.

And these fools thought that four of them could take it away from me. They didn't even want the island, just revenge. Revenge for some stupid thing . . . so I had destroyed their dope. I had probably cut away thousands of dollars of profits from their pockets, but it was only money. Take the loss and go on. There's plenty more dope in the world, but only one Sam. Weigh everything, and I was right. Or wrong. How does one weigh life against money? I had all these thoughts pass through my head, as afternoon followed morning, and late in the afternoon I finally had a large hole dug, enough for the bodies, I hoped.

I had dug it not far from the two fallen men, because I didn't care to drag cold bodies for long distances. I went to the first corpse, the one whose clothing I was wearing. The shirt I had on was matted with dried blood, but I had worn it all day long to protect myself from the heat, from my sweat evaporating too fast and knocking me out. I now removed the shirt and trousers, the cap and the sneakers, and threw them into the open grave, after emptying the pockets of the clothes and putting the contents to one side. Then I lifted the corpse. How strange he felt, or it felt. Cold and already crunched in rigor mortis. I dragged the corpse by the feet and pulled it to the grave, and then carefully rolled the body in. It got stuck because of the bent angle of the body, and I had to force it down with the trenching tool. A bad business all around. I felt myself getting clammy and sick with this work. I wanted it over with. I then got to the second body and emptied its pockets, then dragged it down to the grave and put the corpse on top of the other one. By the time I had both bodies in, I realized that was all this grave was going to hold. Jesus, you needed a huge grave for a body. I shoveled the sand over the inert forms till I could cover them and flatten out the earth, which I patted down with the trenching tool. Then I stood over the bodies and said aloud,

"The lord is my shepherd, I shall not want.

"He leadeth me . . ."

I recited the entire psalm, and then stood silently over the grave and crossed myself. Somewhere there were women mourning for these men, and perhaps children and mothers and fathers. Such was the way of the world. What could I do? What else could I have done, unless I was willing to die instead of them. There was nothing else I could have done.

"Forgive them, oh Lord," I said. "Oh God, forgive them and forgive me."

I was too exhausted to dig the other grave. I dropped the tool and went into the nearby water, washing myself thoroughly. Then I walked with weary steps to the raft and lay down, leaning my head against one of the sides. I fell into a deep, troubled sleep, where wild phantoms assailed me in my dreams the whole night long. When I awoke, I was still tired and bleary eyed. I rubbed my eyes, threw some water on my hands, and washed my face off with the water. I ate half of a ham sandwich and drank some juice, then started back to resume my gravedigging.

Having had some sleep, I found the work easier this time, but still it took till early afternoon to get the grave dug. It was a little smaller than the other, and a little wider. I went into the woods and dragged out the body, which by now was bloating and turning gaseous. It was a distasteful business all right. I pulled the body along the sand, alternately holding my breath and breathing only through my mouth. Then I nearly gagged as I emptied the pockets, and then pushed the body into the grave with the tool. It fell down to the bottom with a thud, sideways. I quickly covered it with dirt.

I recited the Twenty-third Psalm again, and bent my head in silent prayer as I knelt on the earth. I prayed for all those I loved and for the dead men, and those who loved them, and then, finally, again asked God's forgiveness. The burials were over. I went to the water's edge and took off all my clothes, and immersed myself in the water. I wanted to wash my body thoroughly, but mere salt water couldn't wash away my feelings. I felt triumphant now, and this feeling troubled me. I had killed four men with one weapon, and I had taken life from this earth and yet I felt triumphant.

I left the water and walked around till I dried off, then I built a fire and sat by it and sang songs to myself. I sang:

> "Write me a letter, send it by mail,
> Send it in care of Birmingham jail.
> Birmingham jail, boys, Birmingham jail
> Send it in care of Birmingham jail."

And I remembered as a child going to a poor church with some friends, and there, to the same tune, I heard the hymn,

> "Whiter than snow, Lord, whiter than snow,
> Wash me and I'll be whiter than snow."

After singing, I ate another half of sandwich and drank a beer with it. The beer was San Miguel, and tasted really good. I knew beer had some nutritional value . . . perhaps vitamin B, from the malt and hops. I couldn't think clearly about nutrition then, and I didn't want to think about the freshly buried dead, or about myself either. I sang old songs and tried to think about nothing in particular, but it was hard to do. It was so hard to empty one's mind. I had just taken four men's lives with my own hands, and for the moment was contented, and yet it all seemed wrong. But maybe it was right. I had been brought up in America to finally end up in LA, hiding from sheriffs, cursing my fate and the world around me. Now I was in a different world, with different values. It was time to put my house in order, to rethink my life.

I was getting drowsy. I watched the fire die down to embers, then I went back to the raft and lay down. The sky was blue velvet and the stars were bright diamonds in that velvet. I closed my eyes and fell asleep.

29

John Compean, Van Nuys, California, age twenty-nine. Lawrence Hopwood, San Diego, California, age twenty-seven. William Gazzara, Thousand Oaks, California, age twenty-three.

I emptied their wallets and spread the contents on the sand. They each had California driver's licenses, in addition to credit cards, social security cards, some business cards, miscellaneous papers, plus money.

The money was both in American dollars and Mexican pesos. The total came to 246 American dollars, plus 700 Mexican pesos. I guessed they must have kept the bulk of their cash on the boat, or in a hotel safe somewhere, from wherever they had come to invade the island. All three were young men, younger than I was at any rate, and now they were gone. And people who cared about them would never figure out what happened. They'd guess the men were ambushed on some dope smuggling run, or other smugglers betrayed them. They could never, in their wildest imaginings, think that some man who looked like a naked savage had killed them with an M-1 and was sitting right now, like a victor over spoils, sorting out the bits of information that made up their lives.

I put the money to one side, under a couple of small stones, and looked over the other spoils. There was a Swiss army knife, with a lot of gadgets, including a can opener. What I wouldn't have given for this knife a year ago. Now I had nothing to open except a few beer cans and they were self-opening. I examined all the gadgets attached to the knife: a corkscrew, small saw, two sharp blades, cutting tool, bottle opener, small scissors.

There were three opened packs of cigarettes, and two more packs still sealed. All the men had been smokers and their tastes ranged from Marlboros to Salem Longs. I looked at the opened packages, then took out a couple of cigarettes and smelled them. I smelled them again, then put the cigarette packages aside. I pushed the packages even further away, on the discard pile. I didn't want to be tempted by them.

There was also a small box containing marijuana and paper, all neatly packed in cellophane. Three joints had already been rolled. I smelled them and threw them away. No more of these stupid temptations. I had come through and they hadn't because I wasn't worn down by tobacco and dope. I didn't need either to bolster my courage or my nerves. I felt self-righteous and realized how ridiculous my posturing was at this moment, but it was indeed the way I felt. After all, I was sitting and looking through their possessions, not the other way around, and there had been three of them, four of them actually, against me.

I stretched my legs and walked around, then went and had a cold beer. The ice chest was still functioning, and there were twenty more cans and bottles of beer in there, along with another plastic bottle of pineapple juice and some more sandwiches. How I needed this food. After I finished off their provisions, I'd be back on my normal diet of fish and seaweed, but for the time being—for the next two weeks, if I stretched it out properly—I'd make use of their food.

I was sorry they didn't have fresh fruit or vegetables, but the pineapple juice was sufficient for my vitamin C needs. I hadn't had any fruit for almost two years, except for the few cans I found of mandarin oranges and peaches, and I had finished those about eight months earlier. I'd ration the pineapple juice as though I were stranded on a raft in the ocean and had to use it as my sole supply of drinking fluid. I'd make it and the beer go a long way. There were nutrients in the beer. . . . I would have preferred more juice but I'd take what had been given to me by fate.

I went back to my examination of the booty. I had a .45 automatic, with an empty magazine, but with four usable bullets, which I found in one of the men's pockets. I also had a carbine, which still held some bullets, and a small .25 single-shot pistol, which was empty and for which I could find no bullets. They had almost depleted their entire ammunition supply in their stupid attack on me. If I had known, I would have been content just to draw their fire, and then perhaps chase them from the island. No, I couldn't have done that. They'd come back another day, with reinforcements, and I'd be spending every moment of my stay here waiting for the new invasion. Even now I was uncertain. Who else knew of the attack? Maybe no one. Maybe it was their private vendetta. Maybe they hired a boat for this, or was it the same boat they had used before? I wouldn't and couldn't ever know the true facts. I was in no position to make inquiries, and even if I were, it would be more discreet to forget about the whole thing and not stir up trouble. I would be patient and mind my own business forever, but if I was attacked again, well, that was another story. I was still well armed, and had the buried box of ammunition in reserve.

There was another knife, a sharp-edged wide cutting blade in a sheath, about six inches long. It was a finer knife than my old one, and I'd use it instead. There were two flashlights, one of which still worked, but the other was broken, and this went into the discard pile after I ascertained that the batteries were burned out. And letters. There were five letters, all handwritten, mailed to the men at various addresses. Two were addressed to Honolulu, Hawaii; one to Hermosillo, Mexico; one to San Diego, California, General Delivery; and a fifth to Naalehu, Hilo Island, Hawaii. The Hawaiian letters were the most recent, and it seemed a safe bet that I was in the Pacific somewhere, probably west of Hawaii, but not having any kind of map, I couldn't really know.

I read the letters over a couple of times. All were from women, wives or sweethearts who signed them with "love" and sometimes "love and kisses." Sentimental, long letters. I thought of keeping the letters and letting the women know that the men had been killed when I got back to the United States, but how could I do that? If there was publicity about my stay here, the women's friends could put two and two together. No way I'd leave myself open for retribution. No way.

There had been six men in the first boat, and that meant that at least two were still on the loose. Would they come after me? The world was very small in certain ways, and I didn't want to spend the rest of my life as a target for some embittered dope smugglers. I put the letters on the discard pile.

There were four sets of keys, all on key rings. Two were of leather and were embossed with automobile makes—Porsche and BMW. The others were just key rings. I threw the keys on the discard pile, wondering if they could be of any use to me here. Metal rings might come in handy, but for what? No, I didn't want any part of them, or any evidence of former owners.

The rest of the things were worthless scraps of paper, pieces of string, a box of matches from a Honolulu club on North Hotel Street, more matches, with a Sunset Boulevard restaurant imprinted on the cover. I wondered if I had passed any of these men in the street in my aimless ramblings around LA. Probably; little did we know we'd meet again, thousands of miles away and under these conditions. A crazy world indeed.

I started a fire and burned everything that could be burned. I then spread out the remains, which were fine ash, and dumped sand over them, till nothing showed. Then I looked over the other things. I decided to keep the knives. As for the guns, the flashlight, and other metal objects, there was no point in hanging on to these things. They were unclean as far as I was concerned and I didn't need more arms. I wasn't looking for more battles, for more deaths. I had had enough killing.

I dug a hole and buried everything but the knives. Into the hole went the guns, key rings, wallets, and two wrist-watches, neither of which was a calendar type, so I had no way to ascertain the exact date. What use would watches be for me? Time meant nothing on this island, and I didn't want their things anyway.

That left the raft. I examined it thoroughly. There were two life preservers on board, which would come in handy in case I wanted to take a trip to that nearby island. I also found a waterproof flashlight, two paddles, some lengths of rope, and a few boxes of raisins I had previously overlooked. I carried the raft all the way up the hill, for I meant to use it as a roof for a new shelter. My new shelter, I decided, was going to have sand and dirt walls, reinforced by poles. It wouldn't be very sturdy, but my time here was running out. According to my calculations, the date was May 16 and just over three months remained of my stay.

I now had to resettle myself on the island. First, I needed some kind of head cover. I had gone for two days without a hat, and the sun was too much for me. If I had a hat, I could function during the hot part of the day; without it, it was best that I rested in the shade. Luckily, I found my helmet liner. It was a little charred, and had been cracked when the men destroyed my possessions and shelter, but it still fit and still gave shade. I put it on my head, adjusted it slightly, and began to tour the island, thinking about my new shelter.

I went down to the forest and started cutting down trees, aware again of what tedious and hard work that was. It took all day to cut through some of the trees, even with my new knife, which was rapidly turning dull under the work. I was no better off than before. I spent a week cutting down trees and trimming them of branches and leaves. I set the new poles in the ground and used them as reinforcements for the earth barriers I built as my walls. I had to build the barriers quite thick, for they were of loose earth and sand, and part of them continually blew away under the slightest wind. But right now, having little time left on the island, I was in no mood to build a firm, powerful shelter again. For one thing, I had no canvas at all, and only the raft would be my roof.

May turned into June. I still fished and boiled seaweed and drank my one beer a day. But soon all the food I had taken from the men was gone, and I was back to my old diet. I was hungry for a while, but then, as I settled into my dried fish and seaweed soup routine, my hunger passed. I had held my weight from the meat and beer diet, but was again losing it and getting very thin. I needed more food than I was getting.

On June 23, I looked like a scarecrow, so thin had I become. With two months left, I had to find more food. That mysterious island to the north beckoned to me. There must be something worthwhile on that island, something I could make good use of. I decided to journey there. I removed the raft from the top of my shelter and carried it down to the north beach, for I was afraid of dragging it and possibly tearing the bottom accidentally. Then I thought about my thirty-mile or so trip across the water. I sat in the sun, wondering what kind of trip it would be, how dangerous, whether I would ever get back here . . . for I knew, if I was stranded on the other island, I might very well be stranded forever.

30

Four times I equipped the raft with water and dried fish, ammunition, my rifle, and other supplies, and four times I unloaded the raft and returned it to its place as the roof on my shelter. And after I unloaded the goods, I'd climb up on the palm tree and look out toward the north through the field glasses at the mysterious island, which was never more than a grayish black rock jutting out of the water. Maybe that's all it was, and it was so far away, at least thirty miles, I estimated. To take this kind of trip alone, in a raft I'd have to man by myself, using only paddles, was clearly dangerous. If anything happened to the raft I might well be stranded on that island, or worse still, thrown into the water, to be at its mercy. There were sharks everywhere in these seas. While spear fishing I had seen them several times from a distance, their dorsal fins prodding the water, their presence malevolent.

Still, I wondered if I could live on my present food supply. Not only wasn't I maintaining my present weight, but I was growing progressively weaker, day by day. I felt it when I walked around the island instead of running from place to place, and when I took more and more frequent naps during the day. If men were to invade the island now, they'd easily claim me as a victim. I was in no position to run at full speed across the island to the shelter of the trees, to stay awake for three days and nights, and come out fighting. No, things were subtly changing, and I didn't know whether to blame my inadequate diet or possibly a general deterioration of my health and well-being, foreshadowing another kidney stone attack. I feared another attack more than anything else, because I didn't know if I could survive one more bout of that intense pain. And then the fever. I prayed to God to spare me from one more seizure.

Yet, I was surviving. I was eating fish and seaweed, and occasionally catching small crustaceans, crabs and what appeared to be a variety of crawfish. I'd boil these up and then remove the shells and eat them with my fingers. They were extremely tasty and a good change of pace, but I missed the condiments that made them so much more palatable. I was starting to think of food again, all kinds and varieties of food, and sometimes, for days on end, my time passed in fantasies of perfect menus. I knew it was a bad sign, and that I'd have to find more food, and fresh food at that.

Again I went up to the top of the coconut tree. Each climb was more of an effort for me, for, despite my thinness and the hardness of my muscles, something seemed to have left me, some source of energy that had always been in reserve. I scanned the distant island carefully again with the binoculars, looking for something besides that gray rock. I couldn't make out anything else, no trees, vegetation, or life.

June faded out, and July came in, and I started notching the other side of the tree. Thirty-one days in July, and then twenty-three more in August, and I'd be out of here. Fifty-four more days, barely nine weeks. What was eight or nine weeks to me, when I'd spent almost 680 days alone on this outpost? It would be just a few weeks of routine, a few weeks of waiting, and then it would be over. Yet, I still thought of food, of something besides the fish and seaweed. The sun now made me dizzy on occasion, and I knew it was from lack of proper nutrition. I had to make a decision, and make it soon.

On July 8, I carried the raft to the north beach and set it down, and then sat and panted from the effort. I filled two canteens with water, put in a supply of dried fish, and thought of what else I would need. I placed a life preserver in the raft, two paddles, and the waterproof flashlight. I thought of taking the rifle, then equivocated. If I lost the rifle on this trip, that would be a big loss, a terrifying loss, for I would be completely helpless against any possible future invasion. Yet, if I didn't take it and ran into trouble, I'd also be helpless. But what kind of trouble could I have on a raft that would necessitate using the rifle? I decided not to take it. I carefully hid the M-1 and ammunition in a small hole I dug with my hands, then returned to the raft. I took along both new knives and my binoculars. I was tempted to leave the glasses, but they would be invaluable in scanning the island from a distance, or any other island or object I might find in my journey.

I decided that I'd travel as lightly as possible. I took along a spear in case I could do some fishing from another beach on the other island. I looked around the raft carefully. I seemed to have enough provisions for two days on the water. What else would I need? I didn't have a compass, it was true, but I could tell the south from the north by the sun itself, or from the north star at night. However, there was no point in traveling by night. If worse came to worse, I'd dock on the other island for the evening, then return during the day. I examined the rope in the raft, and tugged at it, testing its strength. It would hold well, and there were numerous hooks on the raft to anchor the boat to a solid object. That left only the weather and the sea to think about, but the sky was clear this afternoon, and there seemed no storm in sight. The wind was calm and the water placid. I made a final decision. I'd leave before daybreak tomorrow to give myself the maximum time on the water during daylight. Thirty miles to go. How fast would I travel, that was the question. A mile an hour? Faster? Jesus, at a mile an hour, it would take me almost two days to get there. Now I had second thoughts about the trip. If I had a canvas to use as a sail, that would make all the difference, but I had nothing like that at all. My ragged shirt wouldn't do very well. I decided to get up early and make a decision, once and for all.

It was hard sleeping that night. I was restless, my back bothered me, and I couldn't get into a comfortable position. Before dawn came up, I went to the pond with the ice cooler and filled it with as much water as it would hold, and carried it to the raft, covering it carefully with the styrofoam top. It wasn't the most convenient or watertight method of transporting water, but it held a great deal, probably two gallons of liquid.

I strapped on the life preserver, and pulled the raft down to the shore slowly, careful not to spill the water in the container or to damage the bottom of the raft. I floated it, then got in and grabbed a paddle and sat in the front, paddling against the small waves that broke under me. Then I moved the water container to the front of the raft and sat on the back edge, and with the raft slightly tilted, I paddled in this manner. This was easier, since it was both more comfortable sitting rather than kneeling in front, and the raft seemed to move more quickly in the water.

I headed for the island beyond the horizon, wearing my helmet liner, a ragged shirt, and shorts. I paddled in a definite rhythm, four strokes with my right hand on the top of the paddle, and four strokes using my left hand, turning the paddle from the left side of my body to my right as I changed hands. After fighting the tide near the beach, I found the paddling easier in deeper water, and the raft slowly but steadily made its way northward.

By the time the sun broke in the east, my island was far behind me, and I paused, put the glasses on, and looked it over. It was very small from out here, insignificant, with its beach, its hill, and the random few coconut trees towering above the hill. I turned my back to the island and kept paddling. By the time the sun was climbing in the sky, I had eaten some fish and drunk some water, and my shoulders and arms were feeling slightly sore. I had to stop more and more, rubbing my arms and shoulders. Even my hands hurt, and I saw that I was getting a blister on the thick part of my right palm, near the thumb. There was no way I could cover the blister, as I had no spare cloths with me and didn't want to take off my shirt under this sun, so I clenched my teeth and paddled as best I could.

Midday came. I was moving more slowly through the water now, and my rhythm would break off in fatigue. I took a long rest a few times, then bent to my work, feeling my whole body ache. My legs weren't in a good position and my buttocks, resting on the rubber rim of the raft, were uncomfortable. I felt my legs cramping, and a couple of times I stretched them as the muscles tightened in spasms of pain. This trip was definitely a mistake, I told myself, but I kept the raft moving. The island behind me was still visible, but it was just a slice of land on a vast and dangerous sea, and I realized, in scanning the horizon to the south, just how isolated I had been all these months. I turned and looked to the north again, toward a destination I couldn't yet see. I figured when the island was no longer visible behind me I'd have made fifteen miles, about half the trip there, but the island behind me refused to go under the horizon. It was getting late. Afternoon crept in, and the sun was sinking slowly, and night was coming on with a breeze blowing directly at me. I had forgotten about the north wind, which now made my work three times as hard. It was all I could do just to keep some headway going against the wind.

I told myself, this is crazy, turn around and use the wind yourself, and let it blow you back to your island and to safety. But for some unknown reason, I persevered, even into the night. The sun had long set and I was still at my paddle, still pushing it through the water, which was a little choppy at times, stirred up by the wind out of the north and west. The raft was drifting slightly west as well, and I shifted my position and changed the rhythm to four strokes on the left and eight on the right to compensate for the drift, though in the darkness it was impossible to tell just what progress I was making.

The moon was bright, almost a full moon, giving me good illumination. Still I could see no island in front of me, and now I could no longer see my native island behind me. I was at a point of no return in the night, and I could easily be lost forever on this vast ocean, without any means of guidance except the sun and the north star. If I miscalculated my position, I'd simply miss the island I was aiming for, and turning back, might just as easily miss my own island. A cold tinge of fear possessed me, and I knew it was some kind of inner madness that had drawn me to this insane adventure, to look for an island that was no more than a rock in the middle of an ocean, on a rubber raft that I had difficulty handling. I might end up adrift and lost, slowly dying under the sun. I closed my eyes and rested my arms once more. I was exhausted, and pain was shooting through my entire body. I couldn't give up, and yet I didn't know what to do. I was afraid to sleep, afraid that I'd drift away, out of all recognition of my position, for what landmarks would there be for me in this desolate and barren ocean?

Sporadically I paddled the raft, trying to hold my position, but unsure of whether I was drifting dangerously away from my sea route. I tried to keep awake, but every now and then I'd fall into a half-sleep, then snap awake, looking about me at the sea and then putting on the glasses, looking for the island. Nothing could be seen. Panic was overtaking me. I had done a foolish and awful thing, and I was now going to be doomed. How would I ever find my way back? Where was I at this moment? Thirty miles . . . insanity. I paddled some more, desperately waiting for the sun to come up, to see the light of day, to somehow get my bearings. I sat in pain and waited and moments crept by, slowly and more slowly, it seemed. The darkness stayed on top of me, no light showed. Then, faint trickles of light came over the east, but, to my dismay, the raft was facing due east. I had really strayed off course, and probably had spent half the night paddling and moving far away from my intended destination.

I quickly turned the raft around and headed due west, away from the awakening sun. I had to make up the distance lost drifting, but how much distance? And where were the islands now? I headed west, figuring that I'd spend a few hours moving in this direction to get myself between the islands. Every few minutes I looked through the binoculars but saw nothing. I now turned the raft west by northwest and kept paddling. My strength was rapidly fading. Still nothing could be seen. I thought of giving up and letting fate drift the raft wherever it would. I had run out of energy and hope. I kept the paddle in the water as a rudder, letting the currents move the boat west by northwest. The sun was coming up high in the sky, and all around me, the water, a brilliant blue, reflected its rays like sapphires.

31

I fought to stay awake. The sun charged down, bouncing off the sea as if it were a mirror, and my eyes burned and teared. I couldn't keep them open. How nice it would be, I thought, just to close them and get some rest, refresh my body and mind. I was bone weary from the effort of paddling and wearier still from lack of sleep. My lids drooped, and finally I could fight it no more. I crawled to the floor of the raft and rested my body, keeping the helmet liner over my face for protection from the sun. I shut my eyes, then opened them, for one last effort at wakefulness. But I was no match for my fatigue. My eyes closed, my eyelids trembled as I tried to stay awake, but sleep bound me in its chains.

I dreamed of many things. Scenes passed through my unconscious mind as though I were in the tunnel of a kaleidoscope. Images of my childhood, with my parents fighting, my father storming out of the house after cursing us out; my cries mingled with my mother's cries for him to stay. Stay!

Then I was in a canoe in a cool glade, misty air about me, everything smelling of dank dampness. The walls were beaded with moisture and I was being led down a long stream to a wooden and brick building, where the wood was peeling off and the bricks were red and moldy from the water. I got out of the canoe and approached the building. I didn't want to go in, yet I was curious. I went step by step, then looked down at my feet. They were barefoot and I was caught in oozing mud. I wondered where my shoes were, and why I was dressed this way, in shorts and a jacket and shirt and tie. Where were my pants? I tried to go back to the canoe, but it had disappeared. I was bewildered and suddenly frightened.

Then I was on a train station, still without trousers. I tried to hide my bare legs from the other passengers. Everyone else was dressed well, and reading papers and talking to one another. Now and then one of the passengers would stare at me and look down at my bare legs. I tried to hide them but there was nowhere to hide.

I was then walking in a long, cold corridor; people were rushing past me, but I was in slow motion. I couldn't seem to get any speed going. I knew my destination; it was a ticket window up ahead. I got to the window and asked for a train ticket, but the man behind the counter, the clerk, ignored me. He had fierce brown eyes and a handlebar mustache. He let others get in front of me, and stamped their tickets. When I protested, he asked for my social security card. I told him I didn't have one, but I knew the number. That was not sufficient, he said. I whined that all I wanted was a ticket. Why did I need a card? He told me I was causing trouble and he'd call a policeman. I protested, and then a sheriff came by and grabbed me by the neck and pulled me away from the window. He told me I was a troublemaker, and he dragged me to the wall. I kicked out at him, but couldn't reach his body. I had turned into a small boy, and the sheriff looked like my father. Then he had the same face as the railway clerk. I tried to get free but he told me to take down my pants, that I was going to be whipped for being bad. I tried to get away, but to no avail. I tried, as a last resort, to spit into his face, but the spittle came back to me. I struggled and struggled. . . .

I opened my eyes. The sun was still bright but was making its westward retreat. West to its doom and to night coming on, and I was alone in the boat in the middle of water, seeing nothing but water. I sat up and wiped my eyes, which were running as if I had been crying. I looked around me. Nothing but water. It was so peaceful and yet fear enveloped my heart. I was lost, irrevocably lost in a vast ocean, with no bearings at all and no way of knowing exactly where I was. I could paddle in any direction and it wouldn't matter, because where was I headed? There might be land a few miles away, or no land ahead of me for hundreds and maybe thousands of miles. Where was I? A cold chill pervaded my soul, and I felt more helpless than I had ever felt. Alone this way, alone on the unfriendly sea. I filled an empty beer can with water and drank some and poured the rest back into the container. How long would my water hold out, or my food? It was not only water and food . . . how long could I hold out this way, in despair, lost, afraid, like a child . . . ?

"Sometimes I feel like a motherless child,
A long, long way from home . . ."

I sang aloud, and then thought of other songs to sing. I could only think of old songs, of songs a sweetheart of mine had sung to me a long time ago, a gentle girl whom I had treated with scorn, knowing she cared for me more than I cared for her. The story of love . . . who is stronger? Who will make the other suffer more?

I resumed my seated position on the edge of the raft and got out the paddle. My right palm was one raw blister, oozing fluid, but pain wouldn't matter right now. What would matter would be to find land, to find the comfort of *terra firma*. Land. There must be land somewhere. My vessel had been facing northeast when I awoke; obviously whatever tide ruled this part of the sea was moving in that direction. I paddled west and slightly north, trying to find some sign of land. The wind was starting to blow up against me now from the west, and it was an effort to fight the tide. I sang,

> "I went down to Louisville, some pleasure there to find
> A damsel there from Lexington was pleasing to my mind
> Her ruby lips, her rosy cheeks, like arrows pierced my
>   breast
> And she bore the name of Flora, the lily of the west."

I thought of other songs, songs from my past, hymns I had sung in church, songs from childhood . . .

> "Mr. Froggy went a-courting and he did go . . ."

Oh, for my childhood again, oh to be a boy again, to start fresh all over again, not to make the same mistakes, not to undergo the same agonies and humiliations, not to spend my life running and fleeing from some unknown terror. . . . If I could begin a new novel, if I cared to write again, I'd have the first line read:

"I find myself in the midst of a desperate struggle, but what that struggle is, I have yet to determine."

Yes, the story of my life summed up. Why was I thinking this way now? Why wasn't I self-confident, the way I had been on the island? Why didn't I think positively? I will live. I will survive. I will endure.

Somehow.

Somehow, yes. Somehow. But how, in this mysterious sea, which hid its jewels from me, its land and islands, its places of comfort? I was in peril on the sea, as the old navy hymn went. In peril on the sea. I was a motherless child without comfort. I was in the midst of a desperate struggle I couldn't solve.

I closed my eyes and shook my head as if to ward off these bad feelings, but they covered me the way the sky covered the earth, wholly, unrelenting, unblinking. I shook my head, trying to clear it. Stop thinking like this, think of better things, do something.

I put down the paddle and brought the binoculars to my eyes. I scanned the ocean in all directions. Nothing but water. How frightening that water looked. Endless water. Nothing but salt water. I was scared to death of the water. It was going to be my tomb. One day, maybe within a week, I'd run out of fresh water, then I'd slowly sink into a stupor, then the sun would get to me, and I'd drift into unconsciousness, then my spirit would depart from me, and for one last instant I'd know the true feeling of mortality. Death, stay away from me. Let me live. Let me live. God, let me live. Let me. Let me.

I paddled against the wind and against the tide, and saw that I was going nowhere. Yes, the race is not to the swift, nor the battle to the strong, no . . . time and chance happeneth to them all. To all men. To me.

Night came again, turning the sky black and blazing with stars, sending a chill wind to cool and then to batter my body. I huddled in the corner of the raft, my knees to my chest, and tried to stay warm, to sleep. The raft moved slowly where it would, with a will of its own. I had stopped caring. I closed my eyes. There was nothing to do but sleep away the night, to let it pass over me, carrying me along in time's bosom.

I couldn't sleep comfortably. I got up time and time again, then finally the dawn came, the sun's rays licked the sea with its fire, and I sat up and looked around. Nothing but sea. The raft was facing north. I turned it till it faced east and began to paddle. Then I paddled south. Why not? Nothing made sense anymore, but what was sense anyway, what was skill and knowledge and intellect here in the middle of the ocean? I was looking into the mirror of the world, the vast ocean of this planet, and I was helpless. The rays were bouncing off the water and into my eyes. Warm tears ran down my cheeks.

I paddled south by east. Perhaps I had, in this long two-day journey, gone completely past the island. I wasn't sure now about distance and horizons. Was it really fifteen miles as seen from this raft? That seemed impossible. The whole thing was crazy, and all my calculations made from ignorance were useless, completely undependable. All I had learned in the cities was to hate them, and to hate life. I was in a different existence. The past was unimportant now.

So I continued to paddle south. Perhaps I'd pass the rock island, and run into my own. Perhaps not. Well, there had been nothing in the north, and there might be nothing in the south, but I might as well find out. I'd see what was ahead. It couldn't be worse than empty miles of green sea in the north. Anything was better than that. Anything was better. I shook my head to clear my thoughts again. I had to find something, some landmark in this ocean, some way out of my dilemma. But I saw nothing at all except water and sky and the setting sun. I knew now I was doomed. Well, I had been doomed for a long time. Now the moment of truth was approaching, the moment all men must find in themselves, as Death comes calling, like the Froggy.

Mr. Death came a-calling and he did go . . .

And then it was night again. Night, bringer of calm and cool breezes, harbinger of sleep and of death, yes, of death also. I was now Death's friend. We would plan my demise together. It would be slow and a little agonizing, but in the end, restful. My spirit would be at rest, finally. My bad memories would be at an end. My miserable flesh would melt into this universal salve of salt water. Yes, Death seemed very near, and he wasn't that dangerous or frightening at all. He could be one's friend; one's ally. He could take me by the hand and lead me to a calm, restful place.

Was I dreaming or awake? I didn't know anymore. I saw

the smiling face of a girl I once knew. I knew her when I had been a child. "Tommy," she called to me. "Tommy, I like you so much, Tommy. You're so much fun." And above me loomed my father and mother. They were frowning. Don't frown, I cried, don't frown. I'm a good boy, I'm having fun.

But in my heart I knew I was bad and would always be bad and there was nothing I could do, for no matter how I twisted I was tied to life's tight strings, no matter how I ran, I was tethered to life's prison walls. I was bad and would never be good and nothing good would ever happen to me. I'd be an outsider, an onlooker, excluded from life's bountiful feast of life and love.

32

Sleep, dreams. Waking to the eternal tide of the ocean and the night and its mysteries. Waking adrift on a raft, seeing only water, treacherous, silent water. Where else could a man be so alone, except in his own mind? I sat in the raft and looked about me, too weary to paddle, too discouraged to plot a course. Which course? Nothing but water wherever I looked. The raft was a dot on God's great ocean and I, a smaller dot. Meaningless and expendable. I sank to the rubber bottom and closed my eyes again.

Dawn came with the sun streaming over the water like a slithering snake. I got out the glasses and looked in all directions. Nothing. Once again I was facing the east, and so I turned the raft around and headed south by west, hoping to find something. I had already given up on land; maybe I'd find a stray boat fishing or cruising. Maybe a plane would spot me and radio my position. Maybe some form of life would help me, some human eye would take note of my lonely plight and take me back to civilization.

I paddled with firm strokes. My palms were now raw from the wood paddles, but pain was secondary. What was important, it seemed, was to keep moving, to give some semblance of hope to my own spirit. I pushed the paddle into the water, and with sweeping strokes made the raft move. We were on a stream within streams in the ocean, and I felt the current moving us silently along with my own effort. The raft glideth at his own free will, and all that sleeping heart is beating still. . . . I was paraphrasing Wordsworth, but not thinking of books or poetry or words at all, just one goal, land, and one word, survival.

The wind was at my back, and Death was also at my back, and it was a question of which would get to me first. I bent my body, getting the paddle in deeply, straining my muscles. I was on my own galley, a Jean Valjean of the ocean, a prisoner of this small raft. I pushed the raft forward, faster than I had ever done before, and all through the day, my efforts were rewarded with distance. How far I had gone I didn't know, but I was moving fast and the sun, getting ready to flee westward, was watching me. The ocean and the sun, both eyes of God, both unblinking. The sun slept but the ocean, it never slept. It kept watch continually, its grip never let up, and I was in its thrall.

And then, as night was about to descend, I saw them. Birds. Large, gull-like birds. Were they the fabled albatross? I didn't know about birds at all, but I saw them flying overhead, circling a little and then flying on, in the same direction I was going. I got out my glasses and watched their flight, directly south. I pressed on further, feeling the muscles of my shoulders bunching up with each stroke. I felt renewed vigor. Birds, harbingers of land . . . birds.

"Go, raft," I cried in the night, which was blanketing my vision. "Go."

It was a night lit by a large silver moon and a night in which fleecy white clouds flitted across the sky. I dug in and paddled with all my might. And then, suddenly, as if rising

from the bowels of the ocean itself, there it was. It was formidable. A large cliff loomed ahead of me. It came on so
suddenly, I thought it had risen the way Christ had risen,
sudden, unexpectedly, and yet preordained. I backpaddled for a moment, looking up at the cliff. I stopped and
put my glasses on once more. The cliff was but a part of a
small, very small island. To its right was a sandy beach.
Land. Land. I moved the raft in that direction and steered
my course. The paddle went in right to its top as I heaved
the raft forward. In a short while, we were drifting, the raft
and I, with the oncoming waves breaking against the shore.
I took out my spear and pushed it straight down, trying to
find a bottom. Finally, a short way from shore, I could feel
the firm sandy floor of the ocean. I jumped out of the raft
and pulled it along, standing waist deep in the water. I
pulled it all the way to the beach, and then with one final
effort, dragged it out of reach of the highest waves.

Then I sat down, panting. Sat on firm land. What a glorious feeling, what a feeling of stability, of reassurance. On
land again. I stood up and stomped around on the sand,
feeling it squish between my toes, feeling its wetness and
coolness and, above all, its firmness. Land. I got on my
knees and thanked God for this deliverance. I hadn't de-
served it, really. I had given up, I told God, I had already
made my peace with Death instead of with Life. From now
on, I would be, I swore, at peace with Life. Life would be
my guide, not Death. I would revere all Life.

I wanted to climb up the hill behind me and explore the
entire island, to sing and raise my voice in joyful thanks, but
I was so exhausted from the paddling that I could barely
stand. My shoulders had an inner weariness I had never experienced before. They ached right to the marrow of the
bones. My hands were raw and the palms were covered
with clotted blood and open blisters and wounds, from
which a combination of blood and fluid emanated. But this
was all minor. I was safe for the time being. Safe on land. I

went back to the raft but didn't climb in. Instead, I lay next to it, curled up on the sand, on land itself, and went to sleep.

The next morning, I was up exactly with dawn, with the sun breaking over the distant horizon. The sky looked like a rich brocade of colors, like God's own tapestry with its yellows and blues and reds, and slowly, as the sun rose, all colors faded into one rich blue. A magnificent blue. I went spear fishing, and after a while caught a nice sized fish, and found broken pieces of wood and built a fire and cooked my first hot meal in days. I ate it all, grinding the bones in my fingers, eating every morsel of the fish except the head and tail. Then I drank some of my water, which had been seriously depleted, so that only a little was swilling at the bottom of the large ice cooler. The two canteens were still full, however. I decided to explore the island and look for food and water here, but looking behind me, I could only see a cliff rising to a height of about one hundred feet or more, and the side of the cliff looked mottled and broken, as if it had been formed from some dark and unusual substance. I guessed it was lava, and that the entire island had risen from the sea eons ago during a volcanic explosion. There were a couple of palm trees on the island, near the water, bent like California cypresses by the eternal wind, so that they hung over the water. They were laden with coconuts, and I climbed them and brought down twelve of those beauties. I stored them in the raft, and then decided to go around the island by water, since I was blocked from any other method of transportation by the huge cliffs. I had found no fresh water and wondered if I should dig for some, but first, I thought, I'd explore the island. Who knows that wonders lay on the other side?

I pulled the raft down to the water, floated it, and got in, paddling carefully, staying about fifty feet from the cliffs, trying to spot rocks in the water. The last thing I needed was to cut the bottom of the raft. I moved it even further out from the land, and paddled slowly around the island, but the other side was just rocky cliff, nothing more. I circled the island and came back to my beach. Nothing but this small run of sand, about one hundred feet in length, with its palm trees. Nothing else growing, nothing else to be seen. I beached the raft again, and carrying only my binoculars and a knife, I went to the cliff, trying to find a way to climb its heights. Was I on the island that I had spotted from my own, or had I drifted far away from my original destination and found one of the many unnamed and anonymous islands that must dot this unending ocean? I would know if I got to the top of the cliff. I tried to get a foothold in several places, but saw that the climb would be treacherous, and as always I was afraid of falling, breaking a leg, and then lying helplessly in pain. I did see one thing that had been missing on my own island, and that was birds. I saw them on the top of the cliff, a whole flock of them, cawing and strutting around. Their eggs, I guessed, were up there also. It might be worthwhile to climb for fresh eggs, but I decided not to. It would be a rough climb without any help, and I had no equipment for the climb except for some length of rope in the raft. No, I'd just have to forgo it.

I decided to get off the island with my coconuts and be thankful for the respite and the additional food. I broke open two of their husks and got to the inner shell, drinking the juice of one. Sweet good taste of coconut milk. I wiped my lips with my tongue, and then broke open the shell and cut a couple of pieces of the white meat for myself. I chewed them slowly, my eyes closed, to savor each bite. Then I pulled the raft into the water. I headed the raft due south, which I ascertained from the sun's rise that morning. I did this for two reasons. If this was indeed the island I had seen, then my own island would be in that direction, and also, I would be moving with the prevailing tides and winds.

I got the paddle out and began stroking. I paddled steadily, without stopping, until the sun was high in the sky. After a short break, during which I ate the final half of the coconut and drank the last of the water from the ice cooler, I paddled on. I was dangerously short of water now, and realized that I should have tried to dig for fresh water on the island. I was sorry I hadn't brought my trenching tool with me. I hadn't thought of all eventualities, after all.

Afternoon came on, the sky lit up in glorious colors to the west, streaked by clouds of magnificent reds and yellows. I paused to watch the sight, thinking again of how alone I was, and how I never could seem to share this feeling of awe and majesty with anyone else. Then I bent to my work. Refreshed by my good sleep on the island, I stroked the raft forward through the night. The wind was at my back and it raced along, skimming the surface of the water. We were driven, both the raft and myself, by wind and spirit. The night passed and day came, and early in the morning, there it was. An island. My island. I was sure of it. I picked up the binoculars and scanned the coast, trying to remember what my island had looked like the last time I saw it. Yes, there was the north beach and there were the woods and there was the slope. Land. My land. Home!

It was further away than I had imagined. I paddled and paddled and still it seemed to come no closer. But I was making up distance. Imperceptibly it was growing in my vision. It was becoming a reality. My land. My island. Tears rolled down my cheeks. My own island. I had been truly delivered by the good hand of God himself, given back my life when I had despaired. "Oh God, thank you, thank you, I'll do anything you want, God, thank you," I cried to the open skies.

How can I describe the moment of my landing? I staggered up the sands and fell to the ground, the raft beached behind me. Back home. It was true. This was my home, and I had been foolish to leave its protective comfort. I was home again. I had renewed strength. I walked around the

beach, kicking sand, basking in the comfort of my home-
land. My own island. My own. I took my few things out of
the raft and brought them up the hill to my shelter, which
was merely a raised hump of sand and dirt on three sides.
Then I went back and with a final effort carried the raft on
my back up the hill. By the time I had put it over the walls
as a roof, I was bathed in sweat and my heart was pounding, but what matter? What did anything matter now? Life
had been taken and had been given back, and I was thankful in my heart for this, and swore that from now on I'd
remember this salvation and would carry out the vows to
God I had made in my dark moments of despair.

33

On the tenth of the month, my coconut supply was gone, and I knew I had to somehow grind out the last two weeks of my stay before being rescued. I decided to preserve as much weight as I could by cutting down my exercise to a minimum. This was easy to do physically, but difficult to accomplish psychologically, since time dragged when I did nothing but sit and rest. Time weighed on me, as day by day clicked away. Finally, there was but one week to go. According to my tree calendar, this was the sixteenth of August. One more week. I walked for a short distance among the trees, and came across a few spent cartridges. I picked them up and thought of that bloodbath, shaking my head at the madness of men.

I no longer carried the rifle around with me. What was the point? What was there to be afraid of? It was possible that I could be invaded again, but at best the possibility was rather remote. If they hadn't done it by now, they would never do it. In any event, it was much easier to walk

unarmed, without the constant obstruction of a rifle hanging
on my back by a sling. I still carried the large knife, more
for utility purposes than for use as a weapon.

As the days moved closer to my exit date, August 23, I
thought of what I'd do once I got back to the United States.
If Hildendorf and my agent had lived up to the agreement,
they'd have taken care of my alimony payments for the two
years I was away, and in addition, I'd have another $25,000
due to me. If I decided to write the book, I could raise that
to $100,000, but right now I had no interest in writing any-
thing, and didn't even have a page of writing to show Hildendorf. I could tell him about the storms destroying everything; already I was returning to my prior weak ways,
preparing excuses for work not done. No, I'd tell him the
truth. And the truth was, I was finished with writing. Fare-
well to the pen and the page and the typewriter. I was no
longer going to be a slave to the written word. I'd get my
$25,000 and take off.

Where would I go? Not back to LA, that was for sure.
The thought of living in a city like that again . . . it made
my skin crawl. I'd need a place with plenty of room, plenty
of open space, where I could feel at least a dollop of freedom. Where? There were many places in America still open.
As long as I didn't need an agent and didn't need the mail
and producers and directors and contracts, I could live anywhere. Anywhere. Maybe up in Oregon in a small town,
perhaps a college town. Eugene. I'd look up that woman,
Sarah, there. Anyway, there was time to think of all that.
There was still time, because I'd have to make final arrangements with Hildendorf and the agent before getting my
money. With $25,000 I could possibly buy a small piece of
land. Possibly. I still had the payments to make for support
of my ex-wife. Thinking of her gave me a headache. I decided to think of better things.

I began thinking of the pleasures of being among people
again. Women. I'd find a good woman this time . . . I'd find

a woman who could be my companion and friend and lover, one I could share my life with, or at least, for a while, the joys of living. That would be sweet, along with the good things one could find in the civilized world. They were there, under the blanket of crap that made for modern life. When I thought of my days in Hollywood, choked and smogged out by the fetid air, eating doughnuts and drinking putrid coffee and smoking out my lungs, when I thought of all that, I wondered how I could have lived that kind of life. It wasn't life, it was anti-life. Life was something else. I wasn't quite sure what a good life was, but here, on this island, I had been given hints, indications, of what it meant. Responsibility for one's own self, the struggle for survival, the basic needs of a human being. What was missing was intercourse with others, and all that that entailed; friendship and love, caring and desires, and mutual fulfillment. God, I was sounding like a preacher in some sort of religious temple, with my altar the sand, and my pulpit the sky and water.

By the twentieth of the month, I was feeling rather weak, and it became more difficult to fish, since I was getting dizzy in the sun. I did the best I could, and dried most of my catch, nibbling at the food during the day, drinking it down with fresh water. I boiled up some seaweed, but for some reason my stomach was rejecting it, and I was now limited in my diet to fish. I didn't know how long I could go on like this, feeling dizzy and weak most of the time, and still losing weight, but my solace was in time. Three more days to go. Just seventy-two more hours. I tried to count the minutes, but I was feeling too groggy from the loss of weight to do calculations. My kidney area was again becoming uncomfortable. I spent a lot of time pressing my hand against the left lower side of my back, pushing in the flesh. I drank more and more water, saturating myself with water. I slept most of the day now, and most of the night as well, just waiting.

For the last days of my stay I spent practically all my time in the shelter, waiting out the time, eating dried fish and consuming gallons of water. I had run the full course of my two years here, and now had nothing left. I was staggering to the finish, happy to have it over, happy to have completed this part of my journey through life, for it was time to move on. I had had enough of this life. I was weak and tired now, and wanted out. I waited for the sounds of a helicopter . . . I sat in my shelter and waited.

When August 23 arrived, I was set for my departure. I kept awake, afraid to miss the sound of an approaching plane or helicopter. My thoughts were now exclusively concerned with getting away, or heading to a place where I'd have fresh fruit and some meat and refresh myself and put on clean clothes and once more be a part of the civilized human race. Sometime this day I'd be rescued from here. Sometime this evening I'd be eating fruits and meat. Sometime soon.

The day dragged on. Then the sun went down, and night came and nothing. No word. Nothing. I lay in my shelter, feeling depressed and disheartened. What had happened? I must have miscalculated the days during the feverish period of my illness. That was it. I must have miscalculated. But I couldn't be that far off. One day, two days, maybe three days. Within three days I'd be out of here. Within three days I'd be on my way back. I'd get proper nourishment and food and all the amenities of civilized life. How I hungered for all this now. I wanted to be rid of this island. I had served my time and I wanted to get away. I waited moment by moment in the shadow of my shelter, waiting for the arrival of the plane or helicopter or boat. A few times, dozing off, I awakened to what I thought was a distant motor, and rushed out, only to find nothing. Nothing but empty sky and empty sea.

Three days passed. Instead of approaching engines, I recognized the telltale signs of an approaching storm. The air was full of moisture. The winds were coming off the north and west, hot and humid. My shelter was inadequate for any storm, but I didn't have energy left to do much about reinforcing it. I went fishing and caught but one fish and returned to the shelter, panting. How quickly all my energy had drained away. I might have remained strong if I didn't know that I was to be taken off the island, but once my departure day passed, it was as if that day had pulled everything out of me. Anticipation had robbed me of my strength, and the storm would soon rob me of more, my very life possibly. How could I guard against that storm? I had gone through two before this, but what would I do now? Once it began, winds would probably, in my weakened condition, drive me into the sea. Where was Hildendorf and my agent? Where were they? Had they forgotten? Had they themselves been lost at sea after putting me here? Was I forgotten and forever lost, doomed to spend whatever remained of my life on this island?

I couldn't spend my time brooding. I had to do something about the storm. I had no strength left to build a stronger fortress, and the sand and loose earth I had packed would tumble down after the first blow. I got out my trenching tool and decided, if I couldn't build up, I would dig down. I would possibly dig my own grave, but if I dug a large enough hole, I might stay out of the direct path of the storm.

With the last of my strength, I began to dig. I dug and dug more. I dug out earth and sand and threw it over my shoulder, till all around me the sand was piled with loose dirt. I dug a hole about three feet wide and about four feet deep, then I got in and dug out the bottom, widening the hole as I went along. Meanwhile the wind was picking up, and whitecaps were showing on the ocean. It was going to be a big storm all right; all the ominous signs were there. I dug and sweated out the water I was drinking so freely. I had used up my dried fish and would wait out the storm, hungry and without food, but what was important now was to dig, and have a sufficient hole for myself.

When the rains started to fall on the evening of the twenty-ninth of August, the hole was about six feet deep and about four feet wide. I got in with my canteens of water, my binoculars, and my knife. All else was left to the mercy of the wind. I packed sand over my ammunition belt and my rifle, hoping that somehow they'd hold up throughout the storm and wouldn't be blown away. I took the raft and covered the hole with it, but realized I'd get no air with the raft in this position, so I cut holes into its bottom, deflating it. There went my one chance to leave the island, but I couldn't think in long-term plans now, but in survival for the moment. The winds picked up, and the rains poured down with torrential force. I stayed in the hole, clutching at the raft, keeping it in place as long as I could. If it blew away, there would go my one roof, my one cover.

My head was really muddled. How could I expect the · thin rubber that remained of the raft to stay in place against a wind that might exceed a hundred miles an hour? It would be impossible. This was quickly borne out, for a few hours after the winds hit, I lost my cover as the raft flew away. The rains came pelting down on my unsheltered head and body, but huddled in the hole, I felt safer than in the open as before, for no matter what happened, I couldn't be blown away.

Lightning struck nearby, and the winds howled through a night of terror for me. I huddled in the hole, unable to find a comfortable position. Sand and dirt blew all over me, choking me, covering my face and hair and getting into my eyes. I huddled and shivered with the cold and wetness of the storm, and it lasted all that night and through most of the next day, then it eased off. A misty rain fell through the next afternoon and stopped sometime that night. The following morning I got out of my hole, my body wet and caked with dirt. I was dizzy and feverish. I took off my few things and went to the ocean, practically crawling there on my hands and knees.

I washed in the sea, and then managed to stagger up the beach. I turned my face to the sun, waiting for its heat to warm me, to dry me. I lay in a torpor. My body was burning. I didn't know where my canteens were. I was without water and without food. I lay in the sun all day, and all night shivered and coughed and sneezed, with chills racking my body. I managed to get to the pond by crawling along the sand, and drank from cupped hands, then lay near the pond, unable to move. The sun baked down on me. I lay shivering and chilled, and burning with fever. It was no use, I thought. I couldn't fight this. I needed food. I needed energy and strength. Above all, I needed the will to live, and I seemed to have lost it when the time for my rescue had passed without a sign from the two people who alone knew I was on this desolate island.

34

Slowly, painstakingly, I made my way down to the forest. I knew that I couldn't survive in this condition, racked with fever and chills. I needed some kind of warmth, some kind of shelter. I gathered whatever wood I could find from loose branches and broken vines, and built a fire, warming myself as best I could. I fed the fire all night, though at times I fell asleep and awoke to see only embers. The sun would save me during the day and the fire at night.

The next morning I felt a little better, as the sun burned heat into me, mingling with my fever, but at the same time maintaining my life. Life. I had nothing to eat. I drank water sparingly. What I needed was rest and warmth. The day passed in fits of wakefulness and wild dreams, fed by the fever. I stayed near the forest so that I could spend time in the shade as well. In this way, the day passed, night came, and I built another fire, then went into the water and gathered seaweed. I had lost the helmet in the storm, and ate the seaweed raw. This time it stayed in my empty stomach.

There must be some nutrition in seaweed; there must be nutrition in everything one could put in one's stomach.

The third day passed and the night came again. By this time I had only a vague idea of the date, though carefully figuring the day of the storm and the interval since, I determined that it was September 3, give or take a day or two. Still no word from the men who were to rescue me. By this time, feeling a little stronger, I began to wonder if I ever would be taken off this island. What had gone wrong?

There were many possibilities to consider. Brundage and Hildendorf might have crashed in the helicopter that had brought me here in the first place. In that event, no one would know I was on this island, and my mother's attempt to contact my agent would become meaningless. If that were the case, then I was doomed to spin out my time here unless someone else wandered by accidentally. So far, two groups of people had come in the two years; perhaps, in another year, someone else would stumble on the island. Perhaps. If not, I'd live the true Robinson Crusoe story; without any animals or food supply, however. I'd live the starving story, slowly wasting away, slowly losing my strength and hope, till one day I'd close my eyes forever.

The other possibility was that somehow, both men were dead, and had neglected to inform anyone of my whereabouts. That was a definite possibility. Death could have come in many ways. Perhaps together in a car from the airport, perhaps separately by accident or illness. Both men had been in bad shape, and my fate had been tied up with theirs. They had agreed to let others know about this island, but what were their words worth, when, from the moment I arrived, the agreement had already been broken?

The third possibility was that they had abandoned me purposely, for whatever reason. There could be dozens of reasons. Maybe I was their enemy, or someone else's enemy, and they had been the instruments to get rid of me in this insane way. Again, I thought of my ex-wife. A perfect way to get me out of her life forever. But I had already, I realized, thought about this idea and dismissed it. No, this was too elaborate a plan, just to lose me.

Then, again, who knew Hildendorf's and Brundage's motives? If I could see them now, see what they were doing, have some face-to-face contact, even voice contact, I would know where I stood. If only I could see Hildendorf, see his paunchy face, or could remember all the events leading up to my trip here . . . if I could do this, I'd know what was happening. But it was all a blur, washed over by time, erased by two years in the sun here. All I could remember was Hildendorf eating in the French restaurant, drinking wine, and wiping his mouth with a starched napkin. No matter what I focused on, that image returned to me.

So, I lay by the fire, trying to keep life in my body for a while longer. If I could get back some strength, I could go fishing again and eat solid food and feel better. But right now I was in a cycle of death; fatigued and weary, sick and unable to help myself, sustained only by seaweed and water. That couldn't last long. I got up the next morning and made an effort to fish, but after taking a few steps, I was struck with dizziness. Everything spun around and I was happy to be able to get back to my original resting place in the shade and just lie down and rest my head on my arms.

Still another day passed. I made an attempt again to fish, this time dragging myself down to the water without even a spear. I was going to use my bare hands, which was useless, but I caught a couple of crawfish and took back some seaweed and ate it all together, sucking out the shells. It seemed to put a little energy into my body and I sat up and fed the fire, keeping as warm as I could. As long as I had the fire, I wouldn't perish immediately. I slept during the day and stayed up all night long. How the nights dragged.

And the days were no better. I had nothing right now to look forward to but sheer survival. Nothing beyond that. Nothing at all.

Life at this level meant little. What was it all about? Just to wake and find food and to huddle by a fire and be unable to do anything else? Is that all there was to life? That was all there was to my life right then. And I was sick of it. The best that could happen was that the fever would disappear, and I'd be healthy again and fish and slowly erode away. That was the best I could hope for. I'd drag out my life by weeks instead of days. Alone, there wasn't much hope. My one hope was that someone would stumble on the island and take me off. But each day, only the bare ocean presented itself, an ocean devoid of surface life. No boats, no sails, no planes, no people. Nothing.

Another day passed. I held on, ate seaweed, found some more shellfish. Another day. Another day. I had given up keeping a calendar. There was no point in thinking of months or years. Now it was day by day. And still the fever wouldn't break. My head was always burning and my body, weak, as though my legs were made of soft sand. Perhaps I was blending and melting into the island itself. Perhaps I'd wake up one day and find that I was part earth.

Another storm came that week, a mild one, just wind and a hard rain, and within a day all was sunny and bright again, but for one day I was without fire and without warmth, and once more was soaked to the skin, huddled in the forest. The next morning I shivered on the wet sand, and thought, if I stopped eating, stopped making the effort, I'd no longer prolong this charade I was calling my existence. I'd just drink water until I reached a point where I'd go into a long dark sleep, and from that sleep descend the few steps into death's trapdoor, and shut it over me. I lay on the sand shivering, chills running through me.

I fell into a deep sleep. When I awoke, the sun was shining. The next time I awoke it was night. I drank some water but ate nothing. It was day again. Then nighttime. I was now unable to move. My dreams were of long ago. I dreamed of my childhood, of my mother, of my infancy, of my mother's breast, of me at her breast, of being cuddled, comforted. Comforted by flesh of my mother, of woman, of mother earth. Comforted and kept warm and kept alive. I cried in my dreams, cried for my mother.

"Mama, Mama."

I opened my eyes. Dawn was breaking, the sun was filtering through the woods, leaving trails of light over the overgrown brush.

I closed my eyes again. I wanted only to dream of Mama and not face my life. Not face the chills and the anguish and fever. Just Mama. Just to be in her arms, press my face against her breast. Tears streamed down my face as I held her onto my flesh in the dream. I would go away with her, just the two of us, far away to find peace and happiness.

And then, from the darkest depths of my soul, I realized that my mother was still alive, and that if I allowed myself to die, she would never see me again, or even know what had happened to me. I would have vanished from the face of the earth, forever buried on this pile of malevolent soil.

I struggled to open my eyes, to come back to consciousness. I felt as though I had been drowning in a deep sea, and far above me was the sunny surface of life. It was such an effort to get to that surface, to breathe air again, to fill my lungs with life.

When I opened my eyes, the sun was shining brightly on my body. I touched my forehead. It was cool. Miraculously, the fever had broken.

35

That day I dragged myself down to the water and waded out to my waist, trying to land a fish. Holding the spear above my head, I peered into the clear water, looking for my next meal. I fished for several hours and finally caught a fat silvery beauty, which I cooked slowly in a bed of leaves. Then I ate the entire fish, except for the head and tail, feeling it instantly nourish me and give me strength.

I needed strength. Although I was no longer burning with fever, the quiet effort of fishing alone had knocked me out. I slept all that afternoon and night, waking to an early morning sun that burned down fiercely. The sky was turquoise, and there wasn't a cloud in sight.

The dream I had had of my mother still haunted me. If I were to die here, she would never know my fate, and unless I got off this island, I would never know if she were dead or alive, if she was sick, if she needed my help. I was restless in this prison, restless to be free of its chains, and yet there

was no way I could get out of here. It was enough of a
struggle to survive, to simply stay alive.

I waded into the water again that morning and caught
two more fish. I cooked one immediately and gutted the
other, keeping it fresh in a blanket of green leaves. I ate this
fish slowly, grinding its bones between my teeth. After I
finished the meal, I got up and toured the island.

I gathered up all my possessions. If I were to survive, I
would have to make use of all that was left to me, and what
was left was not much. I still had the rifle, bayonet, and one
clip of bullets. The remaining clips and ammunition had
disappeared, along with most everything else, after the last
storm. I no longer had my field glasses or helmet, but I still
had one Cricket lighter that worked.

As long as I could fish and eat seaweed, I could go on for
a while. Just how long I didn't know, since I lacked fresh
fruit for vitamin C, and probably more importantly, any
source of vitamin B. But there was nothing I could do about
these things. Since I was going to be stranded here, I would
hold out as long as possible. My duty was to life; my obliga-
tion was to living.

For one week I fished and ate seaweed, and tried once
again to eat the grasses that were on the island, but my
human enzymes couldn't break them down as they made
their painful way through my intestines.

Still, I had the fish and the seaweed. I thought of building
another shelter, then wondered if it was worth the effort. I
would find shelter among the trees during the next storm.
What seemed more important was somehow to build a raft
or some kind of flat vessel, to leave here, to get out on the
ocean and trust my fate to the currents of the sea, hoping
that somehow I'd stray into a shipping lane or that an aircraft would spot me from the air.

But how to go about building that boat? My tools were
inadequate, to say the least, and the diet, though it was
keeping me alive, was once again weakening me, not only

my body, but my spirit as well. I was losing strength on all fronts.

A few more days passed. I slept more and more, sleeping heavily through the nights, lost in dreams of childhood, of my mother and myself as a boy. Then my dreams were about my failed life as a writer. I dreamed of editors and publishers and agents, and thought, upon waking from a particularly depressing dream about rejection, that I would never place my reliance upon man again. I would depend only upon myself and my God. Fortified with this thought, my spirit revived, but still the condition of my body deteriorated.

Occasionally I thought of Hildendorf and Brundage but had given up hope of ever seeing them again. Yet I sometimes irrationally spent hours looking in all directions for their helicopter to arrive, but all I ever saw was the blank sky, its blueness stretching to all horizons, a prison without walls.

Another week went by. I notched the days on a nearby tree, but didn't know how long I had really been on this island. Two years and a month, perhaps more than a month, two months. Since my fever had abated, I had notched eighteen days.

One evening, as the sun sank beyond the horizon, as darkness descended like a blanket over the living world, I saw a boat. It was coming in from the west, lighting the water, its sails fluttering in the strong evening breeze. For an instant I stood transfixed, then my mind began to race. Was this a rescue party? Then I calmed down and became quite sober. No, Hildendorf would come by air. This was someone else's boat. And, as I watched the craft, it turned and moved toward the island.

All I could now think of was that I was going to be attacked again by members of the same group that had come to destroy me. I watched the boat with narrowed eyes, realizing that my night vision had gone bad. Everything was a blur, and I had trouble focusing.

The boat moved steadily toward the island. Then it stopped a few hundred yards out, and the sails came down. Yes, it had to be the allies of the men who had attacked me. It had to be those men. Who else would come under cover of darkness to this abandoned island? I had to be prepared for anything now. I retrieved my rifle and put in the clip, snapping the bolt forward, placing one round in the chamber. I kept the safety on, and crouching, moved behind a sand dune near the beach, where I was sheltered in darkness.

If only I had my binoculars. If only it wasn't night. Perhaps I was mistaken, perhaps these weren't my enemies after all, but merely some tourists out on a lark, staying off the island for the night in order to party. Perhaps they'd be gone by morning. That was a possibility to be considered, and if they were tourists or just boatmen, I didn't want to blow my chances at being rescued. I'd have to signal them before they left.

I gathered dried leaves and placed them near me. I could ignite them into a giant flame that they'd certainly see, in case the boat started to move off. I was now prepared for all eventualities. I stayed behind the small sand dune and waited.

How much time passed I couldn't say. But time dragged itself slowly along as I crouched and waited, my weapon at my side. A strange joy possessed me. My body trembled with anticipation. I felt that one way or another, this was the end of my stay on the island. I'd either get off or be killed, but it would soon be all over. I examined the rifle, checked out the sights, and adjusted them slightly.

The boat stayed anchored, its sails down, its motor off, a few of its lights on. What was happening on that boat? I stared at its silhouette till tears came to my eyes. I continually rubbed my eyes till they burned.

Then I saw a smaller craft bobbing on the water. It was a flat boat, a raft. I couldn't tell how many people were on that raft, or whether they were men or women. Nor could I hear their voices, just a silent vessel closing in on the island.

I wiped my sweaty hands on the sand, and put sand against the stock of the rifle to keep it dry and useful when aimed. The raft came closer and closer, and now I could make out the figures of the people, because a couple of them were wearing white shirts. The raft was coming directly at me. I waited with tearing eyes, narrowing them, tightening my cheek muscles, trying to see who was in that boat.

Now they were about a hundred yards out, and I heard a voice carry over the water. "There," the voice said, just that one word.

The night was dark, not a cloud in the sky, and no moon except for a sliver, barely giving light. All was pitch black except for the whiteness of the waves and the figures in white shirts. Then flashlights were turned on, pointing at the island. The raft crawled closer. It was about fifty yards away. It inched its way forward, and soon was about to land. I crouched behind the dune, keeping out of sight. The lights were shining in my direction and would easily pick me up. Whoever was in the boat, whoever had come to invade my island, I would know soon enough, but in the meantime I stayed hidden.

When I looked up again, the lights were still shining, and a single man was dragging the raft closer to shore, wading in the surf with awkward movements.

There were three other men on the raft, one carrying a paddle; the other two, the ones with white shirts, were sitting and holding the flashlights.

I unlocked the safety of my rifle. The man dragging the raft ashore stumbled and fell in the water, and his grip loosened on the vessel. Then he got up again and pulled at the raft, but a voice spoke out and told him to go directly onto the island. The flashlights lit his way as he kicked through the surf. He stumbled onto the island, a few feet from where I was hidden.

"What do you see?" a voice called from the raft.

"Nothing."

"Any fire? Anything?"

"No, nothing."

I had already decided on my plan of action. I'd hold this man as hostage, get the others ashore, and then strand them, paddling back to the larger boat by myself. Once on that boat, I'd commandeer it and head away from here, to freedom. A thrill surged through me. It would be so easy. First, this man.

I got up quickly.

"You!"

He turned, startled, and his eyes opened wide in fear.

"Turn around," I commanded, pointing my rifle at his heart. "Turn around," I said in a tense voice, "and get your hands up."

He did as he was told.

I got behind him.

"Now, tell the others to come ashore, or you're dead."

"Come ashore, all of you," he yelled.

The flashlights were now on both of us.

"Tell them to turn off the lights."

"Turn off the flashlights," he shouted.

Then a man yelled "What's going on? Is that you, Tom? Tom, it's me. It's Ralph. Your agent. I've come to get you."

36

Brundage splashed ashore and rushed up to me, then stopped short. I was still holding the rifle, and unconsciously turned it toward him.

"Tom, take it easy. It's me, Ralph."

For a moment, I stared blankly, then I placed the rifle down carefully on the sand. My agent hugged me. He stepped back and looked me over.

"My God, you're all skin and bones."

"Ralph, where the hell have you been?"

"I'm sorry about being late. I couldn't help it. First of all, you should know, Hildendorf is dead."

"What?"

"He died a month ago, of a coronary. Just when everything was coming together. I'll tell you the whole story on the boat. Where are your manuscripts?"

"What?"

"The journals you kept."

"There are none. Everything is gone. The storms took everything."

"And the dog?"

"Gone also. Killed."

"Come on," said Brundage, "let's get the hell off of here."

I followed him to the raft, where he introduced me to the other man, who was the captain of the sailboat docked offshore. The captain asked how I felt.

"A little weak."

"You spent two years on this island?"

"Yes. What's today's date?"

"Friday."

"I mean, the date."

"Oh. September 24."

"Tom," said Brundage, "once we get back, I'll explain everything to you, don't worry."

When we got to the boat, two other crew members looked me over as I came on board. They examined me as if I were a freak. Brundage hustled me to a cabin, told me there were clean clothes in a suitcase, and showed me where I could wash up. I got rid of the rags I was wearing and changed to a fresh pair of trousers and a shirt, but both things were much too big on me. I had to overlap the belt on the pants to prevent them from slipping off my hips.

After I dressed, Brundage took me to the galley, and brought out the cook, who said he was ready to cook anything I wanted.

I ordered a glass of orange juice and some whole wheat bread and butter. I drank down the juice greedily, dribbling it all over my long unkempt beard. Then I buttered a few slices of bread and gobbled that down, had another glass of juice and more bread. The cook and my agent watched me silently. Then I sat back.

"Do you want anything else?" Brundage asked.

"I could go on eating forever. But that's enough."

We were served coffee, but the taste was too bitter for

me, and I pushed it aside. Instead, I asked for some fresh slices of pineapple.

"Well, feel better?"

"Yes, Ralph, much better. You know, I never thought you'd come. I thought I was abandoned forever."

"Well, let me tell you what happened. First of all, Hildendorf planned it that way. He wanted you to spend an extra month on the island, so that the book you wrote would be more dramatic. It was his idea, not mine; don't look at me that way. He ran the show. There was nothing I could do. And in the meantime he ran around lining up TV appearances for you, then suddenly, poof, like that, a coronary. He died instantly. He was sixty-eight years old."

A dish of pineapple was put on the table and I put a large slice in my mouth, getting my hands sticky. I wiped them off on my shirt.

"Ralph," I said, "forget about Hildendorf for a minute. How's my mother?"

"Oh, excuse me. She's fine. I sent her the money for Christmas and her birthday, just as I said I would. And I have other news for you. Your wife remarried. I haven't sent her alimony payments in over a year."

"Who'd she marry?"

"The man she was living with. She even sent you an invitation to the wedding, which was forwarded to me."

"So I'm a free man."

"Oh yes. And Tom, you must understand, getting back to what I was saying, that between Hildendorf's death and his plans, I couldn't get here sooner. There was also a bad tropical storm, and finally, it was tough to charter a boat to this island. Everyone told me no island was around here. It was hard as hell. So you have to understand. I came here just as fast as I could."

"OK. I understand."

"I know how you must have felt, but there was nothing I

could do. Anyway, let me tell you my plans for the book. I've been speaking to the lawyers for the estate and they've agreed on a settlement that I think we should take. Fifty thousand dollars and they're not obligated to publish the book. That's fifty thousand for us. What do you think?"

"Fifty thousand?"

"Tom, I don't think we can get any more without going to court. The estate doesn't want to have anything to do with the novel now that Hildendorf's dead. And the agreement with the estate will allow us to submit it somewhere else. So we still have the property."

I nodded, finishing off the pineapple, then yawned. My head was drooping.

"I know you must be beat," said Brundage. "Do you want to sleep now?"

"Yes. That's a good idea."

He walked me to my cabin and told me we'd be sailing back to Hawaii after breakfast tomorrow. I shook hands with him and closed the door. There was a small bunkbed covered with a plaid blanket. I sat on the bed, feeling its softness. Then I peeled back the blanket, running my hands over its surface. I rubbed my fingers on the topsheet, feeling its smoothness. Civilization. How soft everything was. I took off my clothing and crawled between the sheets. I turned off the night lamp next to the bed and lay in the darkness, feeling the gentle motion of the boat rocking on the water.

I was dead tired and yet a thousand thoughts flashed through my head. There were so many questions I wanted to ask, but that could wait till tomorrow. There was all the time in the world now.

I yawned again. It was difficult to sleep on something so soft, and I turned over several times trying to get comfortable. I would have to be careful from now on, not to get too used to the softness of civilization.

So Hildendorf was dead. He never did get his dream
fulfilled . . . as if that dream was worth anything when he
had to hire someone else to live it for him. And my ex-wife
had remarried. So many things to think about. I closed my
eyes and soon was fast asleep.

37

The next morning I was up with the sun. I looked around in surprise, thinking it was all a dream, then the events of the previous night flooded into my mind. It wasn't a dream after all; it was reality. I got out of bed quickly, went to the bathroom, and washed up, looking at my face in the mirror. The beard was long, almost reaching the middle of my chest, and my hair was matted and stringy, and just as long down my back. I looked grotesque.

I examined the toilet articles, looking for a pair of scissors, but couldn't find any. After washing up, it took but a minute to get dressed, and I left the cabin and went up to the deck. No one was around.

I went to the railing and looked out at the island. How small and insignificant it seemed from here, just a sliver on the ocean, a barren, empty island. Then I heard footsteps behind me and wheeled around, my hands ready to strike.

"Hey, take it easy," said the man I faced. It was the cook.

"I'm sorry. I guess I've been living alone too long."

"So that's where you were," he said, pointing to the island with one hand. In the other he held a paper bag.

"That's the place."

"And you lived there for two years, alone?"

"Yes."

"Jesus, that must have been something." He held the bag out to me. "Want a drink?"

"No thanks."

"You don't mind if I do?"

"No, go right ahead."

He took a long swig and then wiped off his mouth with the back of one hand.

"Hey," he said, "Jim told me you really scared the shit out of him."

"Who?"

"Jim, the guy with the bald head."

"Oh." He was referring to the crewman who had been the first to land on the island.

"Yeah," the cook continued, "he thought you were crazy. He thought you were going to blast him away."

"It was a mistake."

"I guess so." He eyed me carefully. "Those things happen. You want a smoke?"

"No."

"Mind if I light up?"

"No, why should I?"

He cupped his hands and lit the cigarette, and then dragged in deeply. "Yeah," he said, "Jim was plenty nervous. He figured you used that rifle before. Figured you must of killed some people with it the way you were acting."

He narrowed his eyes, waiting for my reaction. I said nothing.

"Well," he said, "I better get below and get breakfast started."

After he left, I looked back at the island, expecting some final revelation, some illumination, but it was just an island, immobile and silent. After a few minutes, I returned to my cabin.

Later that morning, there was a rap on the door and Brundage came in. My agent was dressed all in white, wearing shorts and a polo shirt.

"How are you feeling this morning?" he asked.

"Much better. I feel pretty good."

"Did you just get up?"

"No, I've been up since dawn. I have my own time since I've been on the island."

"Well, what do you say to breakfast?"

"OK. I'm hungry again."

That morning I had oatmeal, scrambled eggs, whole wheat toast and butter, and three glasses of fruit juice. After breakfast we went on deck and watched the crew mount the sails, and then, in a short while, we were on our way to Hawaii. The island became smaller and smaller and soon disappeared. After it was out of sight, I asked Brundage for a pair of scissors, and he lent me his.

I returned to the cabin and trimmed my beard closely, and cut off most of my hair, leaving it only long enough to cover the nape of my neck. Then I took a shower and shampooed my hair, and later, looking in the mirror, I no longer appeared to be an object of curiosity.

As the boat moved steadily onward, Brundage and I sat in the galley, drinking juice.

"Tom," he said, "I know you must be wondering how Hildendorf got the island in the first place, and just where the hell you've been for the last two years."

"I've been thinking about that."

"Well, one evening, oh, about two months ago, over supper in LA, he told me the story of the island, how he got it, et cetera. Now, it's his story, not mine, you understand."

"Sure."

"It seems he'd been looking for years for an island. This Robinson Crusoe thing really possessed him. And one day in

Washington, a few years ago, he met a Korean national. I never did find out the name . . . and this guy was a wheeler-dealer all over the world. He told Hildendorf he could sell him an island that some South Americans had just rejected as too small and too isolated for a resort operation, which, of course, was just what Hildendorf was looking for.

"It seems the island was so out of the way that no ships or airplanes ever came near it. Hildendorf jumped at this, and came out here to inspect it, then bought it on the spot. Then he flew to South Korea with his new friend, and bought up supplies from the Korean war of the fifties. That's what you were probably eating."

"Yes, pure glop."

"He also said there was American clothing and American weapons and tents and such, from army surplus left in Korea."

"Well, I had an M-1 and a couple of helmets, but the clothing was Korean. I couldn't wear any of it."

"What can I say? That's the way he operated. When he told me you weren't going to get any of your supplies, I really blew my top, but he told me it would be a better book that way. That's the way he thought."

"Why didn't you let me know about the supplies?"

"Why? Jesus, Tom, I . . ."

"I know why. You were afraid I'd back out."

"Tom . . ."

"The truth, Ralph."

"OK, that's the truth. But Hildendorf told me you would have adequate food and supplies."

"He was full of shit. He bought the cheapest things he could get. And hardly enough for one year, let alone two years. And not even a can opener to open the cans, and no fishing gear and no tent."

My agent lit a cigarette and looked away. Then he asked if I wanted a drink. He went to a sideboard and brought back not only a bottle of cognac and glasses, but a folded map as well. He poured out the cognac and we clinked glasses.

"To you," he said. Then after downing the drink, he opened the map.

"I know you must be curious as hell as to where you were."

"It's funny, Ralph. In a way I am, yet if I never found out, that would be OK."

"Why is that?"

"I don't know. That's just the way I feel."

"Well, anyway, here's where you were. I have to give you approximate readings, but about eight degrees north of the equator, and the longitudinal reading is approximately a hundred and twenty-six degrees."

I looked over the map of the Pacific Ocean. The nearest island to the east was Clipperton, and there was a Mexican island to the northeast called Islas Revilla Gigedo. My island wasn't even on the map, but it was located in an area designated as the Clipperton Fracture Area, in the middle of a vast and empty sea.

"According to Hildendorf, you were right between two air routes, the airlanes from Acapulco to Tahiti, and LA to Tahiti. I guess you never saw an airplane go by?"

"No."

"And that's the story. How about another drink?"

"Why not?"

Later that night, Brundage asked me what I intended to write concerning my adventure.

"I don't know, Ralph. I'll be honest with you. I don't want to write the book now."

"Are you serious?"

"I'm very serious."

"Tom, I spoke to a couple of publishers, to a few of the movie studios. There's an enormous interest in all this. You could be a name."

"A what?"

"A name, a celebrity."

"Ralph, right now, I don't want to do it."

"Tom, there's a million dollars still lying around with this story."

"You're probably right, but what happened to me is something I'd rather not write about."

"What do you mean? What happened?"

"Ralph, a lot has happened."

"So it happened. So write about it. You'll get a book published, get a lot of money. Get a name for yourself. This is your big chance."

"No, it's not my big chance. I can't think that way anymore."

"I don't understand."

"It's hard to talk about, Ralph. But I don't think I'll write the book."

He brought up the subject a few more times, but seeing how adamant I was, he finally stopped talking about the Robinson Crusoe novel.

38

We arrived in Hawaii a few days later, and there Brundage gave me an advance on the monies due to me. In addition to the $50,000, there was interest on the money he had held in escrow, and altogether I'd receive about $55,000 after he deducted his commissions. We stayed overnight in Honolulu, and then he took a flight back to New York, while I flew directly to Los Angeles.

I arrived there on a warm September night, and took the bus out of the airport to Hollywood Boulevard, where I checked into a hotel for the evening. It was as if I had never left LA. The crowds on the street; the entire street scene was the same. I walked over to the Pickwick Book Store and thought of buying something to read, but I went away empty handed. I just didn't feel like burying myself in a book now. Instead I went back to the room and watched television. It was all so strange watching the commercials in color, watching the situation comedies and the detective programs. I watched for about two hours, and then turned off the set.

The next morning I called my mother and told her I was back and that we'd spend this Christmas together. That afternoon, I took a flight to Portland, bought a car there, and drove up the coast to Washington State.

Now it is late December, almost Christmas time. I'm living in a rented house very close to the water. Though I'm not directly on the Pacific, I can see it from my upstairs window. The ocean here doesn't have the intense blue I remember so well from the island, rather it's a kind of gray-green, unless the sun is shining and the sky is absolutely clear, and then it turns a pale blue-green. But it's the Pacific, and I'm comfortable near its power. The waves roll in endlessly and break on the rocky shore, or drift in white furrows into the various inlets that make up the Washington coast.

I've done a little writing since I've been here, but it's not about the island. My agent mailed all my manuscripts back and I've examined them carefully, realizing that I had never been able to write what should have been written by me. I had never put down my true feelings, and all my past work was tinged with a kind of commercial flavoring, something I guess I thought the publishers wanted.

Well, that's all behind me now. I've burned all the old manuscripts, burned everything of my past. All I've kept are the tattered remains of the clothing I wore when I was rescued.

I've made a few friends here and I see a woman on a casual basis. My friends know I'm here temporarily and know that I'll probably leave after the Christmas visit with my mother. She's expected any day now. They've asked me about my past and about the last few years of my life. I told them there was something I had to do, and couldn't really talk about it.

Even my ex-wife got in touch with me recently and we

spoke on the phone for a while. She told me I've changed. Well, I guess I have. I guess I couldn't help but change after two years on that island.

Brundage has given up on the Robinson Crusoe novel, but he wants to see my next work. It's a long way off. I have to feel my way back slowly.

I have few books here, but among them is not *Robinson Crusoe*. What I do have is an old family Bible my mother sent to me, and often I sit near the fire and read from it, from my favorite section, Ecclesiastes. I sometimes get into a dreamy state reading, and close my eyes, my face warmed by the fire, and think of that island in the Pacific. I've told no one about it, or about my stay there.

Since I have some time now, I take down the Bible and open it to a time-worn place. I read:

> I returned, and saw under the sun, that the race is not to the swift, nor the battle to the strong, neither yet bread to the wise, nor yet riches to men of understanding, nor yet favour to men of skill; but time and chance happeneth to them all.

To this I say, Amen.